A Little Street Music

Other books by Daniel Stern:

The Girl With The Glass Heart (Bobbs-Merrill)
The Guests of Fame (Ballantine)
Miss America (Random House)
Who Shall Live, Who Shall Die (Crown)
After the War (Putnam)
The Suicide Academy (McGraw-Hill)
The Rose Rabbi (McGraw-Hill)
Final Cut (Viking)
An Urban Affair (Simon & Schuster)
Twice Told Tales (Paris Review Editions)
Twice Upon a Time (W.W. Norton)
One Day's Perfect Weather (SMU Press)
In the Country of the Young (SMU Press)

A Little Street Music

Daniel Stern

Texas Review Press
Huntsville, Texas

FIRST EDITION, 2004

Requests for permission to reproduce material from this work should be
sent to:

Permissions
Texas Review Press
English Department
Sam Houston State University
Huntsville, TX 77341-2146

Acknowledgments:

"The One Thing She Would Not Do" and "The Fellowship"
    were first published in *Prairie Schooner*.
"Use me" first appeared in *New Letters*.
"The Future" was first published in *Hampton Shorts*.
"The Altman Sonata" first appeared in *Southwest Review*.

Cover photograph: ©2004 Man Ray Trust/Artists Rights Society
    (ARS), NY/ADAGP, Paris

Cover design by Paul Ruffin

Library of Congress Cataloging-in-Publication Data
Stern, Daniel, 1928-
 A litte street music / Daniel Stern.-- 1st ed.
    p. cm.
 ISBN 1-881515-61-3 (alk. paper)
 I. Title.
PS3569.T3887L58 2004
813'.54--dc22

                                    2003025948

For my sister, Claire—with love and admiration

Table of Contents

Fabrikant's Way

Everyone knows that music is a blessing. But, sitting in a soundproof chamber in the audiologist's office, Saul Fabrikant, a disappointed composer turned musicologist, reflected that with some blessings you don't need a curse.

It wasn't clear when the non-stop music in his head had begun, a constant undercurrent playing on beneath daily conversation, beneath ordinary personal thought, finally even while he slept. Fragments of phrases repeating themselves over and over, giving way seamlessly to entire melodic lines. At first he registered only a mild persistence of melody, more like a memory than a presence, but gradually it had become more and more insistent. Louder? Well, it couldn't be louder, it was internal, neither loud nor soft, just there; God knows where its actual residence was in the mind. Some doctor could probably find out what side of the brain, what lobe—in fact the M.R.I. was finally invoked; but he wasn't at that point yet. Maybe it would go away as gradually as it seemed to have come. And, to be honest, he wasn't sure how he felt about it. Was it blessing or curse; or mixed, the more usual case?

It amazed Fabrikant, as he grew more aware of his new constant companion, how it could co-exist with the ordinary stream of daily life, thought, talk, work, encounters, perhaps when making love, though about this he was not quite sure, being knee-deep—so to speak—in exploration of passion with his lover, his fiancé, Anna Moores, the tall beauty, the energetic, wandering photographer.

Yes, they were engaged, although Anna did not know this. But Fabrikant had decided and it was only a question of giving her enough time to slough off the old skin of a four-year rotten marriage.

1

"I was so sure Garth was the one. I mean we worked together, played together, we both hated nouvelle cuisine, all that kiwi and stuff being drizzled, the only man I'd ever known who was as bored by football as I was."

"What did he do?"

"Advertising—brilliant. From copywriter to copy chief in seconds flat."

"Then—what?"

Anna went from sunny to dark in one second. "He wasn't there. If it wasn't for having Jason I would have split much earlier. "

"Where was he?"

"I mean he wasn't 'there,' not present, it was as if something else, something inside, or something past or future had his deepest attention. Work, his ex-wife. Absent!"

Fabrikant took a chance. "Even while you were—?"

"Not at first. In fact what I loved—liked—"

Fabrikant eased a smile into the delicate moment. "It's too late to be tactful. I didn't think you were a sacred virgin."

"Well, what I loved about him was that when we were in bed together, God, sometimes men can be off somewhere on their own trip, but Garth was completely in it. I mean, this is getting too thick. Let's just say, after a while he began to drift into himself and he paid attention only at crucial moments when he had to."

"Remind me to pay attention at the right moment."

"Not to worry." She plucked a pen from her purse and began to sketch on the pristine tablecloth: two figures entwined doing you know what. "That's you and me," she said.

"That's a clean tablecloth. Desecration of restaurant property, not to mention pornographic graffiti. You'll get us thrown out."

Anna stood up; she was tall, maybe five-ten to Fabrikant's five-eight. She gazed down at him and said, "Then we can skip dessert and go be pornographic."

It was still April-light out: longer New York cool and sunny days. Walking in the in-and-out shadows was when Fabrikant decided they were engaged. He would tell her later and she would laugh that kind of low-pitched laugh she had and matters would proceed. She would say, "Do people still get engaged?" And Fabrikant would tell her, "It's the new retro formality. People are getting engaged again, preparing for formal weddings, brides in white even for second and third marriages."

If it came off it would be Anna's second, Fabrikant's third; he would not wear white. He was only thirty-four, but he believed in marriage and had begun marrying early and often. There was no way he could tell her about the arrival of this internal loop of music—not yet, anyway. They'd only met three months ago and the arrival of this unexpected mystery was too weird to toss at her so soon. Anna was a photographer—nature, industrial—Alaska one day, Detroit the next; a lover of what you could see, frozen still, as in paintings or photographs, or present and whisking past, as in ballet. Music, invisible, was a reach for her. But with Fabrikant she was reaching.

What kind of music was playing on this unexpected, uninvited jukebox of the mind? What else could it be? Since he was six, Fabrikant had been a prodigy of classical musical memory, also some pop, some jazz. He began to compose when he was ten. By the time he entered Music and Art High School he had written an Orchestral Suite, a touch reminiscent of Debussy, but give me a break, the kid was all of fifteen.

Mort Siegel, his colleague at Columbia, a physicist and medical historian, remembers an amazing ride with Fabrikant in a convertible on a glorious, sunny day when Fabrikant sang the entire first movement of the Mahler *Fourth Symphony*, all orchestral sections, strings, woodwinds, brass, the works, and all between Riverdale and Poughkeepsie. He could perform that same feat with hundreds of pieces: symphonies, sonatas, concertos—even a whole category of pop songs, particularly show tunes for which he had a soft spot— romantic that he was.

And now that they had taken up residence, perhaps permanent, in Fabrikant's head, he was faced with the question: what to do? Ironically, he was also having some hearing loss at the same time, which is why we've found him sitting in the soundproofed testing chamber of Gail Gray, an audiologist at Columbia Presbyterian Hospital, giant earphones clamped onto his head, registering which tones he could and could not hear—tedium touched by anxiety.

"Do you hear these tones? When do these sounds stop being clear? Repeat these words." Released from the space capsule, he sat at the desk, across from the computer on which she was still tapping as she spoke. She laid the computer readouts between them—spreadsheets of a new kind of profit and loss.

"The left ear is more affected than the right, but they both could use some boosting."

"Aren't I a little young for all this—thirty-four?"

"I have a ten-year-old girl in my waiting room." She was congenial, comforting. "Professor Fabrikant, some hearing loss is not the beginning of old age."

He threw a wan smile. For one enchanted moment he rehearsed a confession to this gray-suited, trim scientist of sound, Gail Gray; but it always came out as if I'm hearing things. So the rest was silence, and that night when he met Anna at a gallery opening, the vow of silence ruled still.

Afterwards, he took her to Chez Pierre, two notches above what he could afford—though already thirty-four he was only a graduate student, just coming up for tenure and money was always tight. But in spite of quick, thrilling intimacy, they were still exploring each other, and a little classy ambience could ease the flow.

Over the smoked trout: "How come you gave up on writing music?" They were still at that stage of exploration, every encounter a first date, all questions and answers; only the sex was no longer a question.

"I didn't," he said. "Music gave up on me."

"How does that work? I mean, I love music but I don't know a whole lot about the process."

"It's a matter of style. In a sense everything comes down to that."

He'd not seen much of her stuff and she'd never heard the few existing recordings of his music, but they swiftly agreed. You couldn't separate style from substance. The manner is the matter, that kind of thing.

Over the *poulet aux trois moutardes*, over the *tournedos*, the Beaujolais, he told her: "I was just repeating old stuff. You can't write something if it goes stale under your fingers and in your ear, sounds like a hundred other people."

"You once said you didn't compose at the piano. How do you know what you're hearing?"

She was approaching the forbidden theme. He moved forward quickly. "I can't explain it. You don't need Beethoven's deafness to think about it. Lots of people write music in their heads, first. They say Mozart wrote everything internally first, then just scribbled it all down. Here, hum a melody in your head."

"Okay."

"Now hum it out loud."

"I can't sing."

"Just do it."

"Beatles, okay?"

She closed her eyes and sang a few bars of "I Wanna Hold Your Hand."

"Different?"

"Of course," she said. "Silent hearing isn't really hearing. One's an idea and one's a sensual experience."

Maybe this was the moment. If they were the right combo, he and Anna, then she would understand, not treat it as something freakish. But the check came and Fabrikant was reduced to telling an old musical joke. "So this guy in a bar goes up to the cocktail pianist and says, 'Do you know where my girl went?' And the pianist says, 'No, but hum a few bars and I'll fake it.'" Laughter, public kisses, and suddenly pressing after-dinner plans.

In the cab going to Anna's place, Fabrikant said, "You know, the whole thing's a mystery. Hearing is sensual and there's no substitute for that pleasure. But I remember being damned excited when I was setting something up in my head—if that's where it happens—even before I tried it out on the piano or had some friends play it."

"Do you miss it?"

Her steady gaze was a little unnerving. It told him she was still trying to figure him out; it underscored how new they were to each other.

That night Fabrikant woke sweaty, startled, hearing the plucking of the perfect, melancholy Elgar "Introduction" and "Allegro" for strings, plucking an unbearable sadness from the night. It was the piece he had wooed his first wife with. If that's the word; Christine hadn't needed much, wooing being straight-on, meeting him more than halfway, utterly ready for the sweet life until it turned sour. And this

5

was the piece he'd played endlessly after she'd suddenly vanished—though she'd given warnings, ultimatums for days, weeks. During those post-Christine months he played the Elgar endlessly. Christine, like Elgar, was British; pacing, smoking (he still smoked then, until Martha came along and stopped the Elgar-miseries and the two packs a day of Gitanes, the foul French cigarettes he'd become addicted to as a student in the Ecole de Musique in Paris.)

"Get over it," Martha had said. "It's music to wallow by." But in his memory the Elgar had anchored a special sadness and now it had come back, found a place on this new juke box of memory.

Fabrikant went into the kitchen and tried a soothing sip of jasmine tea. (Christine had gotten him off caffeine, too; the assumption was that they would be together for many years and she wanted a healthy husband; that was, of course, until he met Martha.) But he was eager to throw off these parentheses and find a way to turn off the music, on its third loop by now. Brainstorm! He would just cut the Elgar. Only he found that he couldn't just stop it, he had to replace it. Fabrikant chose the consoling Tchaikowsky fiddle concerto. At last, music to sleep by. God, Fabrikant reflected as he dozed back, what baggage music carried on its back. If it could carry whole marriage/misereres, what other burdens could it call up! This was not going to be all fun.

In the morning he decided he had to tell someone. Maybe other people had the same loop running but just didn't mention it. He called Mort Siegel. They sometimes ran together in the mornings and running would be a good cover for the strangeness of revelation. Besides, Mort was a scientist and what was happening to Fabrikant felt like a kind of science fiction. Fabrikant waited until they were halfway around the Central Park reservoir, panting like a steam engine in a middle-aged crisis—then he blabbed it as quickly as he could. Mort Siegel was known at Columbia as the scientist with a humanist face. He'd won awards for his work in chaos theory, but music, painting, dance, all were important to him. He often sat on thesis committees in creative writing or music as an outside reader. Mort was also a failed writer; two and a half novels in the drawer and a continuing hunger for the literary, the artistic. Anything to broaden his scope outside medical history and the laboratory. But he was

6

also always on the edge of some great scientific project: once a perfect test for some hard-to-classify virus; once a planned paper on science as a mystique—that one called down the wrath of his department head and died a swift death. In his forties he was still finding his way.

"It's everything, Mort. An enormous jukebox with every piece of Western music ever written."

"But it all comes from you. The trouble is you know damned near every piece ever written. Is it terribly distracting? Can you work, talk sensibly to colleagues, to Anna?"

"It doesn't replace the faculty of attention; it sort of— shares it."

A pause for toweling and a water fountain.

"What's playing now?"

"Shostakovich, the *Tenth*: so tragic."

"My God."

Mort seemed as baffled as Fabrikant. Still, it felt good to have it out in the world, to an old friend. In the meantime Fabrikant prepared frantically for his orals, the last hurdle before writing his thesis—the road to becoming Doctor Fabrikant. Anna was sensitive but a touch too insistent, too present for all the pressure Fabrikant was under. On a night when he should have been immured in the library he was immured in a box seat at the ballet. Anna had studied dance and it still had its hold.

At least it gave Fabrikant a chance to try an experiment. How intrusive was the vinegar of the Bruckner *Ninth* against the sugar of *Swan Lake*? No contest. He could turn one down and the other up at will. It felt good, less at the mercy. He was learning new techniques of control every day. The one miracle he could not perform, apparently, was banishment: interior silence. It looked as if he had a companion for life.

At intermission Anna gazed at him steadily, a new gaze not seen before.

"How much for your thoughts?"

"I believe a penny is the usual price."

"You can't get anything for a penny these days."

"Why'd you ask?"

"You look especially thoughtful."

It would have been a good moment, in a public space, her mood softened by ballet. He couldn't get it out.

7

"I have orals coming up in a week."

"Ah. I didn't do graduate school. Are they a horror?"

And the moment passed. Fabrikant was safe; but still in trouble. He gazed at her in return, slim, elegant, easy in her skin, all attentive affection; not being able to tell her made him feel lonely. Out of professional habit he called and checked his answering machine. It was Mort Siegel. "I've got something to tell you. It's quite amazing." Amazing or not, it would have to wait till morning. The night at Anna's beckoned.

She was a downtown person, at home in Washington Square Park, the hip bustle of Bleeker Street, tiny Italian restaurants; Fabrikant was uptown, straighter, Lexington Avenue in the Sixties, French or Hungarian restaurants where Hunter College students and stewardesses hung out. They spent that night at Anna's place on Barrow Street, exchanging lives in installments, making love, telling, making love again, and more telling.

She told him about learning photography—she'd had to support her son after she'd left the husband—who was always nameless—the years of raising her son, who was now away at the Putney School.

"Do you enjoy it?"

"Yes, but it's hard after thirty."

"Everything's harder after thirty." And he told her about his difficulty picking a thesis. It sounded academic but it went to the soul of things. All the usual suspects were taken; also all the far-out nutty ones: conventional: modernism beginning with Handel, I kid you not; on the nutty side: German post-war politics in the piano music of early Stockhausen. "Either way," Fabrikant said, "you might just as well take a Valium. So I'm doing it on Aaron Copland and Leonard Bernstein: Jewish Americana. It's not so bad."

"What would you want to do?"

He wants, beneath it all, the paradise lost; the years when he was writing music, searching for a style, but still doing it. Can he tell her this? Fabrikant feels shaky, maybe a little weepy.

"I want to go back to writing music again. I want to find my own voice, find out what my music is, and then write things that will stretch your mind, will break your heart."

8

Anna sat up in bed sensing something important was being said, touched. "I like ambition in a man," she said.

"I'm afraid it's not just ambition."

"What am I hearing?"

"How about regret?"

He told her how little he trusted himself. Since he'd put the brakes on writing music, he didn't quite know how he felt about who he was—not wanting to be an ex-composer, enjoying teaching budding composers, not without the occasional twinge of envy; but not sure about scholarship, dry.

What he couldn't tell her, of course, was that maybe the One Thousand Greatest Classical Hits, which had taken up residence inside him, might be a punishment—a joke, like a Zen saying: this is what you can't do, but this is what you should be doing.

"Well," Anna said, "Stretch my mind. Just don't break my heart."

Fabrikant had never seen Mort Siegel so excited.

"Listen . . ."

"I'm listening."

"I was reading a journal, I forget which, but I clipped out the piece. Is it still going on?"

"Is what still going on?"

"The round-the-clock inside music."

"Round-the-clock."

"Well, you're not the only one. Some woman in Seattle had it. Here. Read."

Fabrikant read. A mature white female "presenting no other significant symptomology" (as medical journals sometimes describe human beings), had begun to hear, or imagine she heard, musical compositions playing repeatedly.

"Check out the cause."

A stunned Fabrikant read aloud: "Repeated MRI's showed two small tumors on the auditory nerve. After surgical removal of the tumors (benign), the musical hallucinations ceased."

"Jesus," Fabrikant said.

"How about that." Mort Siegel was as proud as if he'd cured the Seattle woman himself. He was, after all, besides being a writer who'd never left the starting gate, also a doctor manqué who'd turned to medical history. Mort was a master of the art of the manqué.

Fabrikant's tears, suppressed last night, arrived now. He began to weep. They were having lunch at The Griddle, a campus hangout, and God knows who from the College of Humanities might see Fabrikant crying into his coffee. Mort sat next to him, his arm around his shoulders, as much to conceal as console.

"Hey, hey. It's not bad news, it's good news. There's a way out."

But there was no way to tell Mort how raw his nerves were; how rehearsing his life, his ambitions and frustrations, his gains and losses with Anna had left him wrecked when he should have been happy. He was falling in love with a smart, sexy woman, moving forward in his academic career, and at the same time he was losing control over his own soul.

By the time Fabrikant had cooled off and was having a second cup of coffee, the "Funeral March" from the Schumann *Piano Quintet* was playing. Could the jukebox make specialized jokes? Could tumors, benign or otherwise, use musical irony? Was the jukebox out to get him?

"What are you laughing at?" Mort was puzzled by the whipsaw between grief and laughter.

"I don't know," Fabrikant lied. "But I can't have an operation now, just before my orals."

"One step at a time," Mort said. "One step at a time."

Doctor Chu, the neurologist, had been remarkably unsurprised by Fabrikant's recital. Fabrikant's internist, Sauerwine, had recommended him because Chu had treated a woman whose husband had died and had suddenly begun hearing Jewish songs from her earliest childhood.

"Did you operate?" Fabrikant asked.

"Nothing showed up."

"So—?"

"We can only hope she learned to live with it. Or maybe it vanished. There are no sequelae; she moved to California."

Chu was a small calm man. "There have been a few other cases reported, one in Sweden, also an older woman. But it's very rare." Doctor Chu was writing in an open chart. Without looking up he asked, "Doctor Fabrikant . . ."

"No. A.A.D. Almost a doctor."

Not listening, Chu said, "Do you have a hearing aid?"

"Not yet. I've been tested and I'm waiting to try it out."

"Ah, it's sometimes associated with hearing loss."

Dr. Chu looked up from his chart-writing as if he had some comfort to offer. "Rare though it is, the disease has a name." He had the grace to smile. "Musical hallucinosis."

There was no sense telling Anna before the M.R.I., so Fabrikant went alone. He'd had one before, a false alarm about internal injuries after a car accident on the West Side Highway, but the incredible loud knocking noise was still an awful surprise. It took forever and shut up in a narrow, slowly moving tube, assaulted by alien drums, he was grateful for the arrival of the Mendelssohn D Minor Trio he'd played by two Juilliard buddies of early youth, Samson, and Levine, neither of whom had made it past early youth. Samson was a prodigy violinist and Levine a cellist with sublime tone. They played Fabrikant's *Piano Trio*, written for them long before doubt and despair had won the day, stopped the flow.

They were going to stay together as soon as they found a name for the trio, start touring the capitals of the world after graduation; they would make Fabrikant's Trio their signature piece, ignoring how much like Shostakovich it sounded. Young, gifted, only early illness and death could put a stop to that foolish dream, before the usual stops of indifference, before learning that the musical world is a ladder without rungs.

Fabrikant felt like a mummy in a sarcophagus. So, naturally, the M.R.I. was an appropriate place to mourn. Though it is not clear if he was mourning the early death of friends or his own prolonged silence starting not so long after. And, as he sat up on the narrow gurney shaken, a touch dizzy, Fabrikant thought, most mourning is probably done after the report is in. Which in his case would be at two, the next afternoon; Dr. Chu was operating all morning. Fabrikant's ears kept pulsing with echoes of the M.R.I. sounds. Had it done something to his already questionable hearing?

In the morning he called Gail Gray but hearing aids apparently took time. He met his classes that morning—over the bitter brilliance of the Bartok *Music for Percussion and*

Strings. The afternoon was his and he sat, warm and tense on a dappled bench on Fifth Avenue, outside the Medical Building waiting for two o'clock to arrive.

"There are two tumors on the auditory nerve."

"Just like the woman in that case."

Dr. Chu was puzzled. "What woman?" His attention was fixed on the radiology report in front of him.

"Never mind. Tell me what it means."

"A textbook case."

"I thought you said it was rare."

For the first time Fabrikant noticed how young Chu seemed. Small, slim, if he wasn't a doctor you could take him for a student. This afternoon he was in a good mood.

"Then maybe we'll write a new textbook."

Both relieved and frightened, Fabrikant wondered who the "we" was. He wasn't sure he wanted be a co-author.

"Forgetting about your extraordinary musical symptoms, tumors on the auditory nerve are not unusual. The operation has a decent rate of success."

And as if he and Fabrikant were ready to get going, Doctor Chu launched into the standard spiel: dangers of operating, dangers of not operating, length of procedure, convalescent period.

It was clearly time to tell Anna, but for some reason it had to be out of doors. It was April, still spring-chilly, but Central Park would be singing. He could sing this new fearful song.

But he had to start at the beginning: the permanent juke-box, the loop. Strangely she got it right away. Like a doctor or a researcher, she asked the right questions.

"No time off, ever? It never stops?"

"Unless I don't notice it sometimes, which is possible."

"You can't control it."

"No. I can change cuts on the CD, to mangle a metaphor, but I can't turn it off. A silence inside is not an option."

The grass was sprawled with young people, dressed brightly: sun-yellow sweaters, heaven-blue woolen sweaters, blood-red caps. Some of the sprawlers and strollers wore headphones. Fabrikant pointed them out, trying a grin. "At least I don't need batteries."

She clouded over. "I always think those Walkman people are trying to shut out the rest of the world. Meaning me. Maybe because of my loony-tune husband, off on Mars while I was stuck down here on the planet Earth."

Then frankfurters and cokes at the zoo and a long silence and Anna finally said, "What dangers are there with the operation?"

"The usual: anesthesia, infection. With one extra zinger thrown in. It might affect my hearing."

"Please talk straight. Do you mean it could make you deaf?"

"You know doctors. They never say it right out."

"But that's what it means."

"That's what it means. Maybe one ear, maybe both. Maybe neither."

"If you don't do anything, can these—things—become malignant?"

"Maybe. Maybe not."

Anna dropped her head onto his shoulder. "Too many maybes," she said. "I know how much music is to you. Is it nice, all that music inside?"

The weight of her head, the shampoo-smelling hair— Fabrikant was overwhelmed with how *there* she was, how absolutely present, and how important that had become, and how quickly.

The operation was scheduled for the week after next. As bad luck would have it Anna had an assignment to photograph an oil rig in Galveston, leaving Fabrikant alone with uncertainty.

At a department meeting, distracted by the boredom of endless grievances, he was suddenly convinced that the music had stopped. Fabrikant's heart practically stopped: anxiety, hope, he could not separate them. This was either a very long pause, or the crazy adventure was over. Good, he thought, stop the music, I want to get off.

The chair was speaking: a tall, nervous fourteenth-century scholar. "We have no funds left for any research travel. Not for the rest of the academic year."

"Except for his MLA trip to New Orleans," the whisper could be heard across the room.

Fabrikant listened intently through his own silence. But it turned out to be only a long pause before the slow, slow, slow movement of the Mahler *Fifth* was to begin. Fabrikant settled down and the slow, slow, slow meeting continued.

The week Anna was away, the waiting week, spring broke open. It was one of those sublime times you get in New York at the end of April: suddenly warm when the city opens and starts to breathe. It was as if the muffling mute of winter had finally been removed. The buses brute braking becomes melodious; the sweaters, scarves and hats come off, and restaurant sidewalks sprout tables and chairs like mushrooms after rain.

Fabrikant was used to eating alone. In between marriages he'd been a bachelor so often that dinner solitude was familiar, comfortable; a book propped up against a glass—or in happier days, a manuscript score open while a martini smoothed the way towards a few good rhythmic bars, an absorbing page, or an appetite. His favorite refuge, La Bonne Plage, furnished the martini, he brought the book—*The Harmonic Revolution,* by some stuffed academic—and he brought the solitude.

Well, not complete solitude. This evening he also brought along the Bizet *Symphony in C.* Then, in the middle of the Bizet, with the gaunt, genuinely French waiter, distracted but courteous waiting for his order, there was an interruption: a piano piece appeared. But wonder of wonders, it was one he didn't recognize. Absolutely strange: contemporary sound, but not atonal, strong but no easy melodic line and electric harmonies that kept surprising. Elliot Carter, no, not that original and bristly; Corigliano, no, too hard-edged for Corigliano. It was in some ways, almost beautiful.

But it was not entirely strange to Fabrikant. He did know it. But what was it? He went around in these circles until a picture appeared in his mind: himself at the piano, pencil between his teeth, hard at work. It was, of course, Fabrikant's own music, his last and best piece, the sonatina, unfinished, drowned in a sea of doubt. It sounded like Elliot Carter, it sounded like Copland's *Piano Variations,* it was/ wasn't original, only aggressive, experimental. It wasn't as subtle as Feldman or as startling as Stockhausen. It was modern sounding wallpaper. It was nowhere. So instead of writing the ending, it *was* the ending. Never finished, but finito anyway.

Other matters, too, were about to be finito. He and Martha had just had their second false alarm: she was not pregnant. She wasn't happy about it, but she also wasn't happy about anything that included Fabrikant. One morning, sick of the sense of failure that had taken up residence in his gut, he'd rented a car and driven all the way to the Vermont border and beyond. It was winter and a hell of a slogging drive through the snow. Fabrikant had no idea why he was doing it—except that despair was in the driver's seat. What did he want—to get stuck in the snow the way he was stuck in his life—maybe freeze to death in his Hertz suicide Ford Taurus rental? Did Hertz give special rates for suicide vehicles?

Instead he drove back to Manhattan, having decided to quit slogging through writing music, the way he'd slogged through the Vermont snow. By the time he got home he felt peaceful for the first time in months. And when Martha said, "I think I've had enough," he said, "That's okay." Then, a laugh, and added, "Easy come, easy go."

Somehow, having given up on music made it easier to give up on his second marriage. Apparently, giving up got easier with practice.

"For every door that closes, one opens," Mort Siegel said.

Not sure he'd heard right, Fabrikant said, "What did you say?" He'd have to call about the hearing aid again.

Mort repeated the line and Fabrikant had said, "Stick to science, Mort. Stay away from self-help," and they tied one on into the smallest hours.

He ordered the *coq au vin* and a Beaujolais and by the third glass the smooth sounds of saxophones, drums, even strings had taken over from Bizet, from early Fabrikant; a cheap way to revisit a youth spent in what they called supper clubs. "Somebody loves me, maybe it's you."

Wine-dark nostalgia took over. Fabrikant was moved. Not surprising, he thought, forgetting who'd spoken of the incredible potency of cheap music, Noel Coward, maybe. But cheap is as cheap does and, finally, it was the things left unfinished that were expensive, that he was paying for, still.

Around midnight Anna called. "How are you holding up? I forgot, it's an hour earlier here in Texas. Were you asleep?"

"I had to get up to answer the phone, anyway."

"Mean," Anna said. "Don't be mean. It's a hundred and three in Galveston and I've been climbing around oil rigs since dawn. "

"Anyway, I'm holding up," Fabrikant said. "How about you?"

"Got some good stuff. But I'm exhausted. Almost asleep and I miss you. As I was dozing off I remembered something."

"Never trust midnight memories."

"When we talked about what you wanted, how what you really wanted was to stop talking and writing about music and to start making your own again. There was one thing I didn't ask. Kids. Would you want to make a kid?"

They tossed it back and forth till one or the other was almost asleep; but she couldn't get a straight answer and Fabrikant couldn't give one. He was hearing his *Variations* again, thinking of how it could be changed so that it could be finished, satisfied; unfinished, it was unsatisfied, like a hungry child needing the milk of conclusion.

Finally: "Darling Anna, never ask such large questions of a musician about to have an operation on his auditory nerve."

Sleepy, almost inaudible, she said, "Sorry. You do seem distracted. Is it the stuff you're hearing, or not hearing—I won't even ask what it is, I don't know half of the titles, anyway, or is it the lurking Dr. Chu?" Of a sudden, sleepy or not, there was a sharp edge to her voice. Concern, anxiety, simple irritation at his *distraction*? There was no simple answer right now, except maybe sleep.

Except now sleep was impossible. He found himself rummaging through piles of manuscript, untouched for God knows how long. It was so hard to find; maybe he'd destroyed it and then destroyed the memory of destruction. But, no, there it was, hatched, cross-hatched with quavers, the calligraphy of failure.

16

Fabrikant placed the manuscript on the piano, open to the last page. He sat there for a moment, waiting, trying to find what might be the next moment of his music. He laughed, thinking of the famous comic song "The Lost Chord." Arthur Sullivan, wasn't it? And, sitting on the piano bench in his navy blue pajamas, risking the security of his rent-controlled apartment, he actually, at one a.m., played and sang with appropriate mock solemnity: "Seated one day at the organ/I was weary and ill at ease . . . ."

A middle-of-the-night vaudeville act, a music hall comedy act, a joke. But what else could you do in the face of loss, possible greater loss, a lovely woman growing more uncertain by the hours; and the tireless assault of the Western Music Top 1,000? The worse times get, the more jokes seem like the only road to truth—or at least at last to sleep.

Fabrikant woke wondering if perhaps, as in legends, he would find that while asleep the piece had been completed, or at least moved forward. No such luck, Berlioz was alive and well inside: the fantastic *Fantastic Symphony*. He dressed quickly, a busy day ahead. Anna was coming home, he had to make out a living will and do about a hundred blood tests and EKGs so he could just zip into the hospital and the operation on the appointed day without delays. The next day: his orals. Fabrikant had asked that they be moved up, in case of post-operative complications. He didn't want to risk losing a whole semester.

At her own invitation, Anna came to listen and to root for the home team, a long, silk bright yellow spring dress, gold earrings. Mort Siegel canceled a class and sat next to her, with, for some reason, pencil and pad in hand.

Gomez led off—a smarmy, eager-to-please associate professor. "How would you connect Copland's *El Salon Mexico* with his Jewish identity?" (*Identity* was the big current word, along with *gender* and *sexuality*.)

Fabrikant—"Jews have inhabited what the Nazis called *host nations* since the Diaspora began in 70 C.E. That is, they are presumed to be in but not of the culture they inhabit. Thus Villalobos could write out of his native Brazilian tradition, while Copland wrote in the style of Mexican folk music, transformed by modernism. But he wrote as an American-born Jew, a cosmopolitan wanderer, an outsider/

insider." He saw Anna beaming at him from her seat along the wall.

Next, Jakob Behr—a nurturing senior professor with an endowed chair. "Bernstein wrote *West Side Story*, American Pop with a Puerto Rican theme, and also the *Kaddish Symphony* with some Hebrew text, a work of Jewish mourning. Which one speaks more to his Jewish identity? And in what ways?"

Nurturing or not, Fabrikant knew a trick question when he heard one.

Fabrikant (without a beat)—"I'd say *West Side Story*. Celebrating the minority Puerto Rican culture, Bernstein did what Jews often do: he appropriated elements from another immigrant culture, in this case Latin Puerto Rican rhythms, combined them with Broadway melodic modes (a Jewish heritage starting with Gershwin, through Irving Berlin, all the way up to Steve Sondheim); and by combining cultures and adding a liberal slant, he protects himself by protecting other minority groups. If one group is liberated from prejudice, then all are—including his own group, the Jews. It's simultaneously an emblematic act of generosity and of self-preservation."

Fabrikant could sense surprise and approval in the air. He'd done the smart thing. Emphasized politics more than musical technique. Now he went for a home run. "Hence the old saying: American Jews live like Presbyterians but vote like Puerto Ricans."

General laughter and the rest of the session was a boat ride, complete with the champagne Anna had brought along. Was this what he'd been so terrified of all this time?

Anna: "A joke. You played them with a joke. Would that be a first in these tests?"

Fabrikant: "I don't know. You only have to do one, if you're lucky."

Siegel: "You have a real talent for this stuff."

Fabrikant: "Stuff?"

Siegel: "Musicology, I mean."

Fabrikant: "Don't do me any favors."

When Mort Siegel had left, Anna spread out the photographs she'd taken in Galveston.

"These have texture, mood."

"Don't be a professor."

Fabrikant didn't have much eye for photographic nuance, but there was something powerful about the long shadows of the rigs, the contrast of dark and light.

"I mean these are damned good, and they have texture and mood."

"That's better."

He leaned over, pressing against her. He loved the way she curved, some kind of special sensual slouch, upper back indenting slightly then sliding down to flare out into rounded buttocks; it was a presentation of herself-as-her-body, probably preserved since adolescence. And it was in operation whether just standing or leaning over photographs or even—harder to do—sitting, legs crossed. It was as if she were saying, look at me, all you nervous wrecks of the world: I'm comfortable in my skin.

"Is this like showing me your etchings?"

"Maybe."

"All those giant derricks, so phallic."

"Don't get competitive."

Fabrikant didn't know if Anna was especially attentive, inventive, that night. But the sex melted into love and back again in an easy, excited flow. It was always good, but this promised to be always, always good. Though who can talk about always? Certainly not a man on the eve of an operation.

Nevertheless, as they settled to sleep, he took a deep breath and told her they were engaged, that in his mind they'd been engaged for weeks.

"I know," Anna said. "I've known for weeks." And she was wrung out into sleep.

In the morning, while Anna overslept the sleep of climbing oil rigs, Fabrikant noted that something new had happened. He "heard" the sound he'd been waiting for. His *Piano Variations*, only taken a step further. It was where he'd left off, the break between lives; but this was new, the moment of changing harmonies to a harsher mode, letting the melody sort of choose between them. Somehow it had moved forward. He rolled out of bed as quietly as he could and scribbled down the few bars on the flyleaf of one of Anna's books. He shoved the book into his briefcase and sat in wonder.

This is what worried him: while the *Variations* were playing in his head, the juke box was playing nothing else. So he couldn't figure out if he'd simply started to get back to work the way one did—ideas, figures, followed by development—or whether it was being delivered to him, ready-made on the loop. Later in the morning at home, at the piano, he worked it out a step further. Then: dead end.

He collared Mort Siegel for a late breakfast. "Then it just quit on me and I just quit."

"And what did you hear after that?"

"Lots of pieces too humorous to mention. Or too tumorous to mention. What do you think?"

"I'm glad you can still laugh about this. I don't know what to think." Mort looked solemn. "In my neck of the woods we talk a lot about the mysterious point where science, medicine, meet the arts, artistic imagination and all that. But nobody knows much. I know how badly you want to get back to it . . . . "

"You don't know half how much."

"Paul Valéry says that works of art are never finished, only abandoned."

"Big help."

Still, unusually solemn, Mort said, "Then why not just keep going on it. Forget about inside-outside, heard or imagined. You know, take charge, like Nike used to say—just do it."

From Valéry to Nike in a flash—that was Mort Siegel, the grandmaster of consoling quotations.

There was a saying at Juilliard when Fabrikant was a student—"Don't let the score get cold." Writing music was like being a detective, score equaled spore. You followed a trail of clues, making larger and larger discoveries, following promising leads which turned out to be false, changing direction, then swerving back. But sometimes the trail went cold; the clues didn't add up and you were left—baffled. Fabrikant gave it the old college try, came up cold, then settled down to wait.

But that wasn't so simple, either. There was the matter of Dr. Chu. The operation was scheduled for the day after tomorrow. Further complicating matters, on the heels of his triumphant orals, suddenly he was finding his students' dilemmas of high interest. They were serious, driven, and confused. Fabrikant's job was to clear away some of the confusion without slowing down the drive. A tightrope, a high-wire act, not without its own giddy excitement.

His students' problems, for the moment, stopped seeming jejune; they had depth, possibilities. And the longer he spent working on them, the more he realized that maybe it wasn't so bad being randomly accompanied (the word was not "assaulted" any longer) by the music of the ages, by a continual playing of a concert program with an infinite number of surprises. It didn't interfere; it was an addition, not a subtraction. How much of this came from an irrational hope that his own stuff would grow out of that joyful or sorrowful noise, he had no idea. But maybe he could just go on living with his new inner companion.

Something warned him not to share this with Anna. But it was impossible not to. He could hear the encounter in advance.

Anna: "Skip the operation? But what about the tumors? Tumors aren't musical or imagined, they're real."

Fabrikant: "Dr. Chu says they're probably benign."

Anna: "Is *probably* good enough?"

Fabrikant: "I'm not sure."

Anna: "And will you be happy helping young people to compose while you wait to see what's coming your way? And speaking of students—you're thirty-four. How come it took you so long to start getting your Ph.D.?" (It was becoming an interrogation, fueled by irritation at his stubbornness.)

Fabrikant: "Because I spent all those years cocking around trying to be Lenny von Beethoven, or Ludwig von Bernstein."

After this she began looking at him strangely, at odd moments.

"What?"

"Nothing."

Then she'd do it again; coming out of a movie, that gaze.

"Nothing. I was just wondering—"

He got it and helped her out. "Don't tell me you were wondering if and what I was hearing."

Anna was edgy. "I thought we agreed it wasn't really hearing."

"That's not what I asked."

And over late coffee and doughnuts, Anna had her own surprises. They poured out like water dammed up for too long. "I told you how it drove me crazy that my first husband, Garth, was never *there*; off somewhere behind his eyes. It was always a bitch to get his attention. But that's not the worst of it. My father—Jesus I never thought to tell anyone this stuff."

She stood up and paced back and forth in front of Fabrikant, a surprising sight in a coffee shop, this tall beauty, agitated into perpetual motion.

Fabrikant said, "If it's too close to the bone, don't." As if she hadn't heard, Anna flooded on. "And not just my father, every man—okay, stick with my father for now. You had to explode a stick of dynamite to get his attention. No, not any mythical *you*. I think it was me, his only daughter. Oh, he loved me like crazy. Anna Livia Plurabelle, he used to call me. Only he never saw or heard me."

"Isn't that Joyce?" Fabrikant asked.

"Sure. *Finnegan's Wake.*"

"Pretty fancy."

"Oh, Professor Moores was nothing if not fancy. His Joyce course was signed up a year in advance. Very attentive to his students. But when I spoke, it was like I was on another planet. My brothers never had this problem it seemed to me."

Anna sat down as suddenly as she'd stood. "I think that's when I began to realize that men and women were different. I mean beyond the usual between-the-legs stuff. Haven't you noticed—women listen, men talk, women talk and men interrupt. Men always seem to have another life, women are in *their* life. God I didn't mean to sound off—this isn't politics, if it's a bunch of clichés, they're mine, if it's some crazy theory, it's all mine, but it's pain, and the pain is all mine, too."

And Fabrikant got it. "Anna, is this you telling me that if I don't try to get rid of this *other life*, if I don't pay the musicians and send them home, if I don't have the operation—we're off?"

This seemed to end the storm. Instead of a rainbow Anna gave out a wan smile, tired. "I didn't quite know, but now that you say it, I guess that's what I'm saying." She took his hand, as if he were the one who might need comfort.

"Aside from all that stuff about men and women, how can you live with a sword hanging over your head, okay, inside your head!? No, a pendulum—benign, malignant, benign, malignant, benign . . . ." It looked as if she might never stop. "And all for—what?"

That was when he told her. She was astonished, even a touch contemptuous. This, she said, was some kind of fairy tale he was telling himself. Only in movies did music get finished while the composer slept.

"It's not quite like that." Fabrikant took his hand back. There was no way to make it clear to her or to himself. It was not something you could argue, prove or disprove. It was a tiny crack in a dark window. It was a throw of the dice. If it was a crazy risk, it was his crazy crap game. If her pain wasn't his, then his risk couldn't be hers.

"I have to go now," she said.

Fabrikant didn't ask her where, or why now? When she was almost at the door, he called out. "Anna, I never answered your question, on the phone." She turned, frowning, question, what question? He stood in the doorway, back-lit by the late afternoon sun, her back arched like a taut bow about to be released, sensual, waiting.

"About kids," he said. "Yes, I'd like that." He didn't expect any answer, any turning of the tide. It was just a full stop, a coda so nothing was left hanging. Just himself. When he got home the light on the answering machine was winking at him. Feeling stupid, he let himself hope for as long as it took to play the message.

But it was only Gail Gray. His hearing aid was ready.

"And all for what? That's what she asked."

"Yes."

"And what did you say?" Mort Siegel blinked at him, warily, as if he didn't really want to hear what came next, he was waiting his turn to talk.

"I told her the music I was hearing might some day turn out to be mine."

"Jesus. You can't tell that kind of stuff."

"Too crazy?"

"Listen," Mort grew excited which usually meant he'd read something in a medical journal. "Listen, if you hadn't called me, I would have called you. Some guys at Duke are doing some research, important, about what they call *universal consciousness noise*. In other words what goes on inside everyone's head all the time. It was in this journal, *Nature*, serious place."

"Noise . . . ."

"Well, these guys are physicists, but it's kind of a metaphor. Anything disorganized, things whirling around."

Fabrikant listened. With the hearing aid in, he heard his friend's words more sharply, more distinct, but the actual tone was strange, echoing. Hearing too well seemed to put you on a different planet.

"They're probing at the real insides of consciousness. Think about the muddle inside our minds. Bits and pieces, a snatch of memory, of a joke, of a loss, a predictive thought, in your case music unspooling, vague images, a fragment of dialogue, sudden panics, flashes of well-being for no particular reason. A ground bass—" Mort liked to toss in musical or painting terms for flavor, "—a ground bass of unspecified murmurs, ideas, remembered and distorted dreams, alertness suddenly sharpened then suddenly softened, attention to particular objects, then a shift of attention to others.

Mort had never been so transported. He was like a gambler on a winning roll.

"And get this. What I've just tried to describe is just me, just one man's inside experience. How about the woman standing next to me at the bus stop? I'm assuming mind has the same texture for her. But that's only an assumption. I'll never know anything deeper about her sense of her mind, about the buzzing of her thought, than what she chooses to tell me."

"If she talks to you."

"She will. Everybody talks to me. But I'll never know what it's actually like to be her." They were having breakfast the morning after the breakup, an hour or so before classes. Mort nibbled a bagel while he carried on his—what—speech, tirade, pre-classroom lecture. But no, it was more personal than that, as it turned out.

"I know you're feeling punk because of Anna signing off. But I wanted to tell you something while I was still hot."

"I was wondering why you were pouring this onto me."

Mort slowed his New York pace of talking. It meant he was getting serious, maybe on tricky ground. "I want to write you up. I want to use—what did the doctor call it?"

"Musical hallucinosis."

"Just so. I want to do a paper on it and you and send it to these people at Duke. The condition seems to be pretty rare. And it would give me a chance to bring everything together."

Fabrikant got it. It was the moment Mort had been waiting for; to make himself whole, sew up the ragged fragments of his life, his skills, his passions, his soul. Science marries the humanities and lives happily ever after.

He waited for Mort to settle a bit before he said anything. Then: "I don't mean to rain on your parade but I'm not sure I like calling what's going on with me a *condition*."

Mort got a little tougher. "For God's sake, you've got two tumors on the auditory nerve."

"But Chu's not positive that's the cause."

"He's a doctor. They're not supposed to be positive. Look at their language; they talk about *following* a case. They can't always predict but at least they can act."

"Right. The only way he can find out seems to be by removing the tumor and then see if the concert stops. That's doing it the hard way."

"So is not operating and waiting to see if you die." This was a new Mort. He sounded like he was struggling for his own life. "This is important. I'd do a comparative study: before the operation and after."

Fabrikant had enough. He grabbed the check, stood next to Mort and said, "You're forgetting one thing. There's not going to be an after. There's not going to be an operation." Mort looked suddenly miserable; but he had another surprise for his friend. He took Fabrikant's hand.

"Listen," he said. But it was a different word than the one he'd used to open this painful dialogue: no longer excited; softer, sadder. "Listen, I'm sorry. You're looking for a shoulder and I give you a shove in the ribs. I know it's bad timing. But I'm forty-nine and I haven't done much. I thought maybe—Ah—it was a half-baked notion, anyway. I wouldn't have a control group, finally it would be what they call 'merely anecdotal'. Never would have gotten published. Listen, do you want me to talk to Anna, see what

I can do?" Surprising both of them, Fabrikant leaned down and kissed Mort Siegel, his friend of twenty years, on both cheeks.

"Thanks," he said. "I think that moment has passed."

At twenty after four in the morning, Fabrikant lay, still as a stone, trying to stop one phrase from the Bach *B Minor Suite* from playing over and over again, count it, one phrase. It had begun as consolation, a kind of musical sleeping pill and then wouldn't go on and wouldn't stop; a kind of exquisite drowsy torture. At last he was able to switch it but like hitting any wrong switch, it brought the unexpected. It brought Christine, his first wife, the wife of his first post-college years; kind, round Christine, a glamorous British accent hiding in a short, plain open-faced woman. Or rather, what arrived was not Christine but her own leitmotif—the Beethoven *Fourth Piano Concerto*, with that amazing dialogue between an angry orchestra and a tranquil piano. God, how many women, how many mistakes could he mourn with music. It was lucky he'd only married twice.

Christine had the pianist's gift, but the need for concentration, for single-minded devotion got lost somewhere between their move from New York to Indiana where Fabrikant took a Master's, then to Rochester, where he had a teaching gig, then back to New York for the doctoral horse race. Somewhere on all those planes, in all those new households, her piano life got gobbled up by their (his) life. The piano finally fell asleep and so did their marriage. Tonight, with each chord from the Beethoven *Fourth* what hurt most was how oblivious he'd been to her misery, to her loss. Fabrikant tossed from side to side in painful disgust at his earlier self. If he was going to be at their mercy like this, maybe just say goodbye to the tumors, take a chance. Waiting for his own gift to show up on some mysterious inside tape—what a mug's game.

The phone saved him. No, he thought, foggy, without hope, it's not her.

"Listen," Mort Siegel said, "I can't sleep too well. I feel bad, I'm worried."

"Not to worry, Mort, I'll be fine."

"What's playing right now?"

"Never mind."

"I was thinking about Anna. She's probably at sea because you might be risking your life to hold onto a kind of pleasure most people can't feel—"

"It's not always pleasure," Fabrikant said, and poured out the ruinous sadness the Beethoven had brought with it, all the rotten reliving of his mistakes with Christine.

Even cloudy with sleep Mort was never at a loss for the apt quotation. He said, sonorous, "'Remembrance of a particular form is just regret for a particular moment.' I forget the rest but it ends with 'as fugitive as the years.'"

Fabrikant hadn't heard clearly; he squeezed and pushed his hearing aid and asked Mort to repeat it.

"Yes." Fabrikant said. And the two old friends, each with his own regrets, lay, each in his own solitude, talking the night away.

Finally Fabrikant asked, "Say that phrase again."

"Remembrance of a particular form is just regret for a particular moment."

"What's that from?"

"Proust," Mort said. "The ending of *Swann's Way*."

And what of the ending of Fabrikant's Way? Surgery is the knife that's supposed to answer all questions. But with or without surgery, only questions remain.

As that flawed philosopher-scientist manqué Mort Siegel has reminded us, locked in our own consciousness, which of us can actually know the internal buzz and click of others, the fading in and fading out, the music of rage or regret, the noise of all human thought? Or, more simply, must the mind of that woman at the bus stop remain always a mystery?

And Fabrikant: does he still hear the roll call of the whole of Western music? If he's back writing again, is it still the same mimicry of other musics? Or, with silence having taken a powder forever, has he at least stumbled on a voice of his own; is he himself at last?

And at what cost?

The One Thing She Would Not Do

The imperfect is our paradise . . .
—Wallace Stevens

"So she says to me, all right, we're on—I'm game for anything—but there's one thing I absolutely will not do."

Don't forget, this is Jay Florenz talking to me. Jay, whose life with women—and money—has been the mystery, the irritation, and occasionally the envy of his friends for decades. For some reason he is telling me, openly, naming names, about the strangest sexual encounter of his life. And this is some life we're dealing with here! Rushing to Tangiers, on the tail of a stolen Veronese, being escorted to the airport at Madrid by the Guardia Civilia because he had sold a Goya to a movie producer, all the while knowing that the Spanish government took the dimmest view of allowing the great Spanish masterpieces to leave the country.

You may say, well, this was a commercial, a political encounter, but with Jay, the female element is always lurking around the edges—or at the center—of his experiences. He had, as it turned out, bought the Goya from a Spanish beauty whose grandfather worked for both Franco and the Republicans and was said to still be an excellent shot. A married Spanish beauty, as if I had to add that—there had to be something dangerous, something complicated, something difficult in all of Jay's sexual and romantic liaisons. Oh, he's a Distinguished Professor of Art History now, covered with honors instead of kisses and money. But at the time we're talking about, Jay's moment was mainly a moment of stolen kisses and borrowed money. He was a hot-shot critic, making and breaking reputations in *Art News* and *ArtForum*, occasionally *The New York Times* on Sunday. But that had not yet translated into cash.

When the eighties arrived and gave birth to a storm of art buying, Jay's expertise was much in demand. People who were pushing Jenny Holzer and Julian Schnabel needed a lot of academic backup to help hold up those heavy-duty prices that made the art market of the eighties such a scandal—at least now, from the vantage point of later years. You know, the way you can point out the similarity between Cy Twombly's graffiti and scribbles around the periphery of some big altar pieces. That kind of thing makes a big buyer feel a lot more secure when he's writing out a check with more zeros than he'd planned on. Which is how Jay first met Shirley Schoenberg, the sister of the woman who would do anything except one thing.

Have I mentioned Jay's integrity? The man would slip an Old Master out of a country that wanted to keep it—that was just business. But when it came to artistic judgments, I mean he was infected with it like a virus. He would make such a comparison between a great master and a current artist only if he believed it in his soul and his art historian's intellect. Otherwise, he would shake his head and decline.

He first met Shirley Schoenberg at an opening—where else? Shirley ran the seedy little gallery which bore her name, Shoenberg not Shirley, almost far enough downtown to be called Soho and not far enough uptown to be within scratching distance of 57th Street. The opening, though, was at the Marlborough Gallery: Maurice Lowenfeld, Jay's buddy from his Paris adventure days, was showing those giant canvases, almost empty, just brushed lightly with a woman's shape, or an automobile fender, but drawn and painted with the lyricism of an Ingres.

"I would have loved it if this guy had walked through the doors of my gallery with one of these."

This, to Jay, who stood next to her gazing with that sad straight look of his at the painting. Whether or not she knew who Jay was at that moment is not clear.

"Maybe she knew," Jay told me, "or maybe not. It was the kind of impulsive thing Shirley was given to." And in Jay's ever alert imagination, talking to strangers could lead, finally, to sex with strangers.

But let's not get ahead of ourselves, let's not put carts before horses or beds before paintings.

"I think," Jay said to her, "that when they're this size the artist just brings slides."

She turned to toss him a look of puzzlement. Didn't he assume that, meeting here at the Marlborough, she would know that he would know that she would know all that?

"I have a gallery," she said.

"Ah. Soho?"

"Not quite. A little above."

"Midtown?"

"Not quite. A little below."

Shirley pressed all of Jay's buttons. She was tall, as slender as the most fashionable of models—but there the simile ends. She was a shambles: her skirt was too long and she kept hiking it up during the walk to the Carlyle for a drink. Her hair was brown and the gray streak she affected—or simply permitted—was right in the center; unbecoming, it seemed to be asking not for esthetic admiration but for one's concern. Her lipstick was the wrong shade—Jay was good on color and good on women's lipstick—too dark for her olive complexion. All this was aphrodisiac to Jay. Something in him needed needy women. I'd once called this to his attention, in my typical moralistic way. "You like women when they're in trouble." He grinned, yielding me the field. "But not big trouble," he said.

"But what is that?"

"Damned if I know."

I'd met his mother when Jay and I were both in Bronx Science High School and she'd been a troubled, melancholic woman. But I wasn't about to talk about repetition compulsions, to play analyst with Jay. There was something too successful, too authoritative about him to invite such speculation.

But he confirmed my insight, letting me in on a secret, he loved secrets. "Do you know what my favorite time is with women? I've never told anyone. It's when they're having their period."

"Oh?" I expected something more perverse on the way. But all he said was, "There's something vulnerable in the face, around the mouth and eyes at that time of the month."

Which is what I meant when I spoke of Shirley pressing all of Jay's buttons. Anyway, when she invited him down to her gallery the following week he was amazed. It was a mirror image of the woman, herself: another shambles. Paintings poorly hung, the lighting miserable, almost no visibility from the street. This was even better than menstrual cramps. This woman was in utter trouble and didn't seem to know it. Jay's interest in Shirley grew deeper.

Their involvement stretched through half-lit gropings in small bars on Houston Street; through gallery meetings in which Shirley pushed Jay to write something ambitious about a young Brazilian painter, an artist Jay thought was entirely lacking in talent; through long, wet kisses in even darker bars on Lexington Avenue. They were like inflamed teenagers condemned to a sexual scramble in the outside world because their families occupied their homes like conquering armies.

Have I mentioned that Jay was living with Simone and her son Raphael at the time? Jay loved Simone, but it never occurred to him that love should end an interest in sexual play with other women. And have I mentioned that Shirley had a roommate, a nearsighted music student who actually paid nothing in rent? She was a cousin of a friend who knew the editor of *ArtForum*, and Shirley had hoped to mix charity and ambition in one gesture, but nothing had come of it, except the usual restrictions on sexual activity for two women living in a one-bedroom apartment.

Impasse? Shirley didn't even own the gallery, completely. Mona Kress, a half-assed painter, had invested her mother's small legacy in a half-interest and once, when in desperation Jay and Shirley tried the couch in the cubicle she laughingly called her office, suddenly they heard Mona's footsteps. "Let me see if I can find those drawings," Mona was saying to some co-intruder while Jay and Shirley struggled with underwear, with shoes.

"I can't stand this," Shirley moaned. "God, my sister has a roommate, too. The damned rents in this town."

"Let's—let's go to a hotel."

"Where? Which one? How about luggage?"

So began the period of making love in a series of Upper West Side hotels—dark brick, slightly odorous hotels full of incurious German and Swedish travelers. Jay paid the hotel bills even though Shirley was just as eager as he for sexual privacy. It was an easy time with its own rhythm. The only persistent irritant was Shirley complaining bitterly about money and why wouldn't Jay help her push this or that new artist. But Jay was adamant and that was that.

Then came the switch. The groundwork was laid when Shirley's roommate quit music school and went home to her family in Wisconsin. Jubilant, Shirley invited Jay up for an afternoon rendezvous. Sensitive to the occasion Jay brought a bottle of wine and over the first sip Shirley let him have it.

"Isn't this great, I mean the freedom?" And without a pause for the rhetorical response she said, "That money you were paying for the hotels, how much was it each time?"

"It varied. About a hundred and fifty, sometimes a hundred and seventy-five."

She blinked quickly a few times and said, "Why not keep the same arrangement. Just give me the money, when we come here, instead of paying it to a hotel. I'm much more short of money than people who own hotels."

The switch!

Jay stood up, slowly, as he told it, telling how, slowly, in the way lovers undress each other, he took out his wallet and showed its modest contents to Shirley. Clearly he didn't carry that kind of money every day.

"I used credit cards," he said.

Shirley laughed a little and said, "I'll only take cash." She put her arms around his neck. Was she turned on by the money-talk? "But we'll run an account for you. You can pay me double next time."

"Wow," the usually cool Jay said when telling me this part of the saga, now it was *pay me*. It seemed to fit the casual way they'd come together, her neediness attracting him as it did; here was more neediness, only of a more aggressive sort. They made love that day with extra intensity from him, with extra imagination and inventiveness from her—was she playing the whore? A nice, middle-class Jewish young woman adding money to sex. A new frisson for Jay, certainly and maybe for her as well. That was the day, Jay said, that she decided, on her own, to lick him from head to toe, turning him over like a cake when one side was done. "Around the world" she called it, Jay marveled. "You'd think I'd have heard of that before."

I'd have thought no such thing: first a pale art student, then an even paler graduate student, the artists all around him leading their traditionally crazy lives while his nose was pressed to the grindstone leaving his other parts free, waiting for someone like Shirley to educate him.

"My sister and I were partners in crime," she said. "Sexual buccaneers. We were only a year apart and we couldn't wait, starting at like sixteen." She widened her eyes. "We were slow for our generation. But we made up for it pretty damned quick."

The sister had now been spoken of twice and Jay was mildly curious as to why she was so invisible. Once he asked and was told that she was shy.

"I thought you said she was your sexy partner in crime."

At which point Shirley became elusive, shifting the subject to a new exhibit of Russian émigré painters she was planning, Jay becoming equally elusive. He disliked most Russian painting and was not about to lend his credentials to the show. Shirley's ambition kept poking through but it was this oddball relationship that now compelled his interest— peeling off bills while Shirley peeled off clothing.

It occurred to Jay to ask or even demand certain things of Shirley, now that it felt as if he were in a game: he asked her to wear a particular kind of underwear when he arrived. She had a mirror on the wall of her bedroom—he told her to kneel and take him in her mouth while he watched, alternately in the mirror and in reality. She acquiesced with her usual good cheer. Jay had the feeling that the money made no difference to her, except as a practical help in getting through her financially chaotic life. He sensed that she would have done everything he asked in the same happy way, even if no money changed hands. Was she actually selling, he wondered, or was it only that he liked the idea that he might be buying.

This appealed to the Jay, who was so leery of personal entanglements—just ask Simone who was hanging in, her second year, in the hope that Jay would talk about marriage, a hostage in the long standoff. But Jay had been married once, one of those instant things you did right after college and packed in just after graduate school. He used the experience the way someone might use having been a POW. Too awful to talk about and certainly too awful to take a chance on repeating. Generally, it worked.

"I don't have any illusions about myself," he told me once, after using this ploy to disengage himself. "That is, not about selfishness, anyway. I'm like a porcupine. My bristles are honesty about work, about paintings and sculpture. Everything else is *sauve qui peut*."

And telling me about this new development in the Shirley affair, Jay confessed, "I'd never fully gotten the idea of how selfish I was. I mean the idea of paying a woman who owns an art gallery, who knows the same people I know, for sex, a woman who might, under different circumstances, become my wife, this turned my head around. I began to act a little crazy. I was making more and more extreme demands—and at the same time I became more tender; I brought her perfume; I advised her on her shade of lipstick."

It was a new way of being in the world for Jay. He was obsessed, began to neglect his work. He missed a deadline for a big piece on Eric Fischl for *Art News*—attacking or defending, I forget which; he canceled a class because it met at the only time that week Shirley could make it. That was the day he suggested tying her to the bed and playing bondage games and she laughed and said, "Sure." Counting out the money and handing it to her, Jay felt a touch deflated. Perhaps he'd wanted some shock, some middle-class resistance. No such luck. He was afloat in a pornographic dream but it was tinged with, corrupted by, affection, by professional ties. Jay thought he was in charge, buying, commanding; but actually he was at the mercy of a sexual buccaneer named Shirley Shoenberg.

It may have been, too, the selfishness, the self-regarding spirit that was in the air in those days. Downtown was becoming more than a direction, a neighborhood, it was a kind of industrial narcissism, a religion of money and self. Andy Warhol hovered in the distance like a secular deity.

Part of the trap was the voice of scorn the times were developing in Jay. He despised the Downtown scene: "Julian Schnabel," he wrote, "is less a painter than an art-market solder-of-fortune. But he's not even 007, more like 000." When the self-invented Basquiat rose from anonymous graffiti artist to instant celebrity, Jay wrote, "His is a kind of inside-outside art, like certain varieties of all-weather carpet." And for David Salle, well, Salle pushed him over the edge. "We need an Academy Award ceremony with David Salle the winner as Most Formulaic Artist in the Dull Category."

Years later, when we all remembered it as a time of foolishness and treading air, Jay said, "I didn't quite realize it, but I was doing myself in with all that contempt. I mean I was probably right about those painters but too much bile kills your own digestive system. I needed something to get me out of the trap I was in."

"Like what?"

"I didn't know. I was caught up in some unholy stew of my career—by this time I must have been writing for seven magazines about seventeen artists a week—along with my nutty sexual sessions with Shirley. The way out came in a strange way."

The way out turned out to be the mysterious, absent sister. Shirley and Jay had a rendezvous on a Thursday at three o'clock and Jay was up for it: the prospect lent a sharp edge to his treadmill week, an eagerness just this side of fixation. On Thursday morning Shirley called—she could not make it. This was a first for her, a last-minute cancellation. There were some buyers or sellers in from out of town, or from Europe, Jay was too disappointed to care about the details. She was cool, Jay was sweating—an indication as to who was the pusher and who the addict. He was like a child in a sulk. Taking a beat, Shirley said, "But I have a surprise for you." Like all sulky children he was eager to hear about a surprise.

Of course, as it turned out, and as I mentioned earlier in this tale of the damnation and redemption of Jay Florenz, the surprise was Shirley's sister, Germaine: the sexual partner in crime, the sexual buccaneer who would do anything except one thing.

Germaine Shoenberg and Jay met at the Carlyle for a drink. Germaine was the Uptown sister and worked for Conde Nast. She was large—that was the first thing you registered when you saw her. Maybe five foot nine, a touch more. She was sitting at a small round table when Jay arrived so he would not get to see how tall she was until the drink date was over. Even so, where Shirley's breasts were like inverted champagne glasses, Germaine's were high and rounded, pressing forward above the horizon of her blouse; her cheeks, beneath bright brown eyes, were curved fully. Where Shirley was modestly made, amplitude was her sister's style.

"Shirley told me about your arrangement," she said.

"Arrangement's an odd word—but I guess you could call it that."

She raised her empty martini glass. "I need another drink," she said. "I'm a little nervous about all this."

Jay raised a waiter. "No need for nervousness is there? Shirley's such a free spirit and she said that you—"

"She gave you that buccaneer stuff did she?" Germaine had a broad smile; Jay liked it.

"Not true?"

Germaine twisted the glass, drank and twisted some more. "No, it's true. We've done a lot of stuff. But until you, there was never any money involved."

"What do you do for Conde Nast?" Jay was stalling, trying not to deal with the false implication that he was the one who'd introduced cash into Shirley's bedroom. He didn't want to have an argument an hour or so before he and this new young woman were to make love—if that was what you called it. But he didn't much like being cast as the financial corrupter of young women.

"Junior editor. Tiny expense account, small salary, lots of glamour. I'm working on an interview with Martin Amis. You go to Wellesley, get top grades and you're qualified to make two hundred and fifty a week."

"So, what intrigues you about this *arrangement* is the money?" Jay was hoping the answer was no.

"No," she said. "Shirley's the one with the real financial pressures. It's not exactly the amount. Though it is close to a week's salary."

"Tax free," Jay said. If she could joke about it so could he.

She opened a small smile.

"Then what?"

"The money is kind of the final frontier. I mean, I don't know you and you're going to pay me. I'm curious how it will feel at the moment when I'm . . ." She lowered her eyes. "When I'm undressed and you give me the money."

Jay was getting more than he wanted. He swerved. "Shirley's your kid sister?"

She shook her head. "Everybody thinks so. That's because she's small and I'm—let's say, larger."

There was a rueful, self-mocking tone that Jay found endearing. It wasn't the same as catching a woman with menstrual blues but it would do. He was looking forward to their encounter.

"Do you have Shirley's keys? Because my roommate—"

"I have them. Shall we get a cab?"

"Listen, Jay . . . I should tell you—"

Jay waited, silent in the patient blue air of the bar. Germaine stood up. There was something regal about her movements; she carved out a large chunk of airspace for herself, not heavy—the proportions were attractively spaced—but her body seemed to call attention to itself as she moved towards the revolving door, perhaps simply because she was so aware of how she carried it. She turned back and over her shoulder tossed at him the words he'd been waiting for. "We'll make this fun. But there's just one thing I will not do."

Jay kissed her in the cab—no sense waiting like a fumbling teenager. She responded wetly, breathing heavily through her nose. In the apartment she tossed her jacket and purse on Shirley's dressing table as if she were in her own apartment. When Jay embraced her and started to ease the shoulder straps of her dress down—she was taller than he was and he had to reach up—she stepped back.

"Shirley said to get the money first." And grinned as if to acknowledge that the three of them were playing a game.

He counted out the money into her hand and waited while she did her wallet and purse business. He was not thinking about money, or about tripartite games. He was wondering: What was the one thing she would not do, this buccaneer. Would she tell him as they approached whatever it was, would she just stop, cold? Would she tell him now? Jay's pulse beat out his excitement at the craziness of it all. Her grin had pleased him; everything about her pleased him. If the whole idea had not been this assignation, he might have been happy to just keep talking over their drinks, move on to dinner somewhere, make another date, keep the intensity going by extra anticipation.

At the same time, the perverseness of the swiftness, the unexpectedness of the game had its own savor. When he told me about the next two hours, Jay walked a tight-rope, not wanting to be gross but needing to be clear as they approached the "one thing." I don't recall now if he spoke of parts: vagina, anus, mouth—of domination or submission, of control, of pauses for some kinds of tender touching, of bathroom games, of his temptations to push her as far as he could until he got to the taboo. But clearly it was a feast of get-acquainted sensuality. Germaine's amplitude implied earlier was an over-flowing flood of nakedness, unfashionable fleshiness, just this side of fat, and pleasing to Jay's eyes and hands.

When the refusal came it was astonishingly simple. It seems, as I tell it, inevitable that Jay, whose life was essentially looking at objects, enjoying them esthetically and evaluating them, should move them both in front of the floor-to-ceiling mirror for voyeuristic pleasure. It turned out to be the moment of truth.

Germaine rolled out of his grasp. "No," she said. "Not there. No mirror!"

She stood at the side of the mirror hands fluttering over breasts, stomach, groin, a parody of *September Morn* but genuinely troubled, agitated. "I told you there was one thing . . . ."

"But you didn't say what," Jay said, helpless. Then, refusing to be helpless, determined to regain control, he went to her and held her. He was flaccid now, desire a casualty of surprise, of anxiety. Of all the words available for such a crisis he could find only the simplest one. "Why?"

She blinked at him, almost teary. "Take a look at my sister."

"I have," he said.

Still in his embrace she spoke over his shoulder, into his neck. "Shirley's everything delicate, in proportion, slim. I'm the other sister. The Klutz."

She let go of Jay, slid to the floor and sat against a rainbow scatter of pillows—a modified Malliol. He sat next to her and listened to her stories of Shirley and Germaine, the wild college kids of Toronto picking up a professor—not one of their own—and trying a threesome; there following the trauma, the nuances of making the beast with three backs with the professor clearly giving the best grades to Shirley's lissome attentions; this story to be repeated in various versions, with and without her sister after their emigration to New York.

"I'm not going all weepy with self-pity. But in my high school yearbook, next to my photo they wrote: 'Schoenberg—means beautiful mountain, in German.' I've been shy about mirrors in intimate situations for years." She inched across the floor towards Jay and rested her head on his now un-threatening lap.

"Sorry for the interruption of the festivities," she said. She continued her apology in political terms. She was not naive—she was in touch. She knew it was retrograde of her to think of physical proportions the way men had for centuries; she knew what was in the air: that to be ashamed of having a larger female body than you saw in *Vogue* or *Vanity Fair* was reactionary foolishness—playing into the hands of every schmuck who enjoyed keeping women in their place—but there it was; there she was. Wellesley or no Wellesley.

Jay caressed her hair, loose under his touch, and quickly formulated his plan. He began with consolation, murmurings and touches; this moved to caresses which became pressing. As they moved to resume—I was going to say the games—Jay made it clear that at this point the tone had changed. These touches weren't games anymore, rather they were urgent claims on the other's attention. Jay took advantage of this change in the atmosphere to place the two of them where he could surprise her but somehow control her reaction. They were standing, now, her back to the mirrored wall, supposedly moving past it towards the rumpled bed in the corner when Jay whirled her around: the two of them framed in a reflection like startled children in the dark on whom someone had turned a searchlight.

He held her in a tight grasp, whispering, "Don't move. This is not personal."

"What?"

"This is not about Germaine Shoenberg. God, your mother must have had some fancy ideas with that name."

"Became a French teacher . . . after Shirley was born . . . let me go . . . ."

He ignored this last. "Look at the extraordinary curve of that throat, where it folds downward into the right shoulder. It's like Bellini's *Leda and the Swan*."

"You're crazy," but she didn't move.

"Look at the shadowed fold of this crease of flesh above the navel, how it leads you downward towards the thigh, pulling the eye into the shadowy mystery of the groin." He speaks in his best docent's tone, fixed before the work of art, concerned to be clear about its beauties and their origins. Gone are the years of clever nastiness; all the witticisms about the gulf between the artist's intentions and the results. This is Jay the classicist. "This thigh, larger than it would be

39

in nature, but perfectly in balance for this composition." She is frozen now in the glare of his exquisite attention, confused but hopeful, a rabbit in his headlights.

His hands point and follow shapes gently—breaking the usual rules about touching the works of art—but he no longer caresses. Behind the cool marble of her buttocks, his prick, which he reminds himself as if to help him keep his psychological distance, rhymes with Frick, again lies flaccid, quietly confident that it will be asked to rise again. But the moment has turned from the sensual to the moral, the ethical. Jay has convened a class of one for the perfect purpose of saving a reputation: Germaine's false contempt for her body. It will take all his learning and concentration to bring it off. It will take even more—a leap.

"The breasts," he says, this time touching lightly, coolly, not wishing to rupture the fragile moment with the sharpness of sensuality, "Not as in Rubens, that's the cliché, more Titian. Claiming space for themselves but elegantly balanced against the largesse of the full arms and the two triangles below, the spread tripod of the legs and, of course, repeated by the genital triangle."

Jay notes, in the mirror, that Germaine's legs are indeed apart, tripod-like, supporting her weight, and, more startling, her eyes are now closed. Is she imagining some personal version of his, what they called in grammar school, art appreciation? He shakes her gently and says, "Look!" Her eyes open and he swiftly turns her sideways. In this view she is a condensed version of the self, condemned to carry it around through sheaves of ordinary days. She is, for the moment, perhaps for the first moment ever, standing out-side her own skin, watching, listening as Jay completes the tour of her body.

At one point he smiles, responding to a clever comparison he has made between the curve of her buttock and a particular Franz Hals in the Riijksmuseum in Amsterdam. Jay outdoes himself—and he knows it. He feels a fleeting regret that there is no other audience. Finally, he knows that this is as much about him as the woman he is exposing, angle by angle, to the mirror.

He knows, too, in his heart that he has been heartless, that his art career like his sexual career has been a cold business, exciting, even thrilling but inhuman. He had begun this stage of the Shirley-Germaine adventure in the hopes that it could put her back into bed—the misery gone; let the games resume. But Jay is terribly, cruelly smart, so smart it's difficult for him to lie even to himself. He is changing something but it is no longer a cool trick on a naked, troubled woman. He'd begun by doing what he refused to do for Shirley's painters: tell eloquent lies about them in art-historical terms. He had begun to praise the tall, expansive woman he'd imprisoned in a mirror, as medicine. But as he feels the flexion of her arm muscles relax and go loose between his hands, as her pain recedes, the doctor may be healing himself.

She lies next to him, now, and he is uncertain: Had he actually thought her ungainly, heavy, fat, only masking his feelings with words like *regal* and *largesse*? He has, it seems, certainly lied to his penis. It is not to rise again this particular evening. She touches him there. "Oh?" she says. Is this, perhaps, another form of criticism? Is this what she is wondering? But Jay puts it to rest at once.

"Never mind," he says. "We're past that for the moment. It'll keep." And they lie next to each other doing everything he'd thought of doing at the Carlyle—telling each other their lives disguised as stories. Incidents, comedy, pathos— the usual parade of disappointments, achievements.

She murmurs, at one point in the double narrative, "I'm starved," though she does not move from the protective circle of arms, of legs. Later, the take-out Chinese jumble of fragrant white cardboard containers surrounds them with new comfort and they cram themselves and wash down any possible chagrin with waves of hot tea. The fortune cookies lie unopened in their greasy paper bag; their fortune tonight was in their own hands

"It was my dissertation," Jay said when he told me the ending of the encounter.

"It was—what?"

It was as if, in teaching himself the methodology of praise he was able to throw off the style of scorn that had put him on a certain map, was able to chart out for himself a finer place. Do I have to remind you how swiftly the new Jay was accepted, with fresh authority, in that special way the art world has of turning on a dime? Or that critics have a tendency to fall in love with what they praise?

Still, when Jay finally dropped his balancing act with Simone, when he and Germaine were married, all of us were astonished; the burned child placing his hand with quiet confidence back on the stove. When I last heard, they were still married and working on a family.

Late that night Shirley had found them asleep on the messed up bed, two naked children taking refuge in each others arms—sexual trespassers staying on long after the prearranged deadline. She sat down on the edge of the bed, flushed with one drink too many, flushed with an evening of unaccustomed success with a new buyer or an old artist, loose, lithe, easy in her skin; Shirley, with all her verbal and professional gaucheries, still the favored sister in the fairy tale.

Jay was only half awake but out of the corner of one eye he saw a startled Germaine first pulling the sheets up over her breasts, then dropping them; he heard an embarrassed laugh from Germaine and a trickle of giggles from Shirley. Dimly, he registered the buzz of words and laughter passing between the Schoenberg sisters, hearing Shirley murmur, "Did you get paid?"

And Germaine's reply, "Yes. Yes I did. I did."

The Fellowship

Okay, how's this for luck? When Leo Lipkin arrived to teach at the University of Arizona, no degree, not a Ph.D., not an MFA, no university sheepskin of any kind, and after falling into a hole with his last three books—blame that on his prolonged warlike divorce from Babette and the troubles with his kids, blame it on the lousy publishing world of the nineties—what falls right into his lap but the Pulitzer Prize.

And for not even a novel—for a book of short stories *Gloomy Sundays* which, until that enchanted moment, had languished in the shallow glow of a good *Publishers Weekly* review—good but not great—and a swift assortment of "in briefs" from the likes of *The East Lansing Press* and the *Cleveland Plains Dealer*. With the Pulitzer, of course, the University transformed him, instantly, from a foundling to a King—or at the least a Prince.

Lipkin had been looking for a teaching job since the first letter from his wife's lawyers. As far as income went, his novels had long since played second fiddle to Babette's research job at J. Walter Thompson. And given the state of post-war negotiations, he could not count on any more bread from that particular stone. Even with Lipkin's history as a Wunderkind, publishing his first novel at twenty-two to some acclaim, Book of the Month Club, appreciations by some heavy literary hitters, even with that history he found himself writing application letters from the deep well of silence into which his last three failed novels had plunged him. History was history; now was now.

It was the cool but attractive Saskia Fitzgerald, always a buddy, never a girlfriend, who'd pointed out that maybe he was striking the wrong note, acknowledging how hard it was for him, Leo Lipkin, profoundly New York to his bones, to consider moving to Upstate New York, or Virginia, to Montana, to Wisconsin.

"It must seem like receiving a letter from Julius Caesar—well, a scroll, maybe," she laughed, "offering, reluctantly, to take a job outside of Rome. You don't know academic life like I do. Wrong tone. Very thin-skinned, these English departments. You're asking for a favor, not granting one."

"Sorry," Lipkin had said, "this is all *terra incognita* to me."

"And don't use Latin terms. They'll think you know more than you do."

Saskia was on the search committee for her English department at the University of Arizona, Tempe branch, and she engineered Lipkin's hire. Only a three-year contract, but it was a foot in the door, the camel's nose under the tent, a rung on the ladder—all the metaphors simply underlined his need.

But Knopf brought out *Gloomy Sundays* in September—the first week of classes—and by chance the Pulitzer hit not long after. The Sunday before had brought a review in the *New York Times Book Review* that placed Lipkin somewhere between Joyce and Saul Bellow. The usually scorching August Tempe had been breathing deeply, happily in a rare cool spell, scudding clouds in seventy-two-degree breezes, the sun overhead a benign enriching coin. The weather appeared to conspire, to literally breathe with the new universe of cultural climate, of rewards for years of making sentences into paragraphs, paragraphs into pages, pages into books which offered life to characters, seated ideas in action, all of the above infused with a wise comic vision. Or so said the *New York Times* and who was to argue?

Certainly not his department, who turned the weekly luncheon meeting into a celebration of Lipkin's literary success. It was most welcome as Lipkin was a bit dazed from the strangeness of settling into a new city. Town, he called it—if New York was a city, what was this melange of adobe short-line homes and highway strips, gas stations, and the occasional exquisite Mission from the border-haunted Mexican past?

It was the president of the university himself who brought the Pulitzer news. He'd heard it on the car radio driving to the faculty club for his own lunch appointment. Suave and cheerful, the very model of a modern university

44

president, he tapped Lipkin on the shoulder, a King anointing a new knight. "Great timing, Lipkin," he said. "Every writer should start his teaching career with a Pulitzer."

His colleagues were not the usual cup of faculty tea. Each was achieved: Robin Fox had published six collections of poems; Jerry Hewlett's last had been a Book-of-the-Month and Jean-Paul Singher was a hot number in Paris—only in France could you call an essayist who parodied Mallarme and Rimbaud a hot number. Lipkin's prize was seen as an addition to their collective pride, not a subtraction, a booster, not a threat. Saskia was roundly congratulated for her prescience in searching out Lipkin for membership in the department.

So Lipkin's launch on the new seas of the academy was a smooth one. He was even given a teaching assistant, a charged but oddly languorous young man named Donald Stark: round, tall, something of a hulk who smoked cigarette after cigarette. Smoking had been one of the angry thunderheads clouding Lipkin's marriage. He'd quit but Babette had refused, filling their apartment and their thinning life with smoke. Typically Lipkin had been furious at this and was at the same time half-nostalgic at the remembered sweet-sour smell of the Benson & Hedges he'd used to smoke himself. He had a similar reaction to Stark's chain smoking.

"I'm not sure I need a TA," he told the young man, hoping to ease him off. "My classes are seminars. I read all the papers myself."

Stark flashed him a charmer's smile, a Southern smile. "I can keep things organized for you, take some student heat off." Lipkin relaxed a bit under the reassurances. "Besides you'd be a big help to me. I need the job. I'm broke most of the time. Except when I win."

Stark was a poker player, apparently compulsive; he was cool and seductive at the same time, and Lipkin was on the fence about taking him on. Until Stark gave him a batch of stories to read.

Bold, witty, condensed—everything Lipkin was not. How could he not admire the man's work, even though Stark the man was a piece of unfinished business? Thirty-four and already giving promise of being a life-long graduate student, hanger-on, gambler/writer. As Stark said much later, when they knew each other all too well, "I appreciate your kind words. But the old farts who hand out the Pulitzer Prize don't give it for bold, witty, and condensed." A piece of sharpness that should have put Lipkin off the younger man immediately. But by that time he was too deeply immersed in the *folie-a-deux* that would become their strange connection.

Oddly enough, Stark was a great help. His languorous exterior concealed a raw energy. He not only collected the papers at the end of class and put them in some rough order for Lipkin, he fielded the anxious phone calls at midnight— or later. He had an assurance beyond his years; surprising since his C.V. recorded few genuine jobs. Stark had just drifted and written, putting together a life knitted together mainly by gambling.

But it was Stark's stories, his talent, that bound Lipkin to him. One story in particular seemed to Lipkin to have the seed of a strong novel. He urged him to take it on. Stark waved him off, mock Southern humility. "I couldn't do a novel. I'm a poker player. Enough attention span for one hand at a time."

But he did give it a shot, began a novel while continuing with stories in an extraordinary stream of productivity that rivaled Lipkin's own energetic output. While his colleagues complained of the demands of classes, papers, meetings which aborted their own writing, Lipkin's long, complicated stories, much like the ones in *Gloomy Sunday* which had done so well for him, kept appearing in *The New Yorker*, in *The Atlantic*, in *Harper's*. Everyone he knew, Lipkin included, complained about how few major magazines were left that published serious stuff in fiction—but Lipkin was the darling of the few. Stark would take him out for celebratory lunches or dinners with the particular publication in hand, "Damn it, Professor Lipkin, you're on a roll." The younger man refused to call him Leo, cherishing in some perverse way the unequal relationship. Something in Lipkin did not appreciate the analogy to gambling, to luck. Though he was intensely aware of how thin the arbitrary line was between "yes" and "no," between acceptance and rejection, between the usual dropping of a book into the silence all around like a pebble down a well, and a Pulitzer Prize.

They would have long kaffe-klatches, talking about the experiences that had fed their writing. These sessions, perhaps more than those with his self-absorbed, overworked colleagues, did a lot to replace whatever New York literary camaraderie Lipkin missed here in the desert. Occasionally, however, Stark vanished for a few days of poker holiday, once not even warning Lipkin.

Saskia was quick to note the oddness of Lipkin's holding onto Stark as a TA even after the second and third time he disappeared on these unexpected poker-binges, leaving Lipkin to find revised class lists, missing student papers.

"How can you stick with him when he's clearly not responsible."

"I like him," Lipkin said. "When he's here he takes a lot off my shoulders. Responsible was never a word I would have used for this guy. Smart, gifted, okay. I guess he feeds my ego and he's going to write a better novel than any of my regular creative writing students. If he stays with it longer than a round of poker."

"I think you're just lonely. Post-divorce." Saskia had known Babette and Lipkin's two kids, Joanie and Alexandra. "Your friend-choosing mechanism is off kilter."

"It's not just divorce. It's the bad feeling. The girls don't trust me. Babette kept telling them I care more about my writing than about them—or any other human being."

Saskia shrugged. "True or not true?"

"Please. No romantic silliness." Lipkin scowled. "I tried to be as good a father as I could given what I had to do. I'm a father and I'm a writer."

"So you're not lonely?"

Anybody but Lipkin, hearing those words from that bold lipstick-swatch of a mouth, from the perfume-clouded Saskia, might have made a move. But she was in the category of a friend, and Lipkin thought in categories. Besides, his writing was going well, and when that was the case it was hard for him to focus on anything else. When his agent called and told him *The New Yorker* had turned down a new story, it was a category shift that got Lipkin's attention. In the months that followed, as if by some reverse magic, the major magazines all turned away from him. Nothing much had changed, yet everything had. His classes went well; he took pleasure in the talents of several students and his own writing. It seemed to him that he was more adventurous than ever yet still shaped, still available. But *Atlantic Monthly* turned a cold eye on the new pieces, *Harper's* did not answer

47

his agent's queries about a story for over six months, then confessed that they could not find the manuscript. *The New Yorker* was in turmoil with a new editor who valued brevity and fashion. Lipkin was good at neither.

While planning his next book of stories, he shifted his professional energies to his students. Over a drink at The Private Eye, a campus hangout, Karen Kessler, a young MFA candidate with blonde hair almost down to her knees and a beautiful face still unmarked by experience, was doing one of those "it must have been so amazing to win the Pulitzer Prize" numbers on Lipkin, when suddenly he couldn't bear focusing on the past for one more minute. He moved dangerously, on impulse, into the present, the future. "Listen," he said, "I'm going to send your story to *The New Yorker*."

She was breathless. "You'd do that? You think I'd have a chance?"

Karen Kessler wrote fragmentary, first-person, present-tense short bursts of oblique sensibility, undeveloped, as much prose poem as story. She said, "Don Stark likes what I do."

"Does he?" Lipkin wondered what she did beside write that Stark liked. Not good thoughts to have. Saskia was right. He was getting lonely. "Why do you mention Don Stark?"

Karen Kessler giggled. "He says he's your right-hand man, that you rely on his judgment."

Lipkin swallowed this sourly. "Listen," he said. "Don't have too high hopes. I don't seem to be so in touch with the Zeitgeist of publication these days."

"I'm sorry."

"I'm sorry too," he said. "But let's give it a shot." Don Stark, he thought, would have to be put on a shorter leash.

"Right-hand man my ass," Lipkin said at their next scheduled meeting. "Where do you get off with that stuff?"

Stark seemed suddenly shy. "Karen's a real beauty."

"Big surprise. Well I'll thank you not to use me as part of your seduction strategy."

Stark smiled; it was a curve of the full mouth that spoke of some mysterious complicity between them. "Don't thank me. It's all in the game. We all use everything we can to win. You of all people know that. As long as you're straight in your writing, none of the rest matters."

Lipkin observed the younger man puffing contentedly on the third cigarette since the conversation had begun. What was the source, he wondered, of that content. A soggy word; smugness was closer to it. Lipkin didn't like it nor the sophomoric neo-Darwinism it relied on.

"Why me of all people?"

The smile grew more insinuating. "That story of yours. 'The Rage For The Lost Penny.' It's all in there."

"What is?"

"Hey, you're the professor, not me. Read it again."

"I don't read my own work after it's published. You're the student, remember? Just let me read some of your stuff. You're supposed to be turning that story into a novel. Are you ever going to do it?"

Stark's smile became a seditious grin. He pulled a folder out of his scruffy field jacket. "You know what we say when you pull your cards in draw poker?" He handed the folder to Lipkin. "Read 'em and weep." Then he lit still another cigarette from the stub of the last and took off, tossing behind him, "Besides, it's really that Saskia I'm after. But I think she wants you first."

Later, Lipkin paused in his reading of the absolutely powerful chapters to wonder at "wants you first." But as he read on, he found that Stark's language, his feeling for dramatic situations, had all the subtlety of relations, all the nuance of sexual negotiations that he seemed to have difficulty with in everyday life. The work was damned good and something would have to be done about it.

But not just yet. Because the writer/gambler vanished to nearby Santa Fe for a poker marathon which he hoped would give him enough of a stake so that he could quit graduate school and just write. He'd never made any bones about the writing program—it was a means to an end. Speaking of means and ends, Stark was still away when the news hit that Karen Kessler's story was taken by *The New Yorker*.

Just before leaving for the celebrating party—the students used any excuse for a celebration, even if envy lurked around the edges—Lipkin opened a letter from Babette. It was the usual: her job was demanding, Joanie was not doing well at school, Alexandra was. She needed more alimony, call it child support, call it anything you wanted, they relied on him even though he was out of their lives. He tore up the contribution he was about to make to Amnesty International and wrote an extra check for Babette and the girls.

The students made it clear that they relied on him, too. Jerry Hewlett who had been teaching at Tempe forever, greeted him with champagne and the V for Victory sign. "Jesus, Lipkin," he said, "our brochure says we'll do everything we can to further our students careers—translation, get them an agent, or even better, get them published. But you actually do it."

"Well," Lipkin said, stretching a wan smile, "They've been turning me down. I'm glad they'll listen to me about these kids. Maybe the Pulitzer is good for something."

Karen Kessler, smelling from lavender and champagne, kissed him on the mouth.

"Thank you," she murmured.

Across the room he saw Saskia observing them with a kind of prurient look, the way a woman would gaze at a pornographic film—detached but interested in the inevitable outcome—and he remembered Stark's words: "It's really that Saskia I'm after. But I think she wants you first." That *first* was quintessential Stark. The man had a perverse kind of magic. For the first time, with Karen Kessler's lavender kiss still wet on his mouth, Lipkin began to think differently about Saskia.

Thus began a time when Lipkin began to move backwards and his students forward. Charles Forst, a second year transfer student from Iowa who Lipkin had been nurturing won a Whiting award: fifty thousand bucks. The news came the same day another letter came from Babette, this one threatening legal action unless Lipkin increased the alimony by the following month. The irony was not lost on Lipkin. He had been in the running for a Whiting several times and the money would have helped considerably now with the squeeze on, but the Gods had spoken and Forst was the elect. Jeanette Carson, who was half-Cherokee and wrote a tough prose, had two stories taken by *The Atlantic* and won a Guggenheim for which Lipkin had written one of the recommendations.

Mixed magic, all this was, because at the same time Lipkin began to receive letters from *TriQuarterly* and *Iowa Review*, "soliciting material," as they called it. It was as if the word was suddenly out that Lipkin had taken a dive from the exalted horizontal realms of *The New Yorker* and the

Pulitzer Prize to the vertical, geographical universe of the literary quarterlies, which paid in copies and prestige. The fall was dizzying.

There was, these days, no one to whom he could confide the experience. Saskia, perhaps, but somehow he did not wish to continue the "buddy" style of discourse with her. He had other plans for Saskia. So when Stark reappeared from Louisiana, where he'd been on a poker-binge, damned if he didn't seek him out for drinks, dinner and confessional.

Stark was full of beans, having won handsomely in some riverboat poker marathon. He'd insisted on the most elegant restaurant in Tempe—continental for a change instead of Tex-Mex—his treat. Lipkin sat on the edge of his chair, twirling his martini glass in circles while Stark leaned back and drained a draught beer.

"Sorry I missed Karen Kessler's celebration bash, but it was worth it. About eight hundred dollars worth." He looked at Lipkin conspiratorially. "She must kiss the ground you walk on. Or any other parts that are available."

Lipkin tried not to sound, or actually to feel, prissy about parts being kissed in gratitude. "She's pretty happy," he said. "Not so bad being in *The New Yorker* at twenty-four. Like the two Johns."

For once Stark seemed nonplussed. It was pleasant to watch. Lipkin took his time and then said, as if furnishing the answers to a quiz the younger man should have known, "Updike," he said, "and Cheever."

Having taken the high ground for a moment, Lipkin began to unburden himself. He told the younger writer what it was like to feel your work to be naturally central, an art easy in its skin because it sang in a voice it sensed was being listened to, though the song he sang was not what could be called popular and those who listened were certainly one of a few elites in a country that stared at TV more than it read. It was never a question of not being marginal; it was a question of where the margins were drawn, of how far from any center you were; how far in his new shift to that outer area where colleges and universities picked up a torch dropped generations ago by the "little" magazines, whose readers were so often other writers. It was a gentle lament, one Lipkin felt certain that Stark would empathize with.

Not exactly.

"In every field," he said with that peculiar cool worldliness that made him seem years older than his age, "there's a first rank, a second and third and so on." And before Lipkin could object, he added, "don't get me wrong, I mean perceived ranking. It doesn't necessarily mean better or worse, intrinsically. But I'm sure even among geologists there's a big-time place and a small-fry place to publish research. Your time came and went and now it's time for the likes of Charley Forst, Karen and me." The student's brutality was wonderfully casual, its truth and justice assumed.

Lipkin stared at the slouched figure before him, stared in a kind of amazement. "Jesus," he said, "you don't have any brakes, do you?" Lipkin was breathless in some kind of in-verse admiration. Stark shook the last cigarette out of a pack. He gazed at Lipkin as if the older man were a child in need of instruction in the obvious. "Brakes aren't what a car is about," he said. "Moving forward, getting where you're going is." Lipkin became aware that however many cigarettes the man smoked, his breath was innocent of tobacco odor, fresh.

"Which brings me," Stark added, "to my novel. What'd you think?"

Lipkin hesitated, even though he had long since decided that Stark's novel was the real thing, had decided, in fact, that he would call his old editor, Maureen Steinberg, at Random House and ask her to take a look at it. But there was that in him that didn't want to yield too quickly, that felt the rise of this particular student was in some way connected to the decline of his own publishing career. And this particular student, tonight, had let Lipkin have it "full in the face" with that talk about whose time had come and gone and whose time it was now.

"The novel? Well I think you're onto something," Lipkin said.

"Something? That's pretty cryptic."

"Which is more than I can say for you."

"I'm sorry if I hurt your feelings."

"Don't flatter yourself. Anyway, what's interesting about the novel is the mixture of fantasy and the real—especially in the gambling stuff. But—"

Stark was quick on the draw where his own writing was concerned.

"But—" he said. His eyes narrowed and he seemed to hold his breath.

"I don't want to hurt your feelings—" Lipkin enjoyed the moment. "But I'm concerned about your gambling. How will you be able to work consistently? If somebody gave you a leg up, would you deliver, would you finish?" He could hear the priggish tone in his voice and he hated it. Instantly he compensated by making his grand gesture. "I was thinking of sending it to my editor at Random House, Maureen Steinberg."

Lipkin paused to gauge the effect. Nothing. A few puffs. "Okay," Stark said.

"*Okay*? I don't expect you to fall over with joy but *Okay*? Do you know how tough the marketplace is these days?"

"You've been telling me."

"Don't you want to get published?"

"Of course I do. I figured you wouldn't offer unless you thought the stuff was good."

"I wouldn't."

"But would I deliver, finish the book? That's what you're asking . . . ."

Lipkin was silent, out of it. He'd said more than he'd expected. But Stark stood, as if he were the teacher signaling the end of a tutorial. He leaned over Lipkin, breathing at last a foul tobacco breath. This time it was empty of nostalgia.

"Professor Lipkin, you know what Freud said about why writers write."

Lipkin smiled at the pupil playing teacher. How much ground had he lost here?

"Everyone knows that, Stark," he said. "Fame, money and the love of beautiful women."

"There's a fourth one the old man of Vienna didn't know about," Stark said.

"Oh?"

But that *oh* was a cue Stark was not ready to pick up on. This was to be, for the moment, his secret. A weapon, no doubt, in the ambiguous war he waged with the world in general and with his teacher in particular. In lieu of the answer he reached into his case—the case that he had once told Lipkin held a spare toothbrush, a change of underwear, several decks of cards, condoms, usually a sandwich and his current writing—a total, portable life-support system. He pulled out a manila envelope and tossed it at Lipkin. "Here," he said, "more ammunition pro and con."

Over a drink at the campus watering hole he told Saskia of the extraordinary encounter, distracted by the not-so-subtle emanation of perfume when she shrugged her shoulders. He had never noticed how pungent her perfume was, insistent. "I've seen it a lot," she said. "Some students take you for a guru, some compete. It's part of the game."

"He seems to have some ideas about you as well."

"Ah," Saskia said, "he is sniffing around. But I don't quite get his song. Is he a writer or some kind of luftmensch/poker player playing at graduate school?"

"Maybe all of the above," Lipkin said and he told her about Stark's Freudian theory as yet unrevealed.

"Fame, money and the love of beautiful women," she murmured and then laughed. "I wonder what this mysterious fourth could be."

There was a pause, a moment in which she seemed to lean forward, though she had actually not moved an inch. Lipkin froze. It was as if the figure of Stark, their attempts to figure him out, passed between them and kept them apart.

In the days that followed Lipkin decided to go ahead with the plan to push Stark's novel with Maureen Steinberg at Random House. This new material Stark had tossed at him so casually, almost contemptuously, had been the final touch: strong, witty, dark, a touch brutal, it reminded him of his first readings of Celine, the shock, the seductiveness of the language. Lipkin was suspicious of his own judgment in this situation and welcomed the notion of an outside reaction. Maureen was tough, smart, fair.

In the meantime his own literary life seemed to go in several directions at once. The places that welcomed his work were growing more and more arcane. He thought the final touch came when the *Chattahattee Review* awarded him first prize in a contest he'd never entered. He had no idea where Chattahattee was and he doubted that magazines could get more obscure. Ironically, at the same time Robin Fox, the house poet, well-connected as so many poets are, told him she'd heard somebody in the department was up for a

MacArthur. She assumed it was Lipkin. "We all knew you were a genius," she said. "Maybe now everyone will know." But she would not reveal where she'd heard the word or how reliable it was. Also, Sarah's mother tongue was irony, so Lipkin didn't quite know how to take this.

Maureen Steinberg was eager to read Stark's stuff. "Frankly, Leo," she confided, "I'm under quite a lot of pressure to deliver young writers. Kids with a number of books in them."

"This kid is thirty-four," Lipkin said dryly, and mailed the MS that day. There seemed to be some connection between that action and his next, which was to call Saskia for a date. And Lipkin was determined it would be a date, an end to the buddy-buddy stuff. The conversation would contain no reference to Stark. Things were going along smoothly, discussing the sexual harassment suit against one of their colleagues—any mention of sex in any context seemed to strike the right note—when Saskia, sipping red wine in just the languorous way Lipkin had looked forward to, said: " I hear you sent the bad boy's novel to Random House. You are being Lord Bountiful."

"You can't let personal feelings or irritations get between you and what you think of somebody's writing."

She leaned over the table shedding perfume and giving her voice the edge he'd been hoping for, said, "So—writing's your—"

"It's what some of us have instead of God." And they both laughed and clinked glasses at the Hemingway reference, and at Saskia's place she did not suggest his coming up, and her goodnight kiss was half buddy and something new that neither of them could as yet figure out. Maybe, Lipkin thought later, *The Sun Also Rises* echo has not been such a good idea: a cab ride with an impotent man and a nymphomaniac.

As if to authenticate his extreme response to Stark's transgression, Maureen Steinberg called bubbling with enthusiasm: . . . ". . . real find, powerful, funny, wild . . . He's fresh and unsettling. It will be noticed . . . I'll offer a contract and advance . . . is his address still the same . . .? When do you think he'll finish it?"

"Got me. Ask him."

"I tried. There's no answer and no machine."

Lipkin got the message. Stark was undoubtedly off on one of his gambling binges. But all he said was, "When I see him I'll ask him to call."

"I read about your 'mini' award," Maureen said. "Congratulations. It's all in *PW*."

Lipkin sent a graduate student to the library to get a copy of *Publishers Weekly*, but by that time the letter had arrived. The Association of Little Magazines gave an award each year to the best writer who graced the pages of the various quarterlies, from *Boulevard* to *Zyzzyva*. A far cry from The *New Yorker* or *Atlantic*, but what the hell. In his new incarnation such things seemed to count. The award was called, without irony, the "Mini" and with it came a scroll, five hundred dollars and a bitter taste of doing everything in his life backwards. From the Pulitzer Prize to the "Mini" award in only a few years. He could hardly wait for Stark's reaction.

That night Lipkin, for some reason, stayed up until after midnight working over his book of stories, mysteriously exhilarated. For the first time he saw them as connected: by theme, by occasional repeated character, a seamless whole in the middle stitching stage. It was going to be damned good, and it dwarfed all the new feelings in his life, satisfaction at teaching well, pleasure at discovering a young writer who was the real McCoy, amused irony over getting a "Mini" this late in his career. Nothing seemed to matter except that the new book was going to be original, strong. He worked until four a.m. and fell asleep at his desk for the first time since his twenties.

As it turned out, the "Mini" award came attached to a banquet: one of those academic things that began with cocktails at six (a cash bar), dinner at seven and home by nine-thirty. Naturally the invisible Stark was suddenly most visible.

"Hey, Professor, how does it feel?"

"How does what feel?"

"To be the one-eyed man in the country of the blind."

"Listen, Stark, just because you've been in the *Atlantic* . . . ."

"The magazine of William Dean Howells, Henry James . . . . " His country-boy grin made it hard to gauge the distance between his natural pride and natural wit.

"You've been in it once."

"So far. Okay, forget the country of the blind. Just enjoy being king of a very small kingdom for a night."

It struck Lipkin that these half jocular, half bitter exchanges helped him keep his balance in this unfamiliar terrain. He needed this competitive, contemptuous, gifted challenger to keep him on his toes—a sparring partner who occasionally drew blood, reminding Lipkin he was still alive.

"Listen," he said, "Maureen Steinberg likes your book. But she can't find you."

"In the nick of time. I was in New Orleans. Took a beating."

"How does it feel?"

"What? Losing over five hundred bucks?"

"Having your book accepted."

Stark surprised him. His moon face turned grave. "I've changed a lot of it since. It may not be the book she thinks she wants."

Lipkin put his arm around the younger man. Wise, avuncular; he could see himself acting it out. "It's you she wants. Your take, your slant, your energy. You're on your way." He did not wait for thanks. If you don't have expectations you don't have disappointments. He left Stark to contemplate the change from a writer manqué to an accepted one and moved into the fray.

Some of Lipkin's colleagues had turned out, too. Robin Fox, sans her usual skirt and sweater, swathed in some sort of sari-like wraparound, looked more festive than the occasion would seem to warrant.

"Remember when I told you one of our gang was up for a MacArthur?" Her grin combined with the unusual costume told him all he had to know.

"Congratulations," Lipkin said.

"Tomorrow's papers."

Trying not to figure her age and the consequent dollar amounts it would bring, Lipkin turned back to being the king of a very small kingdom for a night. At the cash bar he encountered Richard Parnell, who'd taught English for thirty years and who had his own special reason for being glad to see Lipkin. It seemed he had a student, quite brilliant but whose final paper had the smell of plagiarism about it.

"Could you help me out here," Parnell said. "It's postmodernism, not something I usually do. I'm Modern British. It's just that some of it sounds so awfully familiar. I've actually brought it. I knew you'd help out."

After a few too many drinks, after his acceptance speech, which Lipkin gave without irony, no big fish in small ponds stuff, he danced with Robin Fox to dispel any shadow of envy; also she looked rather seductive—was it her wrap-around, did success lend sensuality, or was he hungrier than he allowed himself to admit?

Unable to answer himself, he went wearily home and read the paper, which he knew in his heart had to be by Stark.

It was a clever amalgam of several pieces by Bernard Bergonzi and a little-known Romanian critic, Enesco, who'd been obsessed early on by John Barth, Barthelme, and Borges. Only a few essays had been translated and Stark had come on one or two of them. There weren't too many who would have caught it. In its own way it was brilliantly done. It was Stark's bad luck that Lipkin knew Enesco's work. But it was Stark's good luck that Lipkin was too heavily invested in his young anti-protégé to scuttle him because of a term paper. Also, there was enough of Stark's sharp-edge take on the three B's to prevent it from being an open and shut case. Besides, you didn't become a Random House author and get prosecuted for plagiarism in the same week. Lipkin picked up the phone with the sense that he was entering a new sphere—a new way of being—a not entirely pleasant sensation.

"It's okay," he told Parnell, "there are echoes but not serious enough to invalidate the whole paper."

Like a character out of Dostoevsky, he sought out Saskia and confessed what he'd done. "Big deal," Saskia said when he'd laid out for her what he thought of as his defection from some universal norm. "Look," she said in a tone Lipkin felt was more intimate than the one he was accustomed to hearing from Saskia, "you cut a small corner for a guy—I say small because the paper wasn't a total lift—for a guy you think is a real writer, the genuine article."

"I don't think, I know. And now an editor I respect agrees."

She shrugged this last off. This was between the two of them. "And didn't you tell me writing was sort of what you had instead of God."

He grinned. "You knew that was a pastiche of a famous scene in Hemingway."

"Yes," she said. "And the next line is 'Some people have God quite a lot.'" She leaned back, fielded an arch look, and crossed and uncrossed her legs. "Because it's a takeoff on Hemingway, does that mean it's not true for you?"

"I don't quite know. But I'm sure being pushed these days. Babette says it's all I ever paid attention to when we were married. Now I'm writing my heart and head out and I'm as good as I ever was. And after my Maxi-days and Pulitzer Prize I'm King Mini of the quarterlies. And to top it off I've got Stark pushing me to the edge."

"I said you were lonely," Saskia said. "And lonely people sometimes make strange decisions." They'd left The Coffee Grind and were at her door. She paused. "Want to come in?" He practically fell over the lintel following her. Still, after an enchanting preliminary wrestling match she breathed into his ear. "I can't believe I brought an old friend out here and now—"

He waited, having no choice. "But not yet . . . this . . . ," she said. There followed a bout of skirt straightening and erection hiding. Before he left, as if it might have some connection to the evening's events, he had to ask, "Is Stark still buzzing around?"

She nodded. "When he's around he buzzes."

"Has he landed?"

"No, still buzzing. I think he's having a thing with Karen what's-her-name, the one you got published in *The New Yorker.*"

She stepped outside with him in the Arizona night, cool, still damp from the day. "It's a new life for you, Leo. I pulled you out of New York into this desert, I feel responsible."

"Teaching saved my ass. I'm not equipped to do much except write."

Saskia sighed. "God I'm glad I never wanted to write a book."

"But you had to—that one on Blake for your doctorate."

"That was a bookoid. Write one, get your Ph.D., and settle down to teaching. The students aren't bad. It's a good life all in all." She kissed Leo on the cheek. "You guys are involved in some battle of compulsions. I'm glad I'm just a spectator."

"Thanks for salving my conscience, tonight."

Her laugh was distant. "That's me: Superegos repaired on the premises."

The next morning there was a letter from Kim, his Korean adoptee, in his mailbox. As always he thanked Lipkin for the monthly check. He spoke of coming to America. "I would like to go to Columbia University in New York City," he wrote. Lipkin did not want to think about Babette's request that he stop those checks and send them to his own children. God, you had to do something in the world that wasn't about you and your own. There was a world elsewhere. And speaking of money, the advance from Maureen Steinberg turned out to be twenty thousand bucks.

"But I only get half on signing," Stark complained. They were going over some student papers when he dropped the news about the Random House money.

"That's the way it's done," Lipkin told him. "You can't expect them to pay you the whole amount till you've finished the book."

"It would be a hell of a stake."

"You're supposed to live on it while you finish the book, not gamble it away."

Impatient, Stark muttered, "I'll live, I'll live . . . and I'll finish."

Lipkin said not a word about the dubious paper. If you did something, you did it with a whole heart, not a half-ass. But Stark, truer than ever, proceeded to test him even further. The semester was on its way out and students were making plans for the following year when Lipkin found in his office mail a note and an application form.

Dear Professor Lipkin (Stark continued the absurd formality),

I want to apply for a Whittinger Fellowship for next year. It's twenty-five grand and with your endorsement I'd be a shoo-in. Thanks.

Don Stark

The application form had the usual questions: How long have you known the applicant? How would you rate his literary abilities? So far easy enough. Then: tell us what you think of his reliability, responsibility and a general evaluation of his character.

Push was definitely coming to shove. Lipkin had himself won a Whittinger Fellowship when young. Young and, he had to admit, not so buttoned up that he did not require a little forbearance from his recommenders. He was twenty-five, had dropped out of Columbia and Penn State. He had no idea of what he wanted from life except that he had to write. George Barclay, his good gray professor, had blinked at some of the courses Lipkin claimed as his bona fides—several of which he'd enrolled in but did not complete. No one knew this better than his advisor, Professor Barclay. But he wrote the recommendation anyway, The Whittinger had come through (though it was only five thousand then, but five thousand went a long way in the seventies), Lipkin had written his first novel and he was on his way. This memory of his good luck would be Stark's good luck. Not a word about plagiarism or irresponsibility. He would speak of an astonishing talent, already being recognized by a major publisher. He would fudge his way through the rest of the letter and Stark would be on his way (as if he weren't already).

Lipkin made a rough draft and called Stark. No answer and no machine. It was close to term's end and Lipkin also needed him for some scut work but he was nowhere. In desperation he called Karen Kessler, giving credence to Saskia's gossip about their affair. The young woman was stiff, cool. She had no idea where Stark might be.

"I thought you two were—friends."

She laughed, a little hysterically, Lipkin thought. "No euphemisms, Professor Lipkin, that's what you taught me. You mean were we screwing." Then just as suddenly she began to weep, not great heaving sobs, just a kind of wounded mewing. "Screwing, right, he screwed me good.'

"What . . . ?"

"He borrowed four thousand dollars—the money I got from *The New Yorker*—I was saving towards a year in New York to just write."

Sick in his stomach Lipkin said, helpless, "But it's a loan."

"He said he lost it—in a game in Phoenix. You know he'll never pay it back." She breathed more steadily. "And he's broken off with me. It's over. Screwed."

In a fury of frustration Lipkin searched out Saskia in her office at school. Buried behind a mountain of books and papers, she could still not defend herself against a Lipkin pushed beyond endurance.

"Listen," he said, "are you and Stark what you called a thing?"

She looked at him, an unaccustomed pair of horn rims perched on her nose. "Well, since you've bearded me in my den: yes, but only once. Then he went off to Phoenix to a big game."

Lipkin told her about Karen Kessler and she grew somber, not her usual mode. When he pressed her, she gave him the address of the hotel and the apartment where the game was being played. She'd kept track of Stark's whereabouts. The "thing" was apparently not played out yet.

Lipkin threw stuff into an overnight bag and headed for Phoenix. It was night by the time he was on the road, one of those cold clear nights, dark blue but dotted white with a million stars that reminded him the desert was all around; reminded him that he was forty-eight years old and in Tempe, Arizona, a strange new place, embarked on a strange new life, his writing still strong but headed for strange new destinations; he had seen Andrea and Joanie only once in the past year and he thought of them with a distant ache; Babette had now become an adversary and shared no part of this sudden nostalgia.

The ephemerality of things swept into him, a marriage of eighteen years, a New York way of life all vanished in months. He drove with a strong sense of purpose, he would right a wrong, set things straight with this gifted young son-of-a-bitch. What the fuck had happened to the money from Random House that made it essential to take poor Karen Kessler for such a ride? But along with this was a vague sense of something unresolved in his own life, some testing of who he really was, some balance of powers that had yet to declare itself.

It was a four-hour drive to Phoenix, the passing scene — cactus and mesas — as bleak as the prospect before him. The shimmering horizons of heat added to the surreal sense of the whole journey. The hotel came up bare and Lipkin was forced to track Stark down to the actual poker scene. And scene it was, like some bad movie, ashtrays brimming with butts, men in shirtsleeves, beer cans everywhere (and surprisingly one middle-aged woman, plump and smiling, a winner for the night, perhaps). Stark showed no surprise at his appearance and the game appeared to be winding down.

There was a coffee shop nearby (it was extraordinary to Lipkin that after a life of exchanged dinner parties in New York he seemed always to be seeing people in coffee shops and bars). His rage was slightly blunted by actually having to confront Stark in the flesh. He looked more tired than he'd ever seen him. He carried, as always, the case which held his entire life.

"How'd you do tonight?" Lipkin asked.

"Broke even. Which is good because I can use the money." Stark offered up a wan smile. "An old gambler's joke," he said. "What's up, Professor? You're a long way from home."

The bitter coffee fueled Lipkin up again. "What the hell did you do to poor Karen Kessler! Where do you get off fucking up her life, her plans for a year in New York; what happened to the Random House money? Jesus, you are one piece of work."

Stark shrugged. "Karen's a grown-up. She can take care of herself. And the advance didn't cut it. But," he sat up straighter, his bloodshot eyes wider and brighter, "the novel is really moving. It's taken a terrific turn; the energy level is so strong I can hardly keep up with it." He smiled at Lipkin as if he were a child expecting a reward for especially good behavior.

"You're getting too off-the-wall, Don. One bad number after another." And he told him about Parnell and the doubtful paper.

"I was in a hurry for that one and I couldn't stop my own stuff just to do a lot of original research for a term paper. You know how it is, Professor, when the writing's hot, you stay with it, no matter what."

"Don't pull me into your cesspool. You're a cold, manipulating bastard. You don't care who you hurt or what rules you break."

Stark rubbed his stubbled cheek. He waited a long time before he spoke. He pushed cups and a sugar shaker out of the way so as to have a direct view and eye contact with Lipkin and measured out his words one by one, slow and strong. "I don't care about stuff like that," he said. "Because writing is the only thing that matters." He paused, the student teaching the teacher an unpleasant lesson, the next words coming out with a genuine push, none of his usual irony, no sloppy sarcasm: this was all passion, from behind gritted teeth. "Everything except writing is shit."

The rage that had brought Lipkin on his sudden nighttime mission returned instantly, a storm that needed no gathering force. "Everything else is shit? A girl's money, faking papers." What are you, some kind of half-assed, pseudomandarin amoral esthete? What are you, a Raskolnikov of writing? Who the fuck do you think you are? What gives you the right?"

By way of reply Stark reached into his omnipresent case, pulled out a manila envelope and tossed it onto the table. For some reason he could not explain to himself Lipkin jammed the envelope into his own traveling case—an automatic response—regardless of anger, a student gives you a manuscript, you take it. Seeing Stark's fixed expression, the cool resuming of drinking his coffee, Lipkin expected and wanted no further answer.

He slammed out of the bar and drove home in a sweat of anger and confusion. Why not cut off the son-of-a-bitch without another word. Fuck him and his fellowship application!

"What was in the envelope?" Saskia asked. She had made a dinner for them the next night, lobsters. A rarity in land-locked Arizona.

Lipkin was mellower, a few glasses of wine and the sense that intimacy was in the air, the intimacy of a confidante and also something more still to be explored.

"The next piece of his novel: the big center-piece."

"And?"

"At first I was too pissed off to look at it. When I finally did, it didn't cool me off towards this prick . . . ."

Saskia was easy in her silk lounging pajamas, easy in her skin, easy in their shared knowledge of the strange young man. "And it was good," she said. "Very good."

Lipkin tossed off his glass and grinned, bitter. "It was better than that. How'd you know? But can you imagine *everything except writing is shit.* And he meant it—passionately. Can you feature that for a way to justify anything, all the dishonest crap he's pulled, how's that for a world view?"

Later, when the circling was over and the clothing strewn around the bedroom, after the lovemaking, which felt to

Lipkin like the closing of something rather than a beginning, he said: "What happened with you and him? Why?"

She was drowsy and murmured, "When he wants something, he wants it very much."

Lipkin waited and finally said, "And then?"

Her eyes were closed. "And then maybe he wants something else. It doesn't matter to me any more than to him."

She rolled over onto her side facing him, a passionate but cool woman, moving gracefully into middle-age, given up on long-term commitments but still interested in experience. "What is it with you two?" she murmured. "There's something I can't figure out. You don't really like each other, but you're tied together like two men climbing a mountain peak."

"You mean if one falls, the other falls. I don't think so."

"No, there's some stranger connection."

"Don't tell me. Now that we're actually in bed together you're not going to give me the old Freudian hidden homosexual stuff—the two men going through you but really wanting each other."

Saskia was silent. Then: "I think it's something much stranger than that. What are you going to do—about him?"

"Fuck him." He laughed. "But not in the sense we were just talking about."

He did not stay, an early class in the morning had to be met, with material still at home. Saskia was asleep. He looked at her, curved in the bed like a question mark, stared at her long, before he left. She was still the friend who had brought him out here, had changed his life, probably nothing more, even now. Later at home, in spite of the remembered pleasures of the evening, he was restless. He knew that his tough talk about Stark was a kind of bravado. In spite of his anger, his disgust at the casual dismissal of all natural human concerns, it wasn't that simple. He lay in bed for a while wondering why he had gone so crazy at Stark's outburst. Oh, it was ugly enough, but something pulsed beneath the words that pushed and pulled at Lipkin. He felt feverish, got up and splashed cold water on his face. He did not put the light on in the bathroom. He had, at that moment, no desire to see himself in the mirror.

Instead, he pulled out his own work in progress, the book of stories he'd been working on slowly, steadily, the book which was growing longer and taking more chances with narrative structure, letting characters interweave, hanging everything on the voice—he should have his own voice by now, he told himself. He stared at the book, wondering for the first time if it would find a place in the world, that mythical place where people read your sentences and made sense of them for their own lives. He turned the pages in a kind of exhilaration, thinking, *it matters and it doesn't matter*. In both cases it was life and death; almost nobody could know what it cost you to add a line or change a phrase, to give a character a destiny no one had anticipated, not even the character, what it cost to make it inevitable.

But the cost was repaid in full—witness the wild middle-of-the night excitement he and his manuscript were sharing. Towards dawn he heard thunder, followed by one of those cloudbursts you got in Arizona, in exchange for months of dusty, dry heat. It felt like a relief, as if something had been held in for too long and at last was released.

In the morning he knew precisely what he had to do. He went to his desk and wrote the recommendation: Stark was reliable, Stark had genuine character, Stark could be depended on to follow through on any and all tasks, Stark was a major literary talent, an artist: all lies except one.

He sealed the envelope, feeling as if he were somehow sealing his own fate.

The campus bookstore's air-conditioning was barely breathing. There, between poetry and biography, he encountered the subject of so much of his recent turmoil. Stark looked, if possible, even grungier than usual, a stubble of several days growth, a torn T-shirt that read *Jack Kerouac*, smudges of dirt at the neckline.

Lipkin had to give a talk at the library later in the day so he'd put on a shirt and tie, flannel slacks and blazer, the expected uniform, even though the downpour had not eased the awful heat and his collar was already soaked. The contrast in dress somehow made their unexpected meeting even more awkward.

He'd never seen Stark at a loss for words before—a lot of shifting of feet, craning of the neck. Having come a long way since their last enraging confrontation, Lipkin could only say, stiffly, "That letter you needed for the Fellowship. It's been written." He noted his own use of the passive form. In how many classes had he recited the litany: the passive form is dishonest, passing the buck. "The Jews were murdered in the Holocaust." Wrong: "Germans murdered the Jews."

He added needlessly, as if to drive the point home, "I wrote it and I've mailed it." There was no going back, he was saying, but Stark had no way of knowing what he meant.

Suddenly Stark's awkwardness vanished. "Hey, Professor," he said, "great news. Then I'm in like Flynn."

"Don, it's time you called me Leo."

"Sure, sure. Leo. How about a drink to celebrate?" His face was shiny with sweat and triumph.

Lipkin was sure he knew what it had cost him to write that letter. "Okay," Lipkin said. "I've got an hour or so before my lecture." He was feeling sick, a kind of sick despair that settled in the stomach like guilt, like losing more at poker than you could afford, like fear.

The heat outside hit them—a bright wet wall, but the bar was cool, dark. "Here's to us," Stark held up his glass for him to click in ritual toast. *What the hell*, Lipkin thought, *What the hell*, as he raised his glass, the two of them huddled safe against the savage Arizona summer, one of them enjoying the temporary caress of fortune, the other feeling the pinch of loss, one taking on the pleasures of his careless spring, the other suffering the beginning of his winter and beginning to understand his fate. *What the hell*, Lipkin thought, staring at the self-absorbed, moon-faced young man, wondering what it was that drew him, moth and flame-like to this connection, what had made him fill a letter of recommendation to the Whittinger Foundation, a first-rate place of honor, with outright lies; what kinship was it that Saskia had seen, had pursued into his bed, getting, in some odd way, two of them at a blow.

And of course he knew now that it was not so mysterious, that it had been hidden but clear from the start—that this weird flake of a Philadelphia gambler believed, as he, Lipkin, did and had all along, even though they both lived out their daily lives so differently, somewhere beneath the lacquered care of his daily life, his hard-earned child support, beneath the order of his essentially decent behavior, beneath his adoption of the Korean child Kim with his letters of encouragement about school, about some day coming to America, beneath his donations of support to Amnesty International, still what he believed was that writing was everything, that everything else, family, universities, morality, how you treated women, how you dealt with the institutions of the world, even what happened to the writing—The *New Yorker* or the *Grabass Review*—he believed that finally, everything, except the writing, was shit. The two of them, one suited and burnished by the middle class, the other scruffy with grunge, none of these differences counted; extremists of the word, they were like two terrorists of the imagination, men who knew better than the rest of the world what counted, bombs in hand, brothers in a mad prison of their own devising, caring little for the sufferings of other people who were merely real.

What the hell, Lipkin thought, raising his glass and planning the rest of his life, laughing at himself and the silly pun that sprang forward, *What the hell*, he thought, *there's more than one kind of fellowship*.

Use Me

The strange, whispered phrase came at just the right, and just the wrong moment. One of those moments when you are moving from one connection—I won't call them positions because, unless you're a particularly cool character that's not how you think of it when you're in the middle—when say the man is withdrawing, slick, still in working order, still on call, eager to continue, and the woman moves, say to the side or onto her stomach either in response to an inner instinctive urge, or to a request or perhaps in instinctive balletic response to the way the man is turning. I mean where you are, spatially, is important to both, how you move yourself or how your partner moves, where you or your lover (if love is present, and it is very much present here) bend or don't bend, give or don't give; or, indeed, how you may move each other.

Of course, everything depends on how wordless or how verbal the play is. Is it mostly mime or is it drama? (comedy being, for the moment, out); couples and individuals differ. But either way, communication for change in the shifting situation is always possible. So is mis-communication. Anyway, it was at just such a fluid moment, the esthetic, lyric and physical outcome entirely in question, happily nowhere near resolution, that Sarah, turning onto her stomach, murmured the two words, "*Use me . . . .*"

They struck Marcus as some weird kind of demand, but also a sort of confession, perhaps *not* requiring action, perhaps only a psychological state, less even, a mood. Still, it seemed to require *some* response. In these matters, character is everything. By which I mean, who is saying the words and who is hearing them. Bear in mind this speaker—murmurer, actually—is Sarah Sonnenberg, the rising star at the New

York Psychoanalytic, the leader of the non-medical psycho-
therapists, a kind of combined Kohut and Kernberg—she'd
worked with both of them—full of empathy, yet cool,
neutral where appropriate, forthcoming when useful, always
in control of counter-transference (see her paper: "The
Counter-Transference In Dual Reconstruction of a Border-
line Narcissist"—*Journal of Psychoanalytic Studies*, Spring
1997). Sarah Sonnenberg, the first lay analyst ever allowed to
participate in the training process; a new program designed
to broaden the traditional, detached Freudian treatment; a
program to help the Institute reach out into the community
with fresh therapeutic resources and maybe open a road out
of the dead end of insurance coverage. A feminist who had,
in addition, opened up areas of consonance between anti-
Freudian feminists and the analytic community. While, apparently with one hand tied behind her, writing a definitive
study of sexual motifs in the surrealist films of the twenties:
Bunuel, Hans Richter, Duchamp.

This, then, was the extraordinarily accomplished woman,
a powerhouse, who, turning, face down on the bed, her satin-
white skin sheened with sweat, lying in her long bed of
burnished red hair had said, if he had heard correctly, "Use
me!" For an instant Marcus wonders had she said, "Lose
me"? That didn't make any sense. Could she have said, "Bruise
me"? Ridiculous! It couldn't be "Choose me," he'd chosen
her months ago—in truth, of course, she'd chosen him; he'd
been sort of a visitor in his own life, moving in and out of
different situations, had given up on the idea that some day
he might own a life of his own. The trick to that was, of
course, to meet someone like Sarah—a dumb notion, he'd
never encountered anyone like Sarah—in touch with her
own emotions and at the same time plugged into the enormously charged electric current of her career. No, not career,
more than that, an intellectual life so lived that the ideas that
informed it might flow from Winnicott, from Nietszche,
from Freud or just that morning's *New York Times*—otherwise known as reality. Yet it was her intel-lectual life, so at
home with complex thought, Keats' man (okay, woman) of
Negative Capability, holding all sorts of conflicting notions
in balance while choosing between courses of action that
would help patients, help her finish a new book, help her
talk to one of her children's teachers—that intellecual life

consonant with concern over her three children from two marriages, three jobs at two institutions, squeezing in appointments with her broker, with a French feminist theorist in from the Sorbonne, with her hair colorist.

To make things even worse, the sexual melody improvised between Sarah and Marcus, which had begun in the usual imperfect way, had arrived at a fine song; it had taken weeks to clue each other in, wordless, picking up on the way Sarah liked her clitoris touched, not too lightly because that only tickled, preferring a strong stroke, like pizzicato on a string; picking up on the way Marcus liked his ear to be licked, explored by her tongue, while he kissed the broad round target of her nipples. He had been a musician, played sax as a young man to help pay for his education at Wisconsin and later at Columbia for his graduate work, and this had felt like jamming just right. And now Sarah had torn the delicate give and take by murmuring this mysterious phrase.

Marcus hovered over her, thrown for a loss. "Use me!" Since the two—word phrase had arrived at the moment when she'd turned on her stomach, was it a simple matter of a different opening? If he arrived inside her by a different entrance would that be less mutually balanced, would that be *using* her more than the other two more traditional places in which to place one's calling card? Was the anus so much less a particularly responsive part of Sarah that opening it to his attentions would be equivalent to turning her, for that moment, into an object? God! The people who attacked pornography had the wrong end of the stick—the problem was not the proliferation of hateful imaginative acts, of using women as objects instead of as responsive beings with their own pleasures to be taken into account, no, it was the limited resources of the human anatomy.

The sexual life could learn from the medical world. Marcus's Uncle Karl had had an angioplasty in which they inserted a wire into his groin and ran it into his heart—not the first time those two had been connected. Later, a nurse had fed a tube into his stomach through a nostril. All of it much more imaginative than whoever was in charge of the basic sexual arangements; leaving us to the Marquis de Sade and his rage at the paucity of possibilities, with his whips, chains and mutilations, his rejection of the all too few entrance points: vagina, mouth, anus. Some men just can't take three for an answer!

How many variations were possible before you ended up in low comedy? The ear, why not the ear for a laugh? It was concave, allowed for a modest entrance; the nose was too small, too disgusting even for comedy, even for an adolescent boy; the hand too, like the solitary self-education of youth; one could actually wrap the penis in a woman's hair, Sarah's was long, rippling, red for passion and temper, the images justified in her case, a short fuse in anger a longer one in physical love. But hair had no sensitivity for the woman, would produce only another sort of masturbation—ah, were any of these, then, what she had meant—do something in which she would take only minimal part, reducing the encounter to user and usee?

Marcus touched her hair. Use me, lose, bruise me . . . why not soothe me, why only credit the dark, aggressive side, accuse me, or lurking in the blackness of speculation, the worst one: abuse me. After all, he'd only known Sarah for eight weeks; he was a research psychologist, now, with a specialty in genetics—they'd met at a conference at Colgate—but he'd had patients in the past, knew that eight weeks was about right for hidden predilections to show up, confidence established, a modicum of security, and BANG a woman asks you to abuse her, it's what turns her on, only needing the establishment of trust before unveiling the dark secret. A friend of his who taught in a humanities program at a university in the West, had told him of a woman, pulled this way and that by passion, asking him to urinate on her. "I will not piss on a human being," his friend had told him, firm in his humanism but bemused, troubled by the many roads that led to sexual Rome for his beloved humans. Marcus had actually thought of telling his friend that he was being cruel in denying the woman her source of pleasure in the service of a moral position but had thought better of it.

Use me . . . choose me . . . lose me . . . soothe me . . . abuse me . . . It was becoming a problem in ryhme, but not as in a poem, more like the infernal drumbeat of a rap lyric, the endless, repetitious stringing together of rhyme justifying itself without recourse to reason, to understanding. He was falling into the trap of the ruling, irrational notions of the mind. "Sarah," he would say, attacking her religion, "the notion of the unconscious as this great teeming cesspool which determines our lives is just not scientific. You can't falsify it so you can't verify it; you can't prove anything by it. It may even have some truth to it, but that's a hell of a distance from assuming it's a fact." He'd played a seduction game the first time they'd met by telling her of a paper he was writing, debunking Freud's topography of the unconscious. (There was no such paper, but he sensed it was a way to get her attention.) "Where Id was there shall Ego be. Do you really think you can replace parts of the mind with other parts, parts which are present during life but suddenly vanish when you dissect the brain of a cadaver?"

The Prince of Reason, holding the feet of Psychoanalysis to the fire of scientific proof, while Sarah, in her dealing with patients was famous for being one of those Zen masters who learned everything there was to know about the theory and practice of archery and then, at the central moment, just closed her eyes and—bull's eye.

He could, of course, simply ask her what she'd said, but the moment was too fragile for: "What was that you said just now?" Not exactly bed-talk. Or, "Excuse me, did you say, *use me*?" More appropriate for a musical comedy than for a sequence in the sexual poem in the process of being written *a deux*. Amazingly, under the stress of thought, his passion had not subsided, he was still ready to continue. All this took, of course, not the time it takes to read it or the time it would have taken for him to think this—sexual time is not real time, it is, rather, instantaneous as dreams which sometimes seem to take an entire night but are actually measured in a few seconds.

In a sudden inspiration, he realizes he has an unused option: ignore it, act as if he'd heard nothing, it was after all only a murmur. Which option inspires him to resume, *a posteriore*, the momentarily interrupted lovemaking. She seems to both yield and actively respond at the same time, which arouses him still further. They come together, as if in some sex manual of the fifties or an issue of *Cosmopolitan* and he collapses on her sweaty back, his heart still wild but the racing of his mind, for the moment, stilled.

After a half dozen breaths Sarah reaches an arm out from under their tangle of arms and legs and takes the phone. "Have to call Annette," she is still in her murmuring mode but he hears this as clearly as if she had whispered into his ear. Is it only problematic phrases which feel inadequately enunciated? Annette is Sarah's eight-year-old daughter and in the harmonics of her voice she has made the transition from lover to mother in seconds. Marcus does not listen using the moment to withdraw and head for the bathroom. Sarah's children are off-limits to Marcus until Sarah decides where he fits in her life, in her many lives. Two girls and a boy, they are sophisticated kids, having lived, when Sarah was married to her two European husbands, in more capitals than Marcus had ever visited.

By the time he is back she is off the phone. Surprising himself, he actually asks her, what was so unaskable in the heat of sexual play. Sarah, putting on her pantyhose, looks up in that startled way she had of combining surprise with reproach.

She gave a last tug and turned to him. "I said, *Amuse me*. I was trying to lighten the moment, we've been getting so intense. I don't know, I think I just wanted to be playful. Why, what did you think I said?"

"I don't exactly know," he said. "I don't know." He held his breath as if that would help say the words when he finally released it. "I thought maybe you said, *Use me*."

She looked at him under lowered lids, creased forehead. "*Use me . . .* ," she murmured though it sounded quite different now, reflective, analytic. "Did that excite you? That idea?"

He shook his head. "I don't know. I think I was too startled."

"Why? Did you think I was too—what—middle-class, too together, too independent, too feminist, too healthy for that?"

He took a few steps towards her, a long walk under this pressure, and cradled her tightly, as if she might be in some way getting away from him. "All of the above, I think."

She laughed but with her mouth closed. "Are we back in that cesspool you called my precious unconscious. You've just had, it seems to me, a parapraxis. It's not *my* unconscious we're talking about here. Mishearing can be as revealing as misspeaking."

"Oh, God, Sarah."

"I know, you're not a patient, this isn't a session and I never do this stuff. But—" She rotated in his arms to gaze up at him; she was tiny, he was almost six feet. "*Breathes there a man with soul so dead*, he's never wanted the woman of his dreams—I am that, aren't I?—to say something like she's abandoning control, giving up control of her own sexual existence for one moment to become the complete obscure object of his desire?" Ever the film buff using Bunuel to make her point. "And isn't it even more exciting if she's a woman who—well, does a lot on her own, doesn't usually defer much to men?"

"Defer at all . . ."

"Okay, right, at all."

He'd never felt less like grinning but he had to force a grin. "Is this a test?" he asked. "Are you telling me you *did* say it? Or just that I may have wanted to hear it? And don't ask me what do *I* think, Doctor Sonnenberg."

She tapped a kiss onto his lips, not staying, just an exclamation point. "I'm telling you that if we're in this for the long haul, and we may be, then you should know how you feel about me."

"You mean—love?"

"God, no. I'm going to assume that. I mean things like, are you a man who wants a strong woman he can dominate? Can *use*?"

"And are you a woman who wants to be *amused* so as not to get too serious, too heavy?"

"Maybe, I don't think so, but it doesn't matter. What *does* matter is: we should get a fix on the games each of us likes to play in bed and out. If you want to *use me*—figure out what that would be and ask me."

From the first Marcus had felt a little out of his league in the boldness department. Sarah took whatever ball was in the air and ran with it much more swiftly than he. The first evening at a New York Hospital Christmas party for the department, he'd been with a colleague, a researcher, pretty, very tall, very interested. And when Sarah intervened saying, "Take me home," she knew exactly what she was doing. He dumped the researcher as best he could, lame excuses and all, and took Sarah home. The children were away at various sleepovers, fathers and friends, and afterwards Sarah said, "How does it feel to have started whatever we've started with a nasty, unethical act?"

"Strange," Marcus said. "Not my kind of thing. I've *been* dumped but I've never dumped anyone before."

Sarah played a small smile around her slightly bruised lips. "Maybe we'll have things to teach each other."

"Good," he said. "An adventure."

That had been eight weeks ago.

Now, as she headed for the door, watch-driven, appointment-driven, he said, "Since I've just been convicted of unconscious sadistic drives, can I ask you—was it all me? *Could you ever have possibly, in some out-of-control, wet excited moment, said or thought something like use me?*"

She turned, and as a final turn of mystery in an afternoon of mysteries, said, *"Try me."* Then she was gone in a flurry of scarves and perfume, leaving him wondering, still.

Feeling lucky in his discovery of this woman, probably destined to be his wife, her third marriage, his first, Marcus decided he would actually write that paper, a revised road map of Freud's unconscious. Take her on and everything she believed, as well.

Later, having set up his notes next to the computer, he tried to remember the moment at the door, the open-mouthed smile, the toss of her scarves. And had she actually said '*Try me?*' Or had it been, perhaps, *Why me? Buy me.* or even—*Tie me?* Feeling more foolish than ever, he was saved by the bell, the doorbell. It was Sarah; she had forgotten her all-important attaché case; she was of course late but when he hugged her, as glad to see her as if she'd been gone for months instead of minutes, she hugged back and they both began to laugh wildly, neither one sure which of them had started the laughter, adrift in the happy uncertainty of the attractions which confused their bodies and their intellects; attractions which made zeros of opinions, no matter how passionately held.

Holding her close he said, as inaudibly as he could, a touch ashamed of his own contribution to their confusions, "Sarah—When you were leaving, before, at the door—*what exactly was it that you—?*"

The Future

Golden had the sense that they were all, somehow, in it. Not as a plot against him—quite the opposite; he had the sense that they were all in it because they genuinely believed he was about to make some awful mistake. They were of course a vastly disparate group, Gwinna, Golden's wife of twenty years, was the most indirect in her disagreement. Her style had always been to support him. She was a German girl and to be married to the Professor, the Doctor of Literature and Law at NYU and the Department Chair for twelve years, brought with it a heavy load of respect carried over from her childhood in Bonn, where a Herr Doktor was a kind of secular deity. Not to exaggerate though, Gwinna was quite the American woman now; independent in most matters, a tolerant, patient mother with a healthy laugh and a gift for buying and selling antiques, once both children were grown and flown. He wasn't dead sure, but he figured she would stand by him when the crunch came.

He probably shouldn't have told any of them his plan, should have just gone ahead and done it. It wasn't that big a deal, or so he'd thought. Then Andrew called, agitated, ready to fly in from Colorado, having already spoken to his sister Elfrida. The storm gathered so quickly that Golden hardly had time to prepare his defenses. They'd always been close, this second family of his, both kids, plus Andrew's wife, Sophie, and Elfrida's husband Boris. Not a lemon in the bunch.

But a source of great pleasure seemed to be going into reverse.

"You don't want to do this, Henry." Andrew, the older kid, now twenty-six, had never called him Dad or Father, certainly not Pop; always an oddly formal boy. Golden had the sense, and never had the courage to shape the idea, that

Andrew, his first-born, did not quite approve of him; not of his feckless style, not of his heedlessness in money matters; Andrew was buttoned up, Golden did not have a button to his name.

"If I don't want to do it, then there's no problem, is there?"

"Don't kid around. I've talked to Elfrida. She also thinks it's wrong."

"An open and shut case, is it?"

"I've heard it's risky."

"Right."

"Then why do it? You're not a kid."

"Seventy-one these days is not necessarily *finito*."

"Nobody's talking *finito*. Just common sense."

"A lawyer's common sense may not be a teacher's common sense."

Elfrida's call was less of a confrontation. "What will it give you if it works? Compared to the risk. What do you want to hold onto—your passion for running?"

"Yes. And there are other passions."

But Elfrida was too savvy or too gun-shy to fall into that trap.

After a long, embarrassing silence Golden plunged in. "It's hard to explain." He was being ambiguous, but both doctors, the orthopod and the neurologist, had been precise and vague at the same time. An amazing trick that only doctors and writers like Kafka could bring off, combining realism and mystery. Always the professional, even under pressure, Golden filed away the notion for use in class: scientific knowledge as poetry rather than prose. Real toads in imaginary gardens. Could be the basis of a fresh lecture.

Since turning seventy, he'd been cautious about not being repetitious in his teaching and writing; department chair for twelve years, determined to hold on even though his built-in ethical sense, what Gwinna called his super-superego, told him a younger man should be given a chance; someone like Len Levine, damned smart Blake scholar who knew the Roberts Rules of Order by heart.

Anyway, waste not, want not. His memory was quite taut and responsive, but still he reached for a pencil while Elfrida stumbled through a few finishing sentences. She was a shy girl, the only one in the family who seemed to have the shy gene. Now eager to get off, she said, "We're coming in to discuss this, Daddy." Still Daddy's girl. Golden was pleased and amused. "Andrew will check with you about exactly when."

"Always happy to see my kids."

Golden turned to the golden October afternoon. New York was at its best between summer and winter. Actually, Golden thought of himself not so much as a citizen of New York but as one whose home was "downtown." The West Village, the East Village; a small intense and glamorous country with its own mindsets and weathers. He gladly pleaded guilty to the charge of provincialism: Manhattan was the continent, downtown was his country. And this autumn in downtown was more like spring, Bleeker street smooth and sunny, Houston and parts East fragrant with a smell of freshly opened nuts in the air, and in Washington Square Park pianissimo birdsong from those strong or forgetful birds who hadn't fled south just yet.

He was late for his morning run around Washington Square Park and points North, a ritual as sacred as meeting classes on time. But the phone calls had thrown him off.

"Why exactly does it trouble you so much, your kids' objections?" Pat asked. Pat was new, raw, unfinished business. A thrilling fall from the grace of thirty-two years of felicity, of fidelity to Gwinna. Oh, a flicker of desire here and there in his forties; but balance always kept, no fall. Until he passed seventy. What threw so many of his friends off in their forties had shoved him off his feet in his seventies. Golden knew that as you aged, passion was not too far from comedy and he tried to walk the tightrope between the two. Luckily, Pat had been the pursuer; an astonishingly open woman of twenty-nine, divorced, childless. The cliché embarrassed Golden, the old story he'd seen played out a dozen times, the professor and the graduate student. But she had said over lunch, the words coming through that innocent-seeming cupid's bow of a mouth, "You interest me. I'd like to sleep with you." And at a table in the faculty club, for God's sake.

The word choice pushed him over the edge. Not, "You attract me," but "You interest me." The intellect combined with sexual openness. That did it. The sex was fine, fresh and for some weird reason for a man with a super-superego, quite without guilt. Perhaps it was the "last chance" syndrome. A form of entitlement validated by age. He could still run seven miles a day but making love had never been a form of athletics; rather a form of discourse carried on by touch rather than diction. Also, he thought it was the very "too-lateness," the excitement of the wrong thing at the wrong time. He'd been good for so long that a little "bad" went a long way.

Golden's specialty was the dialogue between prose and poetry from the eighteenth century on to today. Pat's specialty was today; a poetry student, hip, up-to-the-minute, helping him move smoothly from Wordsworth to Billy Collins, before or after making love. It was as if, after a simple conversation, one of them might say, "Was it good for you?"

So that now, over coffee, they could break down his anxiety, his irony and his puzzlement over his family ganging up on him to stop a voluntary operation. Pat, herself, was not without concern about dangers versus rewards.

"What would happen if you skipped the operation?"

"It's not clear. The running is getting to be more and more of a problem."

"Then cut down."

"Cut down? I'm practicing for the Riverside Marathon next week."

"Then skip it."

"Have you no heart? It's for heart disease."

"There's enough heart disease around without you. Besides your two angioplasties are enough. You gave at the office. Do you know what finally pushed me into divorce? My husband was one of those wonderboys who was too good for ordinary caution. He was getting chest pains and wouldn't go near a doctor. I took him to the emergency room when the shit hit the fan and then I got a divorce."

"In the emergency room?"

Pat eased into a tight smile. "No, it took a few months. And the heart business was only the iceberg's tiny tip. But ever since then I've been convinced that everyone I care about is going to have a coronary. So maybe you could do your little girlfriend a favor and cut down on the extended runs."

"You're telling a devout Muslem to pray once a week instead of five times a day."

"Henry, running is not prayer."

"That's because you don't run."

"And maybe you shouldn't have anything done to that nice body of yours that isn't essential."

He took a beat. "It's complicated—"

"Is it just normal aging trouble?"

"Yes—and more." Golden was like a criminal or a spy with a guilty secret and who could only speak in obscure codes.

To lighten the moment he leaned forward and spoke their common language, poetry. "Oh heart, what shall I do with this aging body tied to me like a tin can to a dog's tail?"

"Listen, Yeats couldn't wait to be an old man. But you're all about waiting, or denying. So don't throw Yeats at me, dear Henry. And apropos age, I notice you're not driving that crazy limo that looks like a hearse, today."

Golden declined the gambit. "Didn't Yeats go to Switzerland," he said, "for one of those monkey gland things they did in the Twenties? For his potency?"

Pat giggled. At twenty-nine she still did a giggle now and then. "I think he was all of fifty-six. It seems it didn't work below the belt, but his poetry got a fresh force." She gazed at Golden, swiftly solemn. "I don't pretend to understand this whole operation business—but it's probably better than dogs and tin cans. If it's what you want, stick to your guns. It's autumn but if you want to be spring, be spring."

When he stood and scooped up the check, remembering not to kiss Pat, not even on the cheek, she gazed at him a second too long.

"What?"

"Is that a limp? I noticed it last week."

"All runners get a little stiff now and then." He was impatient at having to lie. It was his turn to level a steady gaze. "What's in this for you, dear, dear Pat?"

After lunch Golden walked, a walk not a run, an autumnal walk but with a spring in his step, the limp gone for the moment, thinking how lucky he felt these days, thinking of his late start in everything: stupidly joining the peacetime Navy mainly to anger his father, starting late at Columbia, a freshman at twenty-six; dropping out in his senior year to marry poor mad Jackie, spending three years seeing her in and out of hallucinations and hospitals, holding her hand while she died in bits and pieces and then altogether. Disorder and early sorrow. A line from a poem he hadn't taught for years flashed at him, Auden on Melville, *Towards the end he sailed into an extraordinary calm . . . .*

only it was not simply a calm, it was also a kind of exhilaration, of which running was the emblem, running when he'd had two balloon angioplasties; if not forbidden then certainly unwise. There were also pleasures of sanctioned and unsanctioned sensuality, and the pleasures of power—if only a kind of petty, ironic power: heading the largest department in a great university when he held no degree at all, except his navy discharge; having edged his way in by publishing early and often. And now holding on under fire; plus, not least, the delicious secret of his July-December affair with Pat.

Golden became aware that his measured walk had picked up the pace of his headlong precipitous remembrance of a misspent youth and a triumphant, greedy age; his breath was faster than his heartbeat (pace Pat), and he grabbed a nearby tree and held on thinking, *let them come, Andrew, Elfrida and the others, let them preach caution.* Breathless or not, he felt irrationally safe in his pleasure, in the delight of all things inappropriate, all things unearned, all things simply claimed by force of will.

"Andrew and Elfrida called today."

"I know. Boris told me all about it."

"All?"

"Enough. They think you should think twice about the operation."

"This is no spur of the moment thing, Gwinna. What do *you* think?"

"I think your idea of how you want to live your future is your own decision."

More luck, Golden thought, *my lover* and *my wife understand me.* "It's not just the future; future is a funny notion, anyway. It's a series of nows that starts now. Where it goes—?"

Gwinna moved next to him, standing as if something was on her mind. Something was: she leaned and kissed him, the kind of kiss that said forget about dessert, the kind of kiss that said forget children, forget operations; we're still here—after thirty-one years we're still at the center of it all. She was a stocky woman but lithe in her movements and when she was responsive she was very responsive. Golden rose to the unexpected gift and tonight Gwinna was very responsive.

About two seconds afterwards he turned to her in gratitude.

"You know . . . ," he said and faltered.

Gwinna was actually out of breath. "What *I* know," she said, breathless pianissimo, "is that we're two aging bodies and souls and it's nice how we still get going. That's what I know. What do you know, Professor Golden?"

He dodged the question for a moment with another question. "When did we get so close? Not when did we fall, what the French call a bolt of lightning. I mean was there a moment, was there a year?"

She laughed, pleased at the turn of the talk. "We were lucky. You fell fast, then I sort of tripped and you caught me. I was surprised and delighted. The foreign exchange graduate student and the tenured professor."

"Ah, tenure. There is something erotic about tenure. And there we were, holding each other in your infinitesimal apartment on Riverside Drive."

"Big enough for the two of us and a bed."

Golden upped himself on an elbow and gazed at her. A quick flash of association brought Pat to mind: but oddly without embarrassment, allowing himself to feel foolishly innocent, only carrying the silly sense of repetition. First Gwinna, then Pat. Thank God for tenure and the wonderment of sustained passion over so many years. Later she said, "Everything is fine," as if making love had been both a question and an answer.

In the morning he drove to the department meeting in the long black hearse he'd bought as a joke when Jule MacKenzie, the associate dean of Humanities, and he were used-car shopping one Sunday, over at Mad Mack's in Queens. Jule had said, almost innocently as he inspected a '98 Buick, "Listen, how long do you plan to continue as Department Chair? I mean, Len Levine has been nipping at your heels for the last two years. He's smart, honest and eager," Jule paused, "and young."

"If those are the four criteria, I fit three of them." That was when Golden's eye fell on the long black hearse. "What the hell is that?"

"What do you think? If you've never seen one you're damned lucky."

"Oh, I've seen them. I just wonder what it would be like to be in one."

Jule had a mordant sense of humor. "You'll find out some day. I've heard they give a real quiet drive."

"Yes, but I won't actually know what it's like then."

They'd come in a cab but drove home in Golden's impulse buy. Air-conditioning, automatic windows and doorlocks. And a nice roomy space in the back for luggage—or whatever. After the initial shock Gwinna bent over laughing.

"It was just my way of answering his question about giving up the Department chair," Golden said. "The answer was *never*. Not until one of these comes along for me. I'm not sure he got it."

Gwinna wasn't sure she got it, either. Did he really intend to never step aside? How about the ethics? Making way for new blood, fresh ideas?

Golden turned serious. "It's an old debate, darling Gwinna. Making way for the young, or making use of the elder wise men."

She didn't press it. "As long it's not the elder wise guys."

"I was pretty wise today. They were practically giving the damned thing away. Fifteen hundred bucks. There were no other buyers. And parking in the Village near school'll be safe for once. Who's going to steal this baby? No need to paste a sign on the window: No Radio."

The department meeting began with the usual chaos. Barnes and Schrift from Romance Languages flirting and arguing, unclear as to which was which. The usual discussion over who would keep the minutes. All quite benign, until a tenure case came up and Levine, Golden's successor manqué, challenged the committee's ruling. "Okay, he hasn't published much by bulk weight, but how about the quality of his ideas? How long must we go on doing our judgments by the pound?" Then, as a small tumult erupted, Golden drifted off into a reverie, a strange one; from an old movie about General Patton, the war-loving soldier of WWII. Golden found his pulses racing as the arguments grew heavier; then in a kind of foolish analogy he remembered the actor who played Patton viewing a bloody battle from a hilltop and saying, "Dear God forgive me, how I do love it; love it all." Who the hell could he tell about wanting to hold onto his department.

He was brought out of his reverie by the sudden motion to adjourn, after which Len Levine appeared at his side, suggesting they make a lunch date. Levine had hazy blue eyes and black hair without hint of the pepper-gray that flavored Golden's own hair.

His smile was cool, all teeth and no warming lips. Golden made the date and promptly forgot it.

When he got back to his office and his phone call list, Andrew's name, like Abou Ben Adhem's, led all the rest. He'd left a message, perhaps wishing to avoid another argument. They would be in next weekend. It was the weekend of the benefit marathon. His kids had never seen him in a marathon.

The marathon morning was suddenly fall—the real thing. Crisp, a wind no longer a soft breeze but a real wind with a bit of a bite. Autumn!

Gwinna called out, "It's chilly; you'll need your heavier jog-togs."

"Jog-togs. You're mocking my big day."

Coffee and an English muffin, bottled water, his recently broken-in Nikes and a kiss from a still sleepy Gwinna, who would be along later.

For all his impassioned defense of the fund-raising marathon, Golden thought of it deliberately in lowercase— Gwinna had repeatedly reminded him that it was a penny ante run, not the Boston or New York Marathon. Golden knew few of the other runners. He didn't hang out with the "running community," no Subscription to *Runner's World*, and all that. It was a private passion; the marathon was his annual tribute to the notion that other people ran, too; and to the memory of a snapping bright poetry student, mysteriously attacked by her heart at twenty-six. Golden had never finished in the first ten and didn't care. But he always finished. He nodded to a few neighbors and did his stretching as if it were some personal Zen gesture; then a few steps alert to the possible return of the limp. Nothing.

It happened at about the three-mile mark. No warning, no premonitory tightness, unclear, as it would always be, whether it was some muscle pull, a descendant of the menacing limp, or simple stumble. One of a thousand unperceived roughnessess that Golden had handled a thousand times before, and now, amazingly did not, could not, had not; a swift faltering that suddenly turned into an accident, a misstep that triggered a weird slow-motion fall, as in so many movies where the slow-motion camera had to be invoked to recreate what it was like, for an important instant, to be no longer automatically secure in moving along the surface of your familiar, taken-for-granted earth.

Of course, no camera could capture the twist of hot pain, yes, it had its own heat, this pain; heat, then pins and needles, then numb. Then passivity, the very opposite of running, being carried by anxious hands, then a comforting stretcher, then his bed and Gwinna's sleep-inducing anodyne.

Late in the afternoon–lying on his side Golden couldn't see the clock but the light was afternoon light, picking up shadows and, startling, though expected, picking out the five shapes at bedside.

Mordant, Golden thought, *like a jury, if a jury could be both angry and sad.* At first all Golden was aware of was sound, voices alternately angry, worried and puzzled. It was a jumbled phantasmagoria of voices, different tones belonging to a jury of his nearest and dearest—the prevailing tone being disapproval, anxiety and more disapproval. Slowly the jumble cleared, like a radio being gradually tuned.

It was almost pleasant to drowse, to hear himself being discussed as if he were not there, the way children are sometimes treated as non-existent witnesses to their own fate; pleasant to listen to the distant sound of Andrew's wife Sophie, usually so quiet, so mysterious, telling, in her soft Charleston drawl, how proud she'd always been of Golden's achievements. But that this peculiar operation, a voluntary one, at his age, well . . . . "What is he trying to prove!"

The anxious, critical chorus slowly resolved itself and one voice, firm and clear, prevailed. Gwinna had taken over. Golden registered her sense without taking in the precise words. It seemed to him that she sounded like a defense attorney: she reminded the jury of Golden's history as a bulwark against all the chance and trouble of the family; against Andrew's restlessness, from school to school treated with kindness, and a firm patience, breeding a closeness; a closeness that held on when Elfrida's first marriage to a liar, a thief as it turned out, threatened chaos. The list of mishaps was probably no longer than most, but it felt different. By the time she mentioned Thanksgiving, Golden's head was clearing. Gwinna was passionate now.

Because of him, the usual American nightmare of Thanksgivings was not turkey and recriminations, pumpkin pie with anger and envy—but lively, grateful gatherings. "For God's sake don't push the man to be what you want him to be—just let him be himself! Back him up. He's earned that."

She took a long breath, perhaps she was getting teary, Golden's perceptions were not sharp enough to be sure but he kept his eyes shut; better if they thought he was asleep. "Or would you rather have what most Americans seem to have at Thanksgiving, a kind of poisoned happiness?" Either her early hopeless ambitions to be an actress were paying off, or she was powerfully moved. Golden had never been injured, hardly ever sick in their twenty years. Maybe, Golden thought, maybe she'd been frightened into eloquence. In any case she was his bastion, his first line of defense, his granite wall.

Golden was irritated by the ringing of the doorbell, one of those stupid imitations of Big Ben that you hear on television. More voices—Pat, at least it sounded like her. "Can I see him, I've been away and I heard. Is it is his heart?" Gwinna's voice, inaudible, and Pat was there, weepy, frightened, grasping for his hand. Golden was frightened—alert in terror. What would he tell Gwinna, a research assistant? An overemotional graduate student? But as clearly as in certain surreal but utterly real dreams, he saw Gwinna take it all in: the body language, the choked tears, the hand held an instant too long for academic or friendly concern, the unspoken intimacy.

He saw Gwinna's face, saw the hardening of the soft lines surrounding the gray eyes, saw the supportive murmur of her mouth tighten, saw the silent stare of stone; he was defenseless, lost. Well before Pat's awkward exit, Golden knew he was alone, naked to his loving attackers, his family, and joke as he might by driving an insouciant hearse, he was now naked to the terror of time.

And in that crystalline instant he loosened his grasp on all he unreasonably but passionately cherished: the foolish enjoyment of clinging to authority, the high of running beyond his powers, beyond his endurance, beyond his age, the slightly ridiculous frisson of young woman/older man sensuality, his pleasure, his delight in all things inappropriate, all things unearned, all things simply claimed by force of will.

And Golden saw the future rush towards him with its terrifying force, saying: "No!"

The Altman Sonata

The question of how men and women behave in bed may give us the sense of a time, a place, an era about as well as anything I can imagine. What we expect and what we accept, tells much about us. I'm thinking about the famous orgasm of Jenny Jenkins, followed by the slap administered by her lover, Max Altman, mister avant-garde music, obscure during the Jenny Jenkins slap-period, but famous after his early death; the slap which marked the end of our friendship that had meant so much to me.

It's hard to conjure up the resonance the word "orgasm" had in 1955, an entire culture of hope and obligation surrounding the word, the idea, everyone drunk on the implications, men and women, both. For the middle class, what we quaintly called the bourgeoisie, there was the Grail of the simultaneous orgasm. Not intensity or frequency—simultaneity was the issue, the capstone of intimacy. The possible failure of this timetable lurked in the air like a great cultural catastrophe, a shared guilt and faith in the next time, holding the middle class together like a special sort of sexual glue.

Simultaneously, there existed an entire downtown world of outlaw climaxes: peaks heightened by smoking pot, Orgone boxes, the creation of the renegade analyst Wilhelm Reich, with Norman Mailer doing passionate PR for its properties. The promise was everything from cosmic orgasms to an absence of the common cold, even during the ferocious snow-winter of 1955. Here, unlike the middle-class goals and anxieties, intensity was everything. There was, too, a Zen strain running through the Village (starting there and making its way up through the Upper West Side); a doctrine of emptying one's self to make room for utter pleasure. The Zen doctrine of no-mind, offering not merely sexual pleasure, that was kid stuff; I'm talking about Nirvana.

This era of hoped for simultaneity came long before the era of the female multiple orgasm, which arrived around the time of the early seventies, perhaps as a reward for so much exhausting political activity. If I sound a touch academic, it's because I am: a musicologist with a second major in sociology. I chart movements in the Zeitgeist as matter of habit. However, in the days of the Altman/Jenkins slap I was still an oboist by trade, helping Max to chart the unknown territory, or rather the aleatory, if you'll permit me a small musical joke.

Now Max Altman was not the kind of man to get hooked on any of these social/psychological strains. Max was an egoist of the bedroom. By day he worked in his family's cloak and suit business (as the garment trade was anachronistically called—I don't know when the last time was that anyone had seen a cloak); by night he was engaged in an ambitious attempt to change the future, even the past, of contemporary music. Max had taken the idea of chance which had been breathed into the air by John Cage, and run with it: in his music the players chose entrances and exits, duration and even the pitch of notes.

His song was a restless complaint. One night down at his place downtown on Monroe Street overlooking an angry East River, he sat at the Steinway grand and launched into the Beethoven *Waldstein Sonata*. He played it with full heroics, all grandeur; it was stunning. Then, stopping on a dime and turning to me: "It's a damned prison. They've handed us Sonata Form: theme, second theme, development, recapitulation and conclusion. Give us a fucking break—after two centuries of coercion. All that process—" he slammed into the last few chords—"with its moral conclusion. For God's sake, take off the straitjacket, let everybody breathe a little."

Power to the players was his motto; philosopher of a universe of accident, Max was the Von Heisenberg of music.

But when it came to sex, Max Altman was interested in simple satisfaction, a sensual universe of orderly movement. Over late-night coffee, after our musical experiments in his apartment, he would share details with me. (You could do that, then, without either gay self-consciousness or locker room jock embarrassment.) The sexual life he laid out was conventional, not necessarily in content—positions, experimentation, frequency, but rather in structure. A sexual sonata (no notion of chance here)—beginning, (theme) approach, (second theme), wooing and what Leopold Bloom calls "the old in and out" (development) then, finalement, the climactic conclusion. No ending with a dying fall, either; a major conclusion, the climax as in the sense of the last bars of a Beethoven symphony. All fixed, patterned, full of the satisfactions of the expected. Thus, Max Altman, passionate avant-gardist in music but a classicist in bed.

Of course, he was also a grazer, a "hulker" as one woman confessed to me. "He will wait till there's no space behind you and then he'll lean both hands on the wall and hulk." There was a lot of Max to hulk; a large man in every sense: bulk, ambition, talent, wit. The bulk was the first thing you noticed, round face, painfully nearsighted eyes, pudgy hands pressing glasses as close to his eyes as they could go.

One woman at a time was never enough for Max—perhaps not even two or three. Once, noting my astonished gaze, noting how impressed I seemed by the energy of the hunt, the success of the primitive rite of scenting, tracking and moving in on the latest prey, he took me aside and said with his half-mocking earnestness, "Don't envy me, Oscar. Think of it as someone needing a day nurse and a night nurse." And with that he wheeled back to close in on the latest young woman. No, not necessarily young, I mustn't give that false impression—no cradle-robbing. By the time he married for the third time his major mistress was Marianne, a music copyist—this was pre-computer when people still copied parts from the score by hand. Marianne was smart, witty, and twenty-two years older than his wife, Carla. At the same time he was prowling around a violist, nine years younger. Max was an equal-opportunity luster.

We broke up over the slap heard 'round New York—or at least 'round University Place, Bleecker Street, Monroe Street, everywhere the painters Max hung out with had their lofts, their studios, their patient underground-painting wives and mistresses, cooking, sulking, fucking, entertaining—providing whatever their heedless painter husband/lovers wanted. That's how it was then and maybe still is. I'm frying other fish these days and university life is more hidden. Also, a woman slapped and then the slap told as a triumphant story would result in instant isolation on the campus. I'd always

thought it was a bad training school for Max, all those painters of that moment, Gauguin-clones, with women taken for
granted as career and sexual aids, giving Max a kind of permission to use women—whether well or badly almost doesn't
matter.

To be fair, though, I should point out that when he was
sleeping with Laura James, the poet who couldn't get a poem
published, even in those days when little magazines were
erupting into print every week, he would listen patiently to
her reading aloud, would arrange poetry readings and strong-
arm the painters and their women to come, paying for the
whiskey and the *hors d'oeuvres* out of his own pocket. "Listen,"
he said to me, "If you're interested in the woman, you're interested in her poetry."

The slap didn't do Max any good with his buddies, either.
Not so much because of what he'd done but because he'd
told all about it, had made a small amoral tale out of what
had provoked it and what it was supposed to mean. My own
take on that was that they were all using their sexual lives as
a free ride for impulse, control and power but only Max
spread it abroad. (Some years later Picasso's love/hate stuff
with his women would blow the secret up to the tabloid level
and then everyone knew.)

But at that time it was their secret and only Max, amoralist
that he was, failed to recognize that it was a dirty secret and
should be kept under the covers. Philip Guston was horri-
fied, Lippold and Kline told him he was a son-of-a-bitch.

You might think I am making too much of one slap.
After all, he didn't beat Jenny. Yetta Altman, his mother, the
matriarch of the Altman family and the family clothing business, would have scorched him with her contempt if she'd
heard of that—and Yetta heard of everything. Max's mother
played the central role in the other famous moment, the incident of her phone call when Max and Jenny were in bed that
Sunday morning. All of Max's incidents were famous, partly
because that group of musicians, poets and painters lived in
each other's pockets, gossip as much currency as the whiskey, cheap red wine and nosherai that fueled the constant
gatherings.

Max was shacked up at Jenny's place, moving in just
enough of his stuff to give the sense that he was entirely
involved with her and leaving just enough stuff at his own

place down on Monroe Street so that he could maneuver as needed in the jungle of sexual opportunity. Now, to understand the story of Max's mother's phone call, you must realize what it meant to "shack up" in the fifties. Marriage waited behind every corner eager to legitimatize all male-female connections. Every other arrangement still trembled with danger. Of course, not so much in the downtown world, I'm speaking of the world. The Bronx, Brooklyn, Long Island, and perhaps particularly Queens, where Yetta Altman lived and where the family ran their small textile factory, to which Max made his daily pilgrimage.

It was maybe two months before the slap. Max and Jenny were in bed, sleeping late one Sunday morning, when the phone rang. Jenny answered then handed it to Max. Maybe she was embarrassed at Max's mother joining them in bed via the phone, but as Max and his mother were talking over some business complication to be dealt with the next day, Jenny became playful, teasing him, tickling him, playing with his balls.

Max whispered, "Quit it." But she persisted, playful, probably in love, feeling she had the right. Now louder Max said, "Dammit!" But Jenny enjoyed being in control of the game for the moment. It was a rarity, feeling in control when you lived with Max and she was enjoying herself. Then came more tickling, mock caressing, finally she took his penis in her mouth and an erection was beginning to join the party. Max, strung between the two major women in his life, perhaps afraid he might come while talking to his mother, shouted, "JENNY, DAMMIT, CUT IT OUT!" At which point Yetta Altman said, in gentle prim and firm tones, "Max, remember, you're a guest."

It was all over town the next day—this charming confrontation of the free and the proper, of illicit sex and the middle class, this triumph of good manners over conventional morality in the middle of an invisible blow job. For months the catchword at the bar hangout or the club where the painters gathered was, "Remember, you're a guest."

I was probably the cause of the quick spread, always the first to hear from Max on matters of morality giving onto irony. Since he'd played the bass and I'd switched from flute to oboe in Music and Art High School, we'd been engaged in an odd kind of dialogue/argument, Max always pushing to

93

the edges and myself pulling back. "Oscar the moralist," he would say and I would reply, "Max the Immoralist," at which he said, "Wrong, wrong, it's more the amoralist." Accompanied by a sly, round-faced serious grin. Behind these exchanges lay the specter of our very different sexual lives, me and my tormented eight-month affairs and/or unrequited loves, Max and his endless screwy, screwing balancing act, late-dating one lover for another, even pulling at the boundaries of someone's shaky marriage if he was attracted to the wife. No, that's not right—he was always attracted, a Don Juan of the quotidian; ordinary or spectacular, it didn't matter. What mattered was the chase, the success, the yes, the prize of the day, the orgasm, his, hers, everybody's. He observed my miserable moonings, my falling into adoration frequently followed by dejection, with ironic concern.

"Listen, Oscar," Max said to me one night, after a music-work session, "Women are terrific, and you certainly treat them like princesses but they're not from the moon."

Our disagreements went from sexual ethics (as it's now called) to abstract painting, which seemed to me, then, in my carefully cultivated ignorance, like pissing on the graves of Van Gogh and Monet, my high school heroes. If Max was the Don Juan of the ordinary and the spectacular, I was the Don Quixote of the conventional, lacking even the courage of his aging Jewish mother in Queens.

We were at that time meeting nightly, Max sketching out methods for "open field" music as he called it, more a painting term than music, exactly why he liked it. He would cut up music paper, write phrases, impulses, scatter them, let me choose which pieces to play, and then create the piece we'd put together on paper. It was exciting to try something that had never been done in music before but I must confess I was skeptical, not moved by the music itself. I was a classicist, I knew the Mozart *Oboe Quartet* by heart. Chance abrogating the sense of order I was accustomed to made me nervous, anxious, left me nothing to hold onto.

Still, chance had determined where I was living. I'd played one season with the Kansas City Symphony, second oboe, and when I got to New York in May I did not want to go back to Brooklyn, where my father, mother and kid brother lived. I'd outgrown King's Highway but I had yet to claim or earn my own place in the larger world. Max took me in. This was fine for the musical collaboration that began almost as soon as I arrived. But it made for some crazy nights when Max would bring a woman home without warning.

The apartment had one bedroom and I was assigned to the living room couch. It wasn't so bad just being woken up when Max and the latest acquisition would clumsily tiptoe past me whispering their way to the bedroom. But there was that night when a girl named Sasha, a student at the Art Students League, had drunk more than she could handle and pulled Max down onto the couch in the dark, dress quickly up, panties swiftly down, ready for everything, the three of us rolling around for one wild moment before anyone realized or remembered that there was a third party under them. Max must have quickly known what was happening, he never drank much. Appetite was his natural state, eating was his anodyne. Late night, after-concert Chinese food binges accompanied by oceans of Chinese tea, rarely alcohol, accompanied by seductions; these were excesses but they left him alert. Thus, when, the largest mound on the quivering pyramid started to quake with laughter Shirley must have thought him crazy. But I knew that he knew that I knew that he knew. It was the closest I ever came to an orgy—another popular Manhattan sport of the time—but without any climactic pleasures for any of us.

Of course, in those days everyone was living in someone else's apartment. Even Max's apartment was actually his older brother's place, Abe Altman, who fled the family business for an extended graduate student's life in Ann Arbor, Michigan. Maybe it was youth for all of us, and youth always flees the family home to stand somewhere else on one leg while figuring out its life.

Apropos figuring out your life, did I mention that Jenny and I had been lovers for about a half hour? That was, of course, the way Max and she came together, myself as the rejected lover and unwitting catalyst. I met her at a party for the Village Democrats, dancing, she talked a blue streak about liberal politics and the Farmer-Labor Party back in Minnesota where she came from.

"You've heard of the Four H Club?"

I had.

She flashed a handsome and broad Midwestern grin— open, available.

"Four H's. The healthy, happy, husky hicks," she translated.

At first glance this seemed a fair approximation of the woman dancing in my arms. She was big, taller than me but not as big as Max, who had both height and hulk. I had never understood what they call rawboned in books but Jenny was rawboned. You looked at this big farm-girl and you expected her elbows to be rubbed red. She was independent—picked me up, actually, made the first move, told me where she lived and asked if I was going that way, invited me in.

She was older than either Max or me, not musical or artistic, not Jewish, either; later, this would be a bitter pill for Yetta Altman to swallow. I was absolutely taken by her open style, equally taken by the fact that she had her own place, a perfect little hole in the corner bachelor pad on a dead-ended Greenwich Mews. We stayed up all night talking, or rather me listening.

She'd fled Minnesota for Rome right after graduate school, had been a literary agent for American publishers, then, turning thirty, it was time to come back to the U.S., take a place in the Village, find herself a psychoanalyst. After a year of this she started studying at the New School for Social Research on Twelfth Street to be a lay analyst.

It was her own struggle with the question of orgasms which had brought her to treatment and finally led her into training to join the profession herself. It was an article of faith in the fifties that you could solve anything by analysis and high on the list was the inability to have an orgasm. There was a wonderful name, then, for women who couldn't or didn't come: frigid. How that word evokes the awful, heedless, painful innocence of the time. One could be with the most passionate woman in the world, full of excitement, inventive caresses, wildly open to anything, but if there was no climax—the only language for her was arctic: the first two syllables of the most famous refrigerator. "I'm through with love," my Billie Holiday 78 record sang, "I've locked my heart in an icy Frigidaire . . . ." In the meantime, any dolt of a man could simply pump and pour and he was sanctified: normal, healthy.

After the first evening, for nights on end we sweated and wrestled in her un-air-conditioned apartment, with an invisible wrestling match referee calling out decisions, "no" or "not yet." Oh, those surprise fortunate moments, those young summer New York nights when for absolutely no apparent reason, "no" or "not yet" magically turned to "yes." Suddenly, we were tumbling together towards the middle of the bed, clothes flying, legs parting, closing then parting again. I was lost in the pleasure of being lost in her when she looked up at me with great open eyes—Max always said those eyes could ask anything of a man, so he kept his own shut—and she said, "Oscar, listen—"

Listen, I hoped, didn't mean stop, but I listened. "Yes . . . ?"

"I—" a wave of her big but graceful hand—"I don't . . . ."

She doesn't . . . . For a crazy moment I thought yes had turned back to no and, like a film rewinding, my erect prick would be returned to me, entirely my own again, our legs would unentwine, her bra would rise up in the air and cup her lovely breasts, my pants would reclaim my legs. But, no, she'd only meant the unsayable, the unthinkable, she didn't come, presenting it, not like a temporary lack but like a fate, a life sentence. "I don't." And beneath that, the unspoken reason for stopping the moment to tell me, was: I, the new lover, should not be disappointed, had to be warned that I was to be deprived of my right, a woman who would blow away with ultimate pleasure. For all she knew I might be a complete bust, a travesty of a lover, my caresses awkward, clumsy, my prick might in the end turn out to be made of Jell-O, but no matter what, I must be warned that she would not come. I plunged back in, happy to ignore all irrelevant warnings, Jenny welcoming me now with a clear conscience; a happy meeting of bodies and minds, of parts and wholes.

In the morning she made pancakes and sausages, "About one tenth of a real farm breakfast," she confided from the kitchen, but it was pounds more than my usual toast and coffee. Later she called me from a pay phone at The New School. "I feel safe with you, Oscar," she said. "I trust you . . . ," everything still in the future, the meeting with Max, the betrayal of Oscar, the infamous slap: struggling with her fate: the only woman in America never to come, innocent of the labyrinth she had just entered.

The next night I told Max all about her. I felt vaguely disloyal doing it ("I feel safe with you, Oscar. I trust you.") but I was twenty-two, flushed with failure after failure and this one felt like success. This particular night each of us was feeling ten feet tall for entirely different reasons. Me, re Jenny; Max re the onrushing future.

Ronald Lang at Columbia University, a vanilla, middle-of-the-road Professor/composer, had heard of Max's spicy open-ended concoctions and instead of the familiar conservative contempt, was making noises about a concert at Columbia's MacMillan Theater up on 116th Street. Max's work had made little noise in the actual music world. He was the most unusual cup of Chinese tea anyone had encountered; chance, randomness. And on his scores instead of the usual pianissimo or forte or crescendo indications the markings went from "soft" or "very quiet" to "almost inaudible." He was the poet of semi-silent accidents in music. Yet he strode the earth, or at least the Village, with the sure step of a man promised fame at birth by the angels of confidence and ambition. He knew it was only a question of when and how, not "if."

We moved down Sixth Avenue, towards Eighth Street, lightly, on wing-tipped shoes, heading for the Waldorf Cafeteria: coffee for me, slabs of pie for Max.

"She's a farm girl," I told him. "Not so much beautiful as imposing. A lot of presence." Now, from the reticence of middle age, I find it hard to believe that I told him every detail, ending up with, "Listen," and the final, "I don't."

"Frigid," he said.

"So why do I feel so good?"

"You always feel good at the beginning. When a woman pays the right attention to you it makes you feel valuable." He paused, turned to me under the street light, a small line of people waiting, restless, at a Nedicks for frankfurters or orange drinks. "This, Oscar old friend, is a feminine virtue, feeling valuable because someone likes you enough to want to fuck."

He slapped me on the shoulder to defuse the moment, pressed his thick glasses up against his eyes, staring at me with concern. "Everybody's replaceable," he called out. "Even us." We moved forward and out of the blue he started to sing, "I'm through with love . . . I've locked my heart in icy Frigidaire. . . For I must have you or no one." Pause. "Bullshit. Here's how it really goes: For I must have you or— someone else. It doesn't scan but it's the truth."

Over coffee he expanded: "It's a random world. I'm not doing indeterminate music because I want to. It's the truth.

Random—whoever shows up is as good as anyone else. Well, not exactly. Everything depends on who they show up to and when. Notes, women, men—we just weave a web of value around them, the way we do with a Beethoven sonata. Like the women we get involved with, it comes already crowned with the sacred, possessive. This is it, my lover, my girl-friend, my wife, willed, inherited," he ranted. He yielded to an ironic grin. "The fascism of the emotions. Beethoven, Michaelangelo, Dostoyevsky, the whole idea of melody. Jesus! Like sonata form! All so damned moral." You've never heard disgust in a voice until you've heard Max speak the word *moral*.

But, as far as being so taken with a woman who didn't come, it was a different story. "Pleasure is power," Max said. He prided himself on being able to give and control a woman's pleasure as much as his own. "If you can't get a woman over the mark, something is off in the universe." I warned you, at the start if you'll recall, how large the question of the orgasm loomed in the fifties—and not just for women. At a certain point even Max was a man of his time.

That was how it went between us and maybe between a lot of others, then, sex and art, music and woman and man, a ping pong game with everything at stake but never quite won or lost. I had to laugh and then he started to laugh and we cleared the coffee cups away and started to plan the MacMillan Theater concert we hoped would make Max famous uptown as well as downtown.

In those days the choices of performance were simple. There was downtown, The Village Gate, the impromptu concerts in friends' lofts and there was way uptown, Columbia's MacMillan, 116th Street, practically knocking at the gates of Harlem. In between was midtown, of course, the straight stuff, the big time: Carnegie Hall, Town Hall, later on Lincoln Center. This was never to be Max's domain in his lifetime.

On my wall as I write this, is a poster for a retrospective concert of Max's most complicated pieces at Alice Tully Hall. One of the pieces, a string quartet, is six hours long. Now, however, four years after his death, they're played with the chance removed, still hovering on the edge of inaudibility, fragments of sound floating in consciousness, but played straight. Death has brought control back to Max, who never wanted it, except over women.

I was too dumb, too absorbed in my friendship with Max and his career, which had become my cause, even though I didn't believe in his music. I believed in Max, that was enough. Naturally, I was eager to have him meet Jenny, setting in motion the oldest treason in the world, the best friend and the girlfriend. When they were sitting opposite each other at Lum Fong's on Forty-seventh Street along with a smattering of friends, Howie Kanovitz, the painter, saw what was happening. David Tudor, the avant-garde's house pianist, got the idea at once and Jean Erdman who had commissioned a dance score from Max told me later she got the picture as soon as she sat down.

"Jenny," Max said, wielding a pair of chopsticks like batons, "Let me show you how to play these ancient instruments and still get some food." What did everybody get that passed me by? They saw the Man of Destiny and the Nebraska Farm Girl, ripe for the fall.

Two weeks later, Max came home at about two in the morning, shook me awake and told me I was liberated from the couch; I could sleep in the comfort of the bedroom from now on. He was moving in with Jenny. He sat down on the edge of the couch and said, mock-solemn, "Her therapist told her it was the right move." A pause, as if to underline the fact that we both knew how foolish that comic strip reason was.

As if to console me, perhaps to keep me on the team, Max reported a few weeks later, "She still doesn't come. She can't—or won't. She's quiet in bed. A lot of small, muted sounds but no crescendo." He made it sound like a performance of one of his pieces. Can't or won't. So much for the classic mind-body problem. He was trying to ease the transition by putting on a macho act—though the word hadn't appeared in English yet—you know, that wonderful picture of two buddies passing a woman around, then comparing notes. Except I hadn't passed, I had simply lost. The only gesture I made towards self-respect was to leave Max's apartment—back to Brooklyn, to the prison of my parents' sullen, silent questioning about my future, the prison of the long two a.m. rides home on the BMT.

I told myself Max and Jenny had been honest, no sneaking around; I was young enough so that honesty counted for a lot. It gave me an out, a way to act as if everything was okay. But nothing worked. I was miserable, sick at being rejected, replaced by my best friend. I finally did break with Max—but, strangely, not until the slap. It was as if he could seduce the woman out from under me, literally, figuratively, every which way; but I couldn't get up the steam to break my closest friendship until he betrayed her. I didn't know who I cared about most, Jenny, myself or Max, what a stew of misidentification and sexual pain. I told myself over and over again, it was Jenny's choice, this was 1951, men didn't steal women like cars, transferring ownership by force or stealth. It settled my head but not my soul. That settlement would have to come later.

Still, settled for the moment, we all concentrated on the big concert coming up. Jenny quickly became an artist's consort in the classic mode: Max was everything, which meant that Max's career was everything. All that Nebraska independence was checked at the bedroom door. A few weeks before the concert Ronald Lang, then the ruling panjandrum of academic music, now quite eclipsed in posthumous reputation by Max, invited us to play chamber music at his home. Lang was the kind of graying lion of academe who greeted you at the door in a tweed jacket, pipe in hand, saying, "Welcome to my humble abode," ushering you into what felt like an upper West Side Palace. There, in the old-fashioned, pseudo-British grandeur of his eight room apartment, I was to have my own moment of truth.

With the usual pickup group of Max Altman groupies, a couple of fiddlers and a violist, The Mozart *Oboe Quartet* smoothed us past the first part of the evening. We took a break, awed by the sumptuous space and antique decorations. In a kitchen as big as my family's whole apartment, Lang took me on, directly.

"Tell me, Oscar, do you really believe in this inaudible chance music?"

"It's more that I believe in Max."

"That doesn't answer my question."

"Well, if you don't, then why the concert, the arrangements, the fuss? You're putting Max on a map he's never been on."

Lang searched his enormous refrigerator for more ice. "Because his work exists—at least for this moment in time," he said. "We're including it, temporarily, not selecting it. Giving something a hearing is not the same as canonizing it."

His pipe, his tweed jacket, his sardonic *politesse*, the use of the royal *we*, the cool game-playing with reputation—he was like a man masquerading as what he was. One of those horror movies where at the key moment a mask is pulled away revealing the identical face. He handed me a glass of something I hadn't asked for; it tasted sweet, Cointreau on the rocks, "I think you'll like this. It's not the usual barbarism of whiskey or vodka."

It was from Lang, drinking Cointreau for the first time, at that kitchen moment, that I first heard the awesome philosophy of downtown and uptown, of out and in. He hearkened back to Paris in the 1880s and the '20s, to Vienna in the 1890s and the 1930s. He sang the old sweet song of avant-gardes gobbled up by fashion, of the inexorable movement of style, like a contagious disease, first virulent, cubism, then the flat-planes of Matisse, Bartok's sharpening of folk melodies into the required modernist craggy difficulties, then the taming effects of time, until Bartok took his place behind Debussy in the orderly progression, what had felt like a revolution became an accommodation making way for the next revolution.

"This is a modern phenomenon," he said. "Matisse's backgrounds are already in demand for fashion layouts."

It was an entirely fifties New York conversation. I had a glimpse, for the first time, of the wonderful world of non-commitment—the upstairs-downstairs, who's-in who's-out life of academia. "The trick," he added, smiling at me, knowing he was making mischief between two friends, between a master and a disciple, "the trick is to assimilate, represent all possible ways of making art. Everything a la carte, no *table d'hôte* dinner. I know you think that Altman is riding a thrilling wave of chance, of randomness, freeing the world from the dead control of the past. But, trust me, it's only one way. There was Jesus and then there are all the people in the Vatican who make everything work. Don't tie yourself to a Messiah. Wait till the dust settles, then take over. Of course, for this," he waved his own Cointreau glass at me, "you need a very long view."

Then and there I took a deep breath and set out on the path which has led me, in a steady forward progress, to the endowed chair I now hold at Columbia, to my editing of the *Oxford Dictionary of Musical Style*—Saint Oscar, Defender of

The Faith." It was probably more gradual than that, but I see it now, looking back, as an instant conversion. Not having the courage to step back from Max and his cause because of Jenny, I was to find another route, cool not impassioned, objective not committed. It was the beginning of a way out.

This beginning was interrupted by one of the guests, a delicate blonde actress of the period, Eva Marie Saint, storming into the kitchen.

"My God, Ronald," she said, "There's a man in there who's attacking Beethoven." It was as if she were reporting a rape or a violent assault. It's wonderful how the icons of art get to be like one's family, who must be defended at all costs. She was noticeably pregnant and it was troubling to see her so agitated.

Not to Ronald Lang. "Eva Marie, I think Beethoven can take care of himself," he said, dry, refusing her distress.

She was not amused. "He also said Dostoyevsky is bad news. That's the expression he used, *bad news*." She paused to catch her breath and I stepped in.

"That was Max," I said. "Big man? Thick glasses?"

She nodded.

"He thinks there are two kinds of art: controlled and controlling, moral, preaching at you. That's Beethoven and Dostoyevsky."

She took a breath. "Is that so! Well then who does he like?"

"The other kind. He loves Schubert, Turgenev . . . the kind who just open their mouth and sing their song. It's the light versus the heavy, the moral versus pure experience." I had the litany down pat by now.

Ronald Lang took her arm and steered her back towards the living room. "You see, Eva Marie, it's just one point of view." She seemed calmer, though the last words I heard from her as they left the kitchen were, "What gives him the right . . . ?" And I think, now, looking back, how wonderfully serious, then, we all were about art. We gave it the kind of attention we gave orgasms, it was as personal as that and as cosmic all at the same time. Politics was a distant echo, a subject for anxiety and jokes. Making love and making music, for one long held breath, could be what life was all about.

I recall the rest of the evening in a half-daze, playing the Schubert *Arpeggione Sonata*, transcribed by Max for oboe and piano, and then a new chance piece by Max that we'd put together the evening before. Jenny, comforting Eva Marie Saint, explaining the drill, happy in her new-found mission. Jenny and I spread our subversive gospel, telling the variety of academics, business people, musicians, assorted celebrities from movies and the theater about the concert coming up at MacMillan Theater, the concert that would announce a new age in music. Lang had said there was Jesus and there were the workers at the Vatican—but there was an intermediate category. We were like the apostles among the unbelievers, spreading the good news: that we were all freer than we believed, that there is no judgment coming, only random chance and the accidental discovery of beauty.

At the end of the evening, we were high on possibility and change (me), on love and mission (Jenny), Max high on impending notoriety and MSG—we'd gone out for the inevitable Chinese at the end of the evening. Then, on impulse, Max and Jenny rode with me back to Brooklyn. In the half-deserted subway car, at three a.m., I took out my oboe. Max crouched at my feet holding fragments of phrases he'd just scribbled out, and to the astonishment and amusement of the few late night, sleepy riders, I played a music never before thought of in the history of the BMT. A laughing Jenny passed her woolen hat and collected a few nickels, dimes and pennies, after which I went home to the endless reproaches of my family and Max took Jenny back to the Village and their peak-less (her peak-less) love. We were young and our losses and gains had yet to be counted up.

"I want people who hear my music to feel as if they've lost, not gained something," Max had once said. Which was exactly why the concert was the success de scandale Max relished. He had mustered twelve of the best classical pianists to turn the dials on twelve radios, at intervals conducted by Max, resplendent in white tie, tails and jeans, (a kind of parody of concert dress) from a conventional podium. Simultaneously, Billy Masselos and David Tudor sat, ready to produce gentle, almost inaudible chords from two pianos, center-stage.

The hall was packed, the audience expectant but, unlike the audience at most concerts, not knowing what to expect. Jenny and I sat together, with us a few of the composers also waiting to be heard from: Milton Babbitt, Ralph Shapey, Meyer Kupferman. Across the aisle Lenny Bernstein conferred the glamour of his attention. When Max conducted, sans baton, and gave the signal for the first of the radios to be turned on, a stirring moved through the theater. Fragments of music, a swiftly touching Billie Holiday phrase, a commercial for Rinso laundry soap, none staying long enough to control the attention; behind these shards sang the soft chords from the two pianos. When some New Orleans jazz crossed the air followed by a news broadcast, the giggling began. There was something so precise about the words ". . . threat of war cannot be discounted . . ." that it made people feel anxious and a little foolish at the same time.

But Max the magician dealt with this, as if randomness of radiowaves were only another medium. For a long pause he kept total silence except for one sustained piano chord, as if to clear the air of misinterpretation. In the middle of this timeless quiet a blast of thunder cracked the air outside the hall. It was a gift to or from Max. People seemed oddly moved by the moment. When a remedy for indigestion followed bits and pieces from a Mozart symphony the laughter was a steady undercurrent, a part of the concert, as if programmed by Max. Of course there was laughter and laughter, some of it tinged with contempt, some of it touched with pure surprise. All in all it was an Altman triumph. When Max turned to face the audience there was a smattering of boos, much applause and a few cheers. And fourteen of New York's best trained musicians turned from their radios and pianos to bow again and again.

As if on cue, the wildest storm of the spring exploded as we were leaving the theater. I arrived at Lang's apartment for the after-concert party, soggy but happy. "Well," I said to the master of the revels, "what did you think?"

"Everything changes," Lang said, "Except the avant-garde."

I told this to Max who said, "He's quoting Paul Valery. He's not a man, he's a collage of quotes. Listen, Oscar," he was urgent, "I'm going to ask Jenny to marry me, tonight."

It was always painfully clear why Max was lunging or hulking at this or that woman, the next day or night nurse as he would have it. But it was not quite clear why he married the women he did. Jenny never came and she and Max both viewed this as a great failure. Perhaps he thought marriage, the great comforter, the anti-anxiety drug of the time, would get her over the mark. His motto that pleasure is power was endangered, his pride in giving and controlling a woman's pleasure was at stake.

The party was a mixed bag. It felt like the beginning of something, of everything, for Max, and the end of something for me. Let him marry Jenny, give her his name (that's how it was done then) while that name grew large in reputaion. As for me, I was now adrift in more ways than romantically. No longer so involved with the sensual sounds I could make on the oboe, I'd discovered the pleasures of thinking about music. In short the incipient academic was being born. I must add, here, that I have never regretted this retreat, as some might call it. I have had a good career, I've been happy, married twice, widowed once, divorced once: but the process was orderly, love (at least twice), marriage followed by the birth of my son, Oscar Simon, Jr., teaching, tenure. A process as satisfying as sonata form at its best.

Jenny sought me out. Behind her the floor to ceiling windows were screening the worst thunderstorm I'd ever seen. She was the tallest person in the room; she was always the tallest person in the room. Her farm-bred height and health seemed to announce that she didn't belong here, that she was a four H—a healthy, happy, husky hick. But right now she was a BSA (a brooding, sad avant-gardnick). We had committed a great alchemical change, a minor crime of transformation. Jenny had come East in search of the Great American Orgasm and had ended up in the endless foreplay of the avant-garde.

"Listen," she said, "I think I'm breaking up with Max."

"When did this happen?"

"Hasn't happened. I decided tonight. I'm just finding it hard to tell him."

"Why now? What has he done that he hasn't done before? You know Max."

"I feel trapped. He's so in charge. I'm sure there are other women." She turned her head sideways, as if we were being watched. "And nothing has changed."

She was speaking in a code I understood immediately: she meant the big O.

I had an idea. I stood up and held her by the arms for a moment. "Listen to me. Break up with him, but don't tell him.

That way, you'll know he's not in charge because you're really on your way out, but he won't know it. Knowledge is power. Then, when you're ready, you tell him and you split."

She sighed, uncertain. "I wish my analyst would tell me what to do."

"I'm telling you."

Her gaze was searching, uncertain. "Whose side are you on, Oscar? You seem—different."

Had she found me out? "I have to decide about where I stand with Max, too."

She stood up, wobbly, weary from changing lives. Was that her second or third drink? I'd never seen Jenny drink before.

"Anyway," she said, "we've done a grand job. The big launch is done. Now the whole world can start to decide where it stands with Max."

I smiled at this. "It's what he's always wanted."

Lang came by with a tray of drinks. "Here we go," he said. "Cointreau on the rocks for some, Martinis for the rest."

Declaring myself once and for all, I took his outré Cointreau-on-the-rocks. I was through being "the rest."

That was the night that Max and Jenny, each nursing different agendas for the future, lurched home in a blinded rainstorm to fall into bed and make love, half-wet, half-dry, completely passionate. Each of them sought me out in the next few days to tell me how it had gone. Their stories were reasonably close to each other. In Max's version they started to make love, going at it with a frenzy born, for Max, of relief that the concert was done, the future was on its way; for Jenny it was a wildness born of her new freedom: she was still there, Max's girl, but she was also gone, on her way back to being Jenny's girl, whoever that might turn out to be.

What transfixed them both, in different ways, was when she started to come: a great, roiling orgasm that shook her body and, wherever it was secreted, her soul. She laughed with me, later, and said people always argue about where does it come from, the clitoris, the vagina, whole schools of early political, feminist thought were built around these topographical explorations. "They don't know," she said, rolling her eyes in comic amazement, "it comes from the toes—and doesn't stop at the scalp, just keeps going."

107

I thought, no wonder it takes up so much psychic space in people's lives, at least at certain moments, certain lives, certain decades. As for the slap, where did that come from? From the heart as much as the hand or the outraged deprived prick; a response to her coming, the way she came, the moment her explosion had chosen to arrive after so many months of climaxless, free-form fucking. His sudden rage had arrived from a feeling of being cheated all that time. As if she had been withholding from him the powerful pleasure of being able to give pleasure: a stubborn child refusing a parent's authority.

Here's the moment as it happens: sweaty, amazed, still engaged, Max rears back like a startled horse and, surprising both himself and Jenny, slaps her, hard. She blazes, perhaps still on fire from the moment before, and gives a great heave, throwing Max off the bed; he lands on the floor and on his right wrist. Grunt of pain.

She gathers a confusion of sheets and blankets around her, looks down at him, and says, "Who the hell do you think you are?"

"I think I sprained my wrist."

"Good!"

"I have to play at Virgil Thompson's tomorrow night."

"Fuck Virgil Thompson! You hit me!"

He gazes up at her. "Well, where have you been all these months—coming like that out of the blue?"

"Where? Working to spread the Good News, as we used to call it when I went to church . . . ."

"Good news . . . ?"

"That the Saviour is coming."

"Don't give me that shit. If you didn't want to help out with the concert, nobody was forcing you." He rises from the floor, gingerly, favoring his wounded wing.

Jenny gathers her assortment of sheets and blankets and steps out of the bed: an outraged Queen of Sheba: Nebraska-style. "Wait a minute," she says, a light bulb snapping on. "You mean you slapped me because I wasn't coming all those months and now I did?"

His silent flexing of a painful wrist is all the answer she needs.

"That I was keeping something from you—something that was yours? My pleasure, my responding is yours?"

108

"Every man likes to feel—"

"Oh, now Max Altman is everyman. I've been strug-gling . . . I came back from Rome to go into treatment just so I could—and you think it's yours . . . ."

Max sits on the bed letting her tower over him even more. "Well, why did you . . . why tonight . . . ?"

"Instead of being happy that I could finally let go—you feel like I owed you something and I—I—I—" Jenny has never stammered before or since, as far as I know. "I offend you because I should have paid up earlier. My God, if I ever come again, I'll feel your slap on my face every time."

At which Max, who has solemnly started to gather his clothes, slyly tries to regain control. "If I could believe that," he says, "I'd be the happiest man in the world."

At which Jenny laughs and is still laughing when Max leaves, like Napoleon after Waterloo, having lost the battle, still hoping to win the war, perhaps a day or two later.

He told me about it, despairingly, not amused or trium-phant—the way a man asks a friend to have a drink and talk when he's found out his lover has betrayed him. I couldn't tell him Jenny's secret of hidden flight, that she'd betrayed him with herself, and within a few weeks he was telling it to the painters in quite a different way, a comic story of the orgasm that came too late and the slap that came from the heart, a cry of pain from a man deprived of full passion from his lover.

When Jenny came to tell her version of the slap, it in-cluded her response of sending him flying, thrashing to the floor in a flowering of sheets, and spraining his wrist so that he couldn't play the piano for two weeks.

Pleasure is power, Max had said, and I wanted to tell him he'd missed a chance to accept a random gift of chance, the chance to extend his beliefs from the concert hall to the bedroom. But I was in no mood to preach to Max. I had my own secret flight in mind.

"Men that we know don't hit women," I said. "What would your mother say?"

He scowled at being misunderstood. "I didn't hit her in that sense. It was as unexpected, just as natural, as her coming."

"Bullshit," I said and walked away for good, feeling some-how implicated in something shameful: Jenny through me to Max to the slap. It took me about a week to recognize that I was the bullshitter. The slap was just a convenient way for me to bail out, to jump the Altman ship. I was tired of being the follower, the disciple—I needed a ticket into my new life. Any slap would do.

Instead of the more conventional fame the concert was supposed to supply, Max's underground reputation only intensified. He was so far downtown now that, instead of from midtown, invitations came from Darmstadt, Germany, the current capital of the far-out, from the dark prince of the European avant-garde, Karleinz Stockhausen himself. Then, two years later, darker information arrived. I heard from musician friends that Max was ill, Hodgkin's disease.

It turns out that Max had written a concert piece for four pianos called *Last Pieces*. Some critics have said, since his early death and subsequent fame, that the title demonstrates that he was obsessed with death. But I knew better. It was a reference to Boris Pasternak. *Doctor Zhivago* had come out and Max was blown away by it. Pasternak had written a little book called *Last Poems*, and then went on to write more poems, being by no means finished with life. Max thought it a nice joke, and played his version of it on himself and the world. He wrote *Last Pieces* and his next work was called *Out of Last Pieces*. He would have continued in this way had Hodgkin's disease not intervened. (They can cure that now, and Max would still be alive, no doubt writing *First Pieces* or some such new complicated joke.)

Since I'd detached myself from Max's life, Ronald Lang had thrown me a series of life preservers: first a job as adjunct professor of music, then a tenure track position. My life took predictable shape for the first time while my oboe lip withered.

I was teaching at Indiana University when I opened the *New York Times* and read of Max's death. It was a modest obit but it contained, already, the seeds of the reputation that would finally give him everything he'd hoped for. "I want people who hear my music to feel as if they've lost, not gained something." This was the last line and it was picked up everywhere as the paradox-of-the-moment. In the following months the vagaries of chance which operate on reputations worked their peculiar chemistry. Max's name, instead of being a distant echo became a well-known melody recognized anywhere, anybody could hum it.

The funeral was a harbinger of things to come. Fame was already in the air. Someone from Peters attended, Peters, the big European music publishers, the legendary name on my sheet music of my student days, publishers of Haydn, Mozart, Beethoven. Also, the assistant conductor of the Berlin Philharmonic was in town and showed up at the chapel wearing a yarmulke. If Jenny was there I would have seen her, looming above the rest, but I caught no glimpse of her.

The decade had ended. In the new dispensation orgasms were political: a right, a statement, not a quest. Psychology, psychoanalysis, was falling on hard times. As for Jenny, she became a great success, the author of twelve self-help books. As her first self-help advisor I take some small credit for her vocation. It may be that I should share it with Max's slap; the slap that awakened a soul. Later on she married a hot-shot photographer and the word is of a happy marriage and kids—if such word counts for anything.

Oddly, Max's posthumous success happened by musicians abandoning chance and randomness. His scores were now played as if they were engraved in stone. The enchanted moment of chance had passed. The new moment was impatient of chaos, open only to new verities.

Yet there is one person who clings to the original idea of randomness and accident, still: myself. I testify now to the fact that Max Altman was right all along. I am the proof. What I said before about the happiness, the solidity of my life, was a lie. It's all been ugly brutal chance; miserable, random chance and accident. Max was right—the gods of indeterminacy have ruled. My only child, Oscar Simon Junior, struck by a runaway car, a fluke by all accounts, a confluence of brake fluid and the incline of a particular street—a random joke of a tragedy. "Bad luck," the police said. My first wife dead two months later, not of shock, of bereavement, but a long-present, slow-growing tumor. "Bad luck," the surgeon said. The year my thesis was published two other books on Max Altman and Von Heisenberg were published. "Bad luck," my chairman said. "Bad luck," my publisher echoed. There's an old saying, even to have bad luck you have to have luck. Like most people I've had my share of luck but of course it's distributed like the fall of dice. One good friend has won the

Nobel Prize, another, equally deserving, has won nothing. Max Altman is gone, I'm still here.

My second wife, Lisa, auburn haired and passionate— all the climaxes, the winter evening orgasms, hers and mine, and afterwards the dying light on the wall opposite the bed, the summer afternoon arousals and completions, warmed by each other, chilled by air-conditioning. But none of the astonishing sensual fireworks stayed, none of them can be called up in anything but thin memory. None of them make up for the pain, the losses of the accidental universe.

There are nights when I stay up late, alone in my study, acting as if I'm working but actually remembering Max Altman at the piano, invoking the spirit of the enemy, playing the *Waldstein Sonata*, that glorious working out of theme against theme towards heroic destiny, down to the last magnificent chord. And I remember his bitter complaint: "It's a damned prison . . . Sonata Form: theme, second theme, development, recapitulation, conclusion. Give us a fucking break—after two centuries of coercion. All that process—" He slammed into the last few chords—"with its moral conclusion. For God's sake, take off the straitjacket, let everybody breathe a little."

The *Altman Sonata* would have been truer—fragments of luck, good and bad, falling where they fell, almost inaudibly, pain and pleasure scrambled and unpredictable. I have a score of Max's *Oboe Fragments*, dedicated "To Oscar Simon, with all my love and admiration." My God, why did I desert him to live here in the desert? He'd invited me into his random universe, but it was too frightening. I have the courage to write this, now, but courage has to be summoned at the right time or it's just another form of cowardice.

I tell you I abandoned the wrong ship, signed on for the wrong voyage. There is no sense to be made of anything; and making sense, itself, is a disgusting lie, seating a moral where none exists. In a universe of luck, good or bad, chance is king. That is why I have written this memorial to Max Altman, the uncrowned Emperor of that kingdom.

Goodbye Max. The sonata ends.

The Condom and the Clarinet

Once upon a time—that's how these things used to begin, isn't it?—everything was new. You might remember that time—Peggy Lee singing "Last Night When We Were Young." But I'm talking about a time in New York. (Actually I lived in the Bronx or the lower East Side of Manhattan depending on the fortunes of my struggling parents, my two brothers, older, and my kid sister.) But the time was a Manhattan time, 1954, and it was set to lyrics, before song lyrics became as surreal and combative as the names of the rock or rap groups that sang them. With barely a dime in my pocket I managed to spend a good many evenings in supper clubs though I don't recall ever having supper in one; The Blue Angel, uptown, The Village Gate, downtown, various other expensive watering places, listening to cabaret singers murmur out the sad or lively melodies and rhymes of the time. *We'll have Manhattan, the Bronx and Staten Island, too . . . .*

Oh, what a jumble of youth: an unused condom left on a living room floor that inflames poor Ellen's parents and sends poor Ellen to Newton, Mass., to live with her uncle Harry, a teacher at Radcliff and a composer of art songs and symphonies. In Newton she stays, at first temporary but finally, forever, far from me and my clarinet and my waiting unused condoms. Leaving me to nights spent in smoky Birdland at first flushed with painful Ellen-regret but then, as happens in youth, along comes Anita on a one-night gig; Anita, with her pathological, shy/public singing, her myopic stare into the alcohol darkness, a held breath before she sings, me waiting, holding the same glass of liqueur all night. I thought liqueur far superior to whiskey and it is so important to hold something superior in your hands when you're young and uncertain.

I was twenty, loose in my skin, tripping on my clarinet and skipping any idea of college, to the dismay of my radical, Marxist, but basically bourgeois parents. My father had been a member of the Communist party for a while: still he was afraid of a son adrift in capitalist society with no education and no defense against poverty except the thin reed of a clarinet.

When a buddy from my high school orchestra offered me six weeks with a Charley Parker tour, a Parker known, in the air, but not yet the legend. As my father feared, I was indeed drifting and the gig was a temporary anchor.

Thus, the clarinet. About the condom: those were innocent, condom-secret days. They came in packages of three and Ellen and I had made love twice and I forgot the unused one, leaving it on our bed of love which was the Aubasson carpet on the living room floor of her parents' Central Park West apartment. I quickly learned that the Aubusson carpet was sixteenth century from Lieges, France, probably worth more than my father earned in a year; while my mother was happy to have wall to wall carpeting in our small living room, with an occasional little throw rug bought on sale at Macy's. Aubusson and Macy's—that was Ellen and me.

She was only seventeen to my twenty, a May-July romance, neither of us quite knowing what we were doing. She cast a tall shadow, had a lovely oval face like an antique French brooch held in place by shoulder-length Jewish upper-middle-class brown hair. And about her there lingered the faint scent of something fresh and sweet. Not perfume but a meld of some fragrant soap and delicious shampoo, which I somehow associated with her being rich and me being poor, as in a fairy tale.

We were both panicked, quite certain that her lawyer parents would go through the roof if they thought she was having sex; Radcliffe, early admissions, being at the time an assumed sexual-safety choice; this was nineteen fifty-four, years before sex was discovered. Her father was a leader of liberal causes, open-mind and generous-heart, a lover of justice, her mother, sophisticated, accomplished in law and music. But something more primitive then the liberal, ethical life was set in motion: Ellen, their only child, a musical prodigy, whose art songs were being performed on the local public radio station and at Temple Beth-El on Fifth Avenue, a tall, stylish seventeen, 4.0 grade average, happily early admission to

114

Radcliffe, was sending love letters in Winnie-the-pooh code to a slightly older broke young musician, who heedlessly scattered unused condoms all over Central Park West. Condoms, with their silent promise of future rolls, not in the hay but on the Aubusson carpet, in their (to him, that is, to me) awesomely handsome antiqued living room on Central Park West, several worlds away from the Bronx, and light years away from the smoke and jazz of Birdland.

Here's the trio: Ellen was to be a classical composer—that year Hindemith was a visiting Professor at Radcliffe—but she cherished secret yearnings to write pop songs. I was supposed to be a clarinetist and a bassist, this last a comic instrument to the unmusical, but a profound mixture of rhythm and improvisation to jazz lovers; and Anita was to be a famous singer, after her apprenticeship in supper clubs: The Blue Angel uptown, The Village Vanguard downtown, Upstairs At The Downstairs, midtown.

O, the supper clubs of Manhattan in 1954; blue nights of blues when everything began at dusk, when the nights were safe but dangerous—safe as in gangless, unviolent, street-safe; dangerous as in threatening, complicated relationships that could go from naive to entangled in the turn of a song phrase; when lyrics, the light verse of the times, seemed in our utterly foolish seriousness, to represent our lives.

> *We'll take Manhattan*
> *the Bronx and Staten Island too.*
> *It's lovely going through*
> *the Zoo . . . .*

> *I'll take romance,*
> *While my heart is young*
> *And eager and gay,*
> *(no, gay didn't mean that)*
> *I'll give my heart away,*
> *I'll take a chance . . . .*

And it was true; life followed lyric as we walked through the Central Park Zoo (was it Ellen or Anita I walked with and does it matter, now, so many years and lives later?). Anita loved me; and on the Staten Island Ferry I declared that her shyness was pathological—what was the use of being able to bend a melody with such finesse if she was terrified of an audience. And while she kissed me in gratitude I was already making plans to sneak away to Newton, Mass., to seek out Ellen in her exile; to heal, if I could, the awful results of the tell-tale condom. That extraordinary object, pristine, still wrapped, still holding out the promise of an intimacy waiting to be resumed, even though its destiny was to be melded into a trash compactor on its way to some garbage dump in New Jersey. It was the condom—that protector of my lady love Ellen's ovaries, until they might be ready. We'd laughed and invented the slogan we wanted printed on each package: Sold Only For The Prevention of Pleasure. In my High School they had been nicknamed "safeties," though it was that condom whose existence on the living room floor had shattered an entire upper-middle class assumption of safety—Ellen being an only child, more closely guarded than Rapunzel, if you'll forgive the image used for a shiny brunette.

> *I'll take romance—*
> *while my heart is young*
> *and eager and gay,*
> *I'll give my heart away,*
> *I'll take a chance on romance . . . .*

But irony also held its own: In the few sets at The Blue Angel Anita didn't cancel, her signature song began:

> *Down with love . . . .*
> *give it back to the birds and the bees*
> *and the Viennese . . . .*

A war between romantic naivete and ironic sophistication.

I, too, was at war: with my other self, the one who played the Brahms Clarinet Quintet and read Yeats, who felt the distance between high art and Kitsch as a painful divorce, unsure of which to give allegiance to.

> *When I was one and twenty*
> *(Okay make me a liar for one lousy year)*
> *I heard a wise man say:*
> *Give pounds and pence and shillings*
> *But give not your heart away.*
> *. . . And I am two and twenty*
> *and o, 'tis true, 'tis true.*

Maybe it's not Yeats, maybe it's A.E. Housman, not quite as high art as Yeats but a young man's poet and this is all about youth and its madness. It sort of goes like this: I love Ellen, Ellen loves me; Ellen is forbidden to ever see me again, (being young enough to be under the technical, emotional and financial thumbs of her parents. I have no idea what the fourth thumb was for); short, plump and pretty Anita loves me, but at bottom I am mainly intoxicated with her singing, with the ambience of clinking glasses, the haze of smoky supper clubs; she was temporary anodyne for my Ellen-wounds; in return I would cure her public performance block. Was ever a young man so trapped in a circle of desire, of lost, requited and unrequited love?

I decided to break out. I had a plan.

"I don't know why I'm doing this."

"You're doing this because you have a car and I was born in New York and never learned to drive, because you sing like an angel and because you can fix things with Ellen. She likes you. She respects your singing."

"No! I'm doing this because I'm crazy. Crazy in love with a kid with a clarinet, eight years too young for me, who ruins other young lives by dropping condoms everywhere he goes."

"Turn left at the next intersection. And you're not in love. You're just grateful because I'm curing your stage fright."

"Some cure. I'm still shaking from last night when Dick Rodgers walked in. And my agent was there."

"Your agent's always there. He only has three clients and two of them are out of town."

She drove, quiet and thoughtful, for a few miles, with her window down. The October night was dark and cool. We stopped for gas and she was singing in low tones:

> Dancing in the dark.
> Till the tune ends,
> we're dancing in the dark
> and it soon ends . . . .

"I love that song but I don't know just how to do it, because I don't get it."

I didn't respond because I was selfishly brooding about the success or failure of an impending singing in the dark. Maybe it was a crazy notion. While the pump pumped, she said,

117

"You know Ralphie wants me to concentrate on a recording career. He says that way I won't be performing in public. So I can play hide-and-sing for an invisible audience."

"What kind of man calls himself 'Ralphie'? He must be forty and still Ralphie. God!"

She took a *luftpause* and hid behind the lighting of another cigarette, then said, "I think he wants to marry me."

"I think your Ralphie just wants to get into your pants. And I thought the royal road went the other way. That no record label would take a chance on a singer unless she had a public performance rep."

"Actually I'm still afraid—even of a microphone. But Ralphie says he'll take a chance if—"

"Don't tell me. I know what the *if* is."

"If I find the right song, wiseass."

When we started out the sky had been mad with prodigies of stars. But now the New England night had clouded up. I lit two cigarettes and gave one to Anita. Soon the car was filled with smoke. It sounds awful now but back then cigarette smoke was the innocent air we breathed. Inhaling helped us postpone precipitous action; it helped us see ourselves and the exhalation gave weight to our words.

"What are you going to do when we get there? For God's sake, she won't talk to you on the phone, she won't answer your letters. And her uncle will probably want to kill you."

"He's away at some academic conference. I asked to speak to him; Ellen told me before she hung up on me last night."

"It's still a crazy idea."

"You're her idol, her role-model, her—"

"Okay, she likes the way I do a song. Does she know how I feel about you?"

"She's very smart."

We drove on and I said, "But you're going to melt her heart by singing her own love song, for me, in the dark. Have you ever read Cyrano de Bergerac?"

"Who?"

"Never mind."

"But if anybody comes out to listen, I might freeze up as usual. It's been getting worse."

"Nobody's going to come out. Probably not even Ellen. But you'll be singing her own song . . . ."

118

"The song she wrote for *your* birthday. Good luck."

"I think she gave it to me hoping I would get you to sing it." Either love or youth makes you prone to hope; when you're not sunk in despair, that is. I was high on hope.

Some invisible cosmic director contrived that Anita should stand in a peculiar splash of starlight surrounded by a spattering of other stars. I know—if you have a cloudy sky you're not supposed to get stars, too. But this was no ordinary night. I'd rung the doorbell—having called and been hung up on twice en route. No Ellen, only silence. Then Anita sang. She sang like a myopic angel, twisting and curving phrases in un-expected ways, ways the composer could not have imagined. Have I mentioned that Anita was tiny and round, as tiny as Ellen was long and slim? And relevant or not, I was chunky as I have been ever since; three different shapes in a magnetic field. As I listened I fancied that I understood why three has always been a magical number—trinities repeated eternally. The eternal triangle was not just a convention of novels or musical comedies; it was the hidden truth of all human relationships.

Okay, give me a break. I was twenty, Anita's voice was as husky and sad-warm as it has been during those later years of her fame. And somewhere behind the redwood door of her retreat, my condom-haunted young Roxanne was hearing, all unwilling, her song.

The first drops of rain barely distracted either of us. I was waiting for a light to go on in a window, any window. It was a mild windless shower at first. Anita sang on, eyes closed; she seemed oblivious to rain or dark, concentrating only on making a seamless web of phrases. But soon a wind was added to the rain. Anita's eyes opened and just as he was coming to the end, she rushed a bit, startled by the realization that she was singing into a gathering storm. The purpose of the enter-prise, if one can call a loony parody of Cyrano de Bergerac with love-music replacing love-speech a purpose, was being drenched out of existence.

Then the house was startled into light, it seemed, from every window and the door opened. Ellen appeared in night-gown and robe—matching pink as I recall, looking so young, younger than her seventeen years.

"My God—what are you doing?"

"Anita's singing the song you wrote."

"Not that, you jerk. I have ears. I mean you can't stand there. She'll get soaking wet. She'll catch a cold. Come inside." And getting herself wet, too, she came out, grabbed Anita's arm and yanked her inside. I could, it appeared, stay out in the rain or come in if I wished. It was irrelevant. I stepped inside as the whole evening's enterprise collapsed around me.

"What kind of silliness was that? Don't you know singers are delicate?" At least she'd noticed me enough to lecture me.

"You wouldn't talk to me or answer my letters and it wasn't raining at first and—" She was shedding that sweetish soap-scent into the air and breaking my heart.

"That was beautiful," she said to Anita, pouring her a medicinal cup of hot tea with lemon. My eternal triangle was becoming a duet. I began to sneeze. That was the start of my solo. After about an hour in the kitchen with Anita, Ellen decided that we could not drive back to New York, that death and destruction waited for us on I-95 in this rainstorm. Since singers were delicate, Anita got the one guest room bed. I got Uncle Harry's couch, a pillow and two of his blankets.

The dark Massachusetts night felt strange. I'd never been outside of Manhattan, except on tour with the band, and that was always bandland, not really a city or state. I fell asleep in my underwear, immediately. No restless twisting, no dark dreams; just exhaustion. I have no idea how long I was asleep before Ellen knelt beside the couch and woke me.

"What the hell do you think you were doing?"

"Winning you back," I said, awake as quickly as I'd slept.

"By playing that scene from Cyrano? You are a nut."

"I miss you so much, I couldn't stand it."

"I miss you too. It's my folks, not you. I can't stand hurting them. Move over."

I rested my head in the nest of hair. "Anita's so nice." She whispered. "I'm going to write a song for her."

"You'll never hear it. She's too scared."

"She'll cut a record. There's this fellow Ralphie who owns a record company. Does she love him? I think she loves you."

"It never matters who loves you," I said with my twenty-year old wisdom. "It only matters who you love."

"Good idea for a lyric. Maybe I'll use it." And she giggled into my shoulder.

Night conversation became nuzzling, holding, holding became kissing, kissing became wandering hands. Then there came the inevitable stage business of condom-out-of-wallet, of unrolling and rolling on—only then could love make its claim. Uncle Harry's couch was more confining than the Abausson carpet but it didn't matter, here was my banished princess in my arms again, fragrant with expensive-smelling, fragrant soap. Murmuring strange, arousing seventeen-year-old sounds.

Afterwards—that unavoidable word when telling about sex—afterwards I lay listening to Ellen breathing into my neck, thinking not about triangles any more, but about dualities: Ellen's richgirl versus my poorboy, about Radcliffe versus Birdland, about Anita versus Ellen—about jazz versus the Mozart *Clarinet Quintet*, about song lyrics versus classic poetry. How split my life was; my post-lovemaking thoughts rambled on while the rain splattered furiously against the window near the couch. But I held Ellen firmly as she dozed half on, half off the couch and I was happier than I'd been for months.

> *Blow, blow thou winter wind*
> *That the small rain down might rain.*
> *O that I were in my (something something)*
> *And my love in my arms again.*

Ellen stirred. "Listen, I've been thinking . . . ."

"Is *that* what you were doing?"

"After that. I mean just now, this minute, this second—I think maybe I can get my Uncle Harry to calm my folks down. He's my father's older brother and Daddy trusts him."

"Tell me, this is true," I breathed.

"I can't. But it's possible. I've been working on him." A swerve. "Isn't Anita like much older than you?"

"About eight years."

"My God," said the half-naked seventeen year old.

"It is odd, I guess, to love a guy so much younger than you and to come and sing just to get him back with another girl . . . ."

But she was on a different track, entirely. "No, I mean shouldn't she be much further along in her career? She's so damned good; she made my little number sound like Cole Porter or somebody."

I parroted into some detail about anxiety, fear of exhibitionism, stuff that Anita's therapist had told her.

"I'm going to write another song for her."

"If you do, now," I said, "you're going to make romantic, musical, psychological and sexual history." But she'd dozed off in my arms, leaving me to thoughts of all my dualities coming together at the slightest words of comfort that Uncle Harry might say to his almighty, rich and stuffy younger brother. Ellen had been such an unanswered question for so many months that now she seemed like the answer to all my questions. We would marry and I would probably teach music to keep her free to write her songs, during and after college, our two sets of oil-and-water parents would meet and befriend each other—a sort of Romeo and Juliet in reverse. I would still be soft touch for a cabaret song, I might even play some jazz in the evening with friends, but I would probably go to graduate school first, and then teach music at a college, and play the Mozart and Brahms quintets with students; I would calm Ellen's parents. My folks dreamed of a dentist or a lawyer; but still, maybe a professor would make the grade. I was leaping through a college and graduate school career I hadn't even laid a glove on. But passion had given way to fantasy, I was loony with hope.

That was when I heard the door slam and a man's hoarse voice, ratcheting: "Goddam rain . . . shit . . . ." My heart tried to leave my chest by pounding it with a hammer. Apparently Professor Uncle Harry had made a surprise return. Ellen was wide awake on the instant.

"Omygod. Quick, get under the blankets." And in seconds, pink nightgown and velvet robe arranged rough and ready, she was in the foyer spinning out some tale of friends, orphans of the storm, spending the night. But apparently Uncle Harry was more concerned with getting into some dry pajamas and talking to some pillows. Minutes later I heard an upstairs door slam. Ellen left me to an uneasy sleep on my solitary couch. And upstairs, Anita slept the sleep of the shy, safe, for the moment, from the eyes of others.

A sleepy Uncle Harry joined us for breakfast, asking me ambiguous questions about my clarinet playing—so he knew I was the banned boyfriend, but that was all. When we left Ellen kissed me at the door, but she held Anita in a tighter embrace and thanked her about fourteen times before we got into the car. After ten minutes of silence, I said,

"Thanks . . . thanks for doing me this nutty favor. You got me face to face with my lost ladylove." I didn't mention the more intimate sequel on Uncle Harry's couch, or my own fantastical post-sex plans for a new life. We'd arrived at a tollbooth on the interstate and she said, "No, it's me who gets to thank you."

"What for?"

"I had a big moment last night. Singing in the dark—"

"And the rain . . ."

"Never mind the rain, it was singing in the dark, and I realized that maybe I should stop torturing myself in clubs. Maybe singing in a recording studio is a little like singing to an invisible girl for a boy who's carrying a torch . . . maybe that's what singing torch songs in a recording studio must be like. I'm going to call Ralphie."

I wasn't quite taking this startling information in because in searching my wallet for the toll I found an astounding absence: the package of condoms. Who was it who said if you don't understand history you're condemned to repeat it? Never mind. There was no way to understand how I could have done it again. Another incriminating condom left behind; I was apparently bent on leaving a trail of them, like bread crumbs in a fairy tale, this time on a couch, instead of an antique rug. Who would find it, Ellen or her ace-in-the-hole Uncle? On that tiny swing vote by the gods of chance, my whole future life dangled.

I was on the edge of confiding in Anita, but she wasn't next to me, in the driver's seat, she was on another planet.

"Anita, you know what I did . . . ?"

"No," blithe and confident, "but I know what I'm going to record with Ralphie. Just listen to this lyric. It moves me, but I'm not sure how to make sense out of it. Tell me what you think." And my anguished condom-confession was swallowed up in her intense, *sotto voce* singing

> *Dancing in the dark—*
> *till the tune ends*
> *we're dancing in the dark-*
> *and it soon ends,*
> *we're dancing in the wonder of why we're here.*
> *Time hurries by—we're here—*
> *and gone . . . .*

I was, for an instant, distracted from my misery by the soft, dark tone she gave the words. "I mean," she said, "it's a romantic picture of two lovers, but that's all—it's not enough."

In a grim, mordant insight, appropriate to my mood, I said, "It's about love and death."

"What—death!"

I was implacable. I said: "That's where we all are, dancing—or in your case, singing—in the darkness collecting around us, or waiting for us. Listen to the words—the wonder of *why* we're here . . . time hurries by . . . we're here—and gone. Get it, we're here and gone. Forever."

"Omygod."

I relented a bit. "It doesn't make it less beautiful. It's more like a real poem."

She was silent, taking it in. And I stared out at the passing landscape in my own despair. Which turned out to be entirely justified.

"How could you do it again?" Ellen's phone voice was equally despairing, though hers was mixed with anger. "Harry showed it to me just before he called my folks. Jesus. Anyway, it's all over now." My tongue was tied in a knot of shame. "Do you have Anita's number?"

I gave it to her as if it were a farewell present. She took it down carefully, then said, "Two strikes and we're out."

She was treading delicately around a voice full of tears followed by the saddest dial tone I've ever heard.

By now the fruits of that connection between the two women in my life have become pretty well-known, if you follow the pop music world. They became the closest of friends, the launching pad of two important careers. Ellen's song "Dancing In The Rain," became Anita's first runaway hit for Ralphie's new label. From that moment on Ellen chose the low road—Hindemith was forgotten in exchange for Cole Porter and company. And I chose the high road: exchanging Charley Parker for Mozart and Brahms. My couch-fantasy born in Uncle Harry's house, became a reality, sans Ellen. First NYU then Columbia Graduate School and a tenure track job in Indiana. I teach students everything from William Boyce to Phillip Glass, with Mozart and Brahms in between. In the evening I play chamber music with colleagues and students. My parents' dream of a dentist or lawyer, smoothly incorporated the title of Professor. And my father says, as often as he can, how safe and secure he feels now that I have Vitamin T—that is, tenure. They come to visit their grandchildren when they're well enough.

But no one, not even my wife Miriam, or our two musical children, Ben and Sarah, as we play, perhaps, the Faure *Piano Quartet*, knows my secret: the foolish stirrings that take place in the vicinity of my heart when I hear Sinatra sing, "I've got the world on a string, sittin' on a rainbow . . . I'm in love." When I long to sit in the smoky darkness of the Blue Angel (no one smokes any more and the Blue Angel is long since closed) my hand curled around a glass of Cointreau on the rocks waiting for Ellen—or the chanteuse of the moment—to sing: *Dancing in the dark . . . in the wonder of why we're here . . . time hurries by/we're here and gone.*

These are some of the ways youth and death collaborate, with the help of what someone calls "the incredible potency of cheap music."

And speaking of life or death, time has worked its magic, too, on the condom, taking it from an adolescent joke, to a sacred, life-saving object.

This may all appear to be just my own ancient history but "once upon a time" will happen to everyone; and however old or young you are—some remembered youth, joy, disappointment and nostalgia are probably in the cards for you—and more than likely they'll come wrapped in music.

It doesn't matter *what* music—everyone has a music-memory hidden away—it can be a Schumann song, Rock or Rap; something soft as soup or hard as rocks, but some refrain will trigger a time or place, a happiness or a hurt. We're hardwired for song and our lives are rounded with melody.

A Little Street Music

Now, here I am, Zachary Roth, after some years of being lost and then found, here at seven p.m. on Fifth Avenue between 52nd and 53rd Street. Snow is swirling everywhere, a beginning blizzard. I pause and listen: a ripe violin sound, strong, clean double-stops and chords and a vibrato just eloquent enough for the Bach *Chaconne*—that *Chaconne* I sweated over, without hope, so many years ago. The style is rich, Christ you could melt snowdrifts with that passion. At the same time the playing is cool, controlled, a nice trick combination if you can bring it off; just right for a street-performance here on Fifth Avenue among the swirling ghosts of twilight snow.

In front of 666, in the slight shelter of the building's overhang, a young woman, perhaps more a girl than a woman, stands, her violin case open, bills and coins scattered on the purple satin lining, playing as seriously, with as much concentration and skill, as if she is playing at Lincoln Center instead of a sidewalk in midtown Manhattan. I stop and stare. She's tall, with a startling waterfall of hair dripping below her waist; she wears only a light cloth coat against the bitter night. Her eyes are mostly closed as she plays, but when she opens them from time to time, I see a beauty straight out of a Norse legend. Blue eyes, blonde hair, statuesque. What my poor father Karl Roth would have called the quintessential shicksa. What I call, in the abstract, magnificent; forbidden, but definitely magnificent.

I've always thought of this central moment of my life as a scene from a novel by, say, Schnitzler. The winter street could be in Berlin or Vienna and the listener a wealthy burgher, as indeed I guess I am, though the wealth is brand new and isn't mine but my wife's; this burgher is hurrying home in the snow only to be caught suddenly by a blast of thrilling wintry music. He listens long enough to start shivering in the cold, but is totally taken. Then he removes a business card from his wallet and writes a few words. *If you would like to play chamber music, please call me.* In the unlikely event that she might call a stranger's number on a card, she would be a wonderful addition to the Friday nights of music, friends, wine, coffee, talk. Of course, since he is only a wealthy burgher in an imaginary Schnitzler tale it is impossible for him to know that she will change the destinies of all concerned.

He steps forward, places the card, along with a twenty dollar bill, in the waiting violin case, and since cabs are hopeless in the oncoming storm, hurries towards the subway some blocks away.

I knew an extraordinary player when I heard one. A consuming love for music was my inheritance. I was the only child of Lottie and Karl Roth, Hungarian refugees from the 1957 uprising whose passions included the playing of string quartets and Orthodox Judaism: Mozart and Moses. Making money took second, maybe third place. As a result, their marginal jewelry business suffered. Lottie and Karl, the failures of Forty-seventh Street. Perhaps that's why I never caught up with money—until three months ago, when it caught up with me.

Grace Freund and I married in haste after a zip-zap courtship only three months long. I had been hacking around Paris, taking courses in philosophy and, so help me, philology; she was doing a stint as a docent in the Rodin Museum trying to pick up the pieces of an interrupted career.

I was eager to tell her about the street violinist. Indulging my penchant for writing with the invisible ink of imagination, I rehearsed the scene in which I would tell her of my discovery of musical beauty on a sidewalk. I would describe the beginning blizzard, add a ferocious, non-existent wind; then the mixture of snow and sound. I would create a Schnitzler novel on the hoof, romantic, impulsive: contrast between the rich burgher and the poor violinist—though that would have to be underplayed since the money in my life came from Grace. She would be gently skeptical, putting some humorous spin into it. I couldn't envision it in detail, but it would probably include caution and some autobiographical touches. We were three months old and catch-up autobiography was still in progress.

Grace: "She won't call."

Me: "I don't know . . . ."

Grace: "I wouldn't. I'd be scared to call a stranger in a strange city." A pause. "I'm cautious—once-burned twice-shy, isn't that how it goes?"

It was not the first time she'd hinted at painful early experience. But she'd never come out with it.

"Also, I play a rotten piano. And you can't put a piano out on Fifth Avenue. Just let's wait a while before we tell Daddy about entertaining street-strangers." And laughed a pale laugh to show whose side she was on.

The snow-waif called three days after the snowstorm.

"Yeah," she said, "Here is Grete."

Grete? German, Swiss, Austrian?

"In my case your card you left."

"Yes, yes. You play very beautifully."

"Thank you. I am student still. We shall play?"

It was as simple as that. And yet in the end it turned out to be terrifying.

"A street player." Paul Dubay, our perennial second fiddle/professor, laughed. "I knew we were hard up for fiddlers but—"

Suzanne Leff, the lawyer-cellist whose grandparents had died in Auschwitz, did not look happy.

"German?"

"I think," I said.

Suzanne was silent. Tony Romano, the chemist-violist, thought it was a romantic story—but improbable. "She's probably mediocre. Listen, it was at night in the middle of a blizzard. Not the perfect moment for razor-sharp musical judgment."

We'd been at dinner in the village, Rocco's, one of our hangouts. We lived in each other's pockets, close as ever and still played together every week; the four musketeers. In those first months of my marriage, the more mysterious my marriage seemed, the more I clung to the group.

It had been important for me to sketch my friends for Grace about three weeks into our precipitous marriage.

"Each of these guys—one was a fiddler, one a violist, and one a cellist. For violin read pathologist, for viola read playwright, and for cello read save-the-world lawyer. All with big dreams."

"What happened?

"Well, Tony Romano, the pathologist, wanted to find a cure for cancer. But all he could do was get a job in low-end research at Sloan-Kettering. Paul Dubay, our playwright, had his name on a few off-Broadway flops. He teaches playwriting at the NYU school of the arts, and our cellist didn't make partner at her law firm, and turned into a store-front lawyer in Soho. You'll meet them. We'll have them over, I hope, for quartet evenings. Like me, they all still play. A terrific bunch of guys. Anyway, when each of them was finally tested, they took a dive and regrouped, went on, finding different New York paths of their own."

"Guys," Grace said, "I thought there was this woman, a lawyer, Suzanne."

"Suzanne is sort of one of the guys."

Suzanne was not only one of the guys, she was the most skeptical, the toughest, refusing to believe in midtown musical miracles.

"I'm telling you she's good. And it's no accident she should show up on a New York street. Great cities are magnets."

I floated the idea that a sense of destiny was the natural property of only a few cities in the world: New York, Paris, Rome, London.

"How about Baghdad, Tokyo . . . ?" Paul Dubay asked.

"I'm confining myself to the West for the moment."

"In any case," Suzanne, dry, taciturn, said, "None of us found what we came for."

"But we've found other things."

"Other things are always second best."

"That doesn't change anything. You win some, you lose some. But destiny is in the air, even in the small talk you overhear in coffee shops or bars. It's not a question of who finds one. It's general property."

"So she was drawn here for a destiny as a street-player?" Suzanne Leff was unyielding.

"Who knows what her story is? Maybe Berlin fizzled and New York beckoned."

Suzanne Leff said, "I suggest you drop Berlin, for the moment."

Grete showed up exactly at the invited hour, eight p.m., carrying her violin case slung over her shoulder, student-style. She looked even younger than I'd remembered, wearing the same too-thin cloth coat for the bitter New York winter, a skirt and a pale-blue middy blouse with a bow in front. The whole effect innocent and alien. Her mouth was painted in some aggressive shade of red; it curved, puffy lips parted, a quick flash of nervous pink tongue appearing and vanishing. She smiled at each of us in turn, her mouth a little crooked, a downward slant at the right side. It marked her lips, exotic, wounded or just that slight imperfection that lends what we call beauty a helping hand.

Grace performed her sunny welcoming number, but it was sort of awkward for the first half hour.

"Where are you from, Grete?"

"Germany."

"Where in Germany?"

"Dresden. You know about it? The war bombing."

"Yes," I said. "Everyone knows about Dresden."

"But I am student in Paris. It is the Conservatoire de la Musique."

Maybe it was her youth, or the intensity with which she played, but Grete flared a raw sensual energy into the air. Her fingers were oddly stubby for making such quick magic. She seemed to have a dozen of them, flying over the strings. I didn't sit in because we had a full complement without me, so I crouched behind Suzanne's cello, watched with my ears and listened with my eyes. The string quartet, two upper voices, one middle voice and one lower voice has always seemed to me to be the human situation worked out in song: all the argument, all the claims of a lyric quarrel with self and others, resolved, satisfied—the way they can never be once the playing stops.

This particular evening an unexpected comedy began almost at once.

I could see Tony Romano fixing passionate attention on Grete; he was taking a dive—Italy falling immediately into the arms of Germany yet again. During a break over white wine and *hors d'oeuvres*, we took turns drawing the newcomer out.

"What brought you to America?"

"Job, boyfriend."

"What kind of job?"

She paused before her reply, distracted, her eyes roaming across the grand living room, the seven-foot Steinway, the Aubusson carpet, the rich lacquer of the Louis XIII antique porte-cochere, the exquisite balletic armchairs, the general grandeur of the living room of a nine-room apartment for two people on Fifth Avenue; the same perfectly wrought artifacts, the same spaciousness that spoke a language of ease and money's understated power. I was still caught by surprise, some evenings, returning from the foundation, as if I surely must be an invited guest viewing this richness, this ease, instead of a man walking into his own home.

"I come with ballet orchestra," Grete said, at last. "Touring. I must have money for conservatory, for concerts. In music, someone must always pay."

It was as if we were hearing poetry in a foreign language. Behind the tightly wound sentences there seemed to be a torrent of something hidden waiting to be released. When she played, she didn't sway or close her eyes, she made a dazzlement of fingers and song, her gently slanted mouth half-open, tongue peeking in and out again and again in concentration.

The whole effect was erotic, or so it seemed to me. Perhaps not to the women present. Grace was gracious as usual, everyone there was almost as new to her as the German girl and she watched carefully. Estelle, Tony Romano's wife, was tense, sitting close to Tony. She was trying to seem amused at the whole incident—seeing Grete as a sort of found object. Suzanne Leff treated her as if she were an unexploded bomb: Germans were Germans. We had a conversation the next evening.

Me: "I could see you were uncomfortable. I'm sorry. But she was probably born thirty years after the war ended."

Suzanne: "And her parents and her grandparents?"

Me: "My God, Suzanne, do you want to be held responsible for everything your family ever did?"

Suzanne: "Don't make it trivial. We're talking about enough total horror for a thousand years. I'll play with her. The violinist is quite amazing. But don't ask me to be delighted with the person. What about you, Zach? You were raised super-orthodox. How does all that sit with you? I noticed you didn't marry a shicksa."

Me: (a swerve) "I married Grace because of Grace. These days I'm a card-carrying agnostic, citizen of the world. We were lucky. My family all came here in the twenties, except for one aunt. Your family got the worst of it. Forgive me, you don't have to be so damned reasonable."

Suzanne: (Pause) "She's very beautiful. If she didn't have a violin she might be doing something entirely different on the sidewalks of New York."

At this I gave up. There was something so tailored, rigid, almost tough about Suzanne, that I wondered if she wasn't simply jealous of Grete, who was feline female while Suzanne was tailored, tight. What I'd told her was true: I had married Grace because of Grace, falling, dizzy, headlong. But in the tight circle of Jewish self-protection, Suzanne had raised the stakes. The German taboo took precedence. No one had ever fought a war over a shicksa. Except maybe for Helen of Troy.

Over coffee at Starbucks one evening we wondered if Grete would be back playing on the street between Fridays. There was no reason why not, although I offered to pay her for playing with us. After all, even though a student, she was to be a professional and we were okay but still, eternal amateurs. She'd accepted, though it took me a little hemming and hawing to figure out how much or how little to offer with-out being insulting. A hundred dollars seemed to do the trick but that wouldn't go far in New York. For the rest of that week I checked the Fifth Avenue spot but it was empty. Which didn't mean she wasn't playing somewhere else.

Once I was even late for a dinner party Grace was giving because I found myself wandering midtown listening for that thrilling sound. At the next Friday get-together we grilled Grete. Under pressure, her sentences became longer, less gnomic. Between a Haydn and a Schubert, over a glass of wine, Tony Romano asked about the boyfriend. "He was fool," Grete said. "And liar. He played clarinet, good. But the job he said was six months for tour . . . ."

"And?"

"Six weeks."

"And then?"

Her first laugh, bitter but a laugh. "And then another girl. Job ends. I make money playing on street."

"But what will you do? Especially now in the winter."

This was the moment when I and perhaps the others first realized we had someone here much more implicated than we'd imagined. She shook a cloud of red hair around her shoulders, hunched forward, displaying long eloquent legs. "It does not matter. I was born for . . ." she waved a hand in the air. "Pencil?"

Bemused, Grace produced a pencil and a sheet of paper. Grete scorned the paper.

"Big, please, I make poster."

Grace, ever resourceful and patient, produced a pad. Grete spread her legs, nestled the pad between them and printed in great block letters:

> HEUTE ABEND
> GASTEIG HALLE
> GRETE MUELLER—
> SPIELEN: BRAHMS VIOLIN CONCERTO
> BERLIN PHILHARMONIA
> DIREKTOR LEONARD BERNSTEIN

Then, perhaps seeing she had her audience startled, she added, below:

> CE SOIR
> SALLE PLEYEL
> GRETE MUELLER
> PROKOVIEV VIOLIN CONCERTO #1
> DIREKTOR HERBERT VON KARAJAN

So this was the concealed torrent behind the monosyllabic, tight-lipped autobiography: a world-class concert career waiting in the wings. Then, in the first hint of the trouble to come, Tony Romano grabbed the pencil and made it a *folie a deux*.

> TONIGHT
> AVERY FISHER HALL
> GRETE MUELLER
> BEETHOVEN VIOLIN CONCERTO
> DIREKTOR KURT MAZUR

"*Shicksal*," Tony said.

She beamed at him. In confusion, Tony dropped the pad and pencil to the floor.

"Easy does it," I murmured, a phrase I picked from Grace.

"What?" Suzanne said. "*Shicksal*—that she's a gentile girl?"

I was silent. I would not touch that issue, but I thought I saw a sly glance from Grace.

"It means destiny," Grace said. She had taken several languages at Wellesley, German for a semester when it looked as if she might take her junior year in Berlin. She went to Paris, instead.

"Ah," I said. "A new member of our club."

"I think she means to have it, still," Grace said. "It's a different club."

Estelle Romano carefully retrieved the pad and pencil and returned them to Grace. There was something laughable about Grete's solemnity as she took us on her imaginary whirlwind concert tour. At the same time she compelled a kind of weird attention. Apparently I was looking at the real thing. Destiny was no simple fantasy to this girl, it was a personal possession, something natural like breathing.

So that was the way you did it. Pick a career, choose the high road, and invoke your will. Of course you had to assume the talent, but lots of people had talent. Professor Grossberg at Stanford had spoken of my talent for creative writing; one long story in particular, the one I'd used for my entrance sample had evoked that magical word. After graduation I'd never written a word of fiction again.

But Grete had apparently held on. Behind the calm assurance of *shicksal*, of a destiny, had to be piled up hours, days, months, years of relentless practice. Still, there were so many who performed the necessary rituals of preparation and had no such a vision, no such will.

I could see I was getting carried away. Maybe it was just a German thing, *shicksal*; maybe it had an ugly side, from Schopenhauer's *The World As Will And Idea* to Hitler's destiny of the two thousand year Reich. My reactions were getting loonier and loonier.

I was oddly taken and troubled.

"The question is," I said to Grace later as they we were gathering up wine glasses and cheese plates, "Is she crazy or just enormously ambitious?"

Grace waited a long time before she answered. She never shot from the hip, answered and asked with caution. My guess was: burn them early on with a scary first marriage and caution is built in. She'd waited a long time for a second try, a long time considering all that money, considering all her smarts and soft blonde symmetry.

She was thirty-one, graced with good looks, her figure was still *Vogue*-elegant; she had a sharp, intelligent smile involving crinkling blue "gentile" eyes and a downturned cupid's mouth, albeit not fully used. That smile was perhaps her best feature, but grace-like it invited you in and at the same time held you off.

She paused at my question. "It's hard to say. Crazy,— or maybe just terribly young. Or maybe," she said, "maybe we should ask Tony."

Recalling the public electricity between Tony and Grete gave me a charge as well. Softly settled in the great canopied bed, I turned and reached for Grace, spur of the moment, ran my hand up her long tennis-muscled legs.

I think perhaps we made love that night in the afterglow of Grete and Tony's click, at least I did; I had a sharp edge for Grace and it didn't need any sharpening.

Often after making love she would express the hope that we'd just made a baby.

Her anxious joking told a lot: "Am I so inconceivable, am I impregnable?"

Tonight she lay in a pleasure of sweat and said, "Baby or not, it's a lovely way for us to pass the time." Then, in a panic, "Zach, where does the time go?"

She had a degree to finish, a thesis to write: a comparative study of Balzac and Henry James, two peas from different pods, you'd think. But, full of enthusiasm, she'd remind me that James, the delicate Mandarin used to lecture on the rough-and-tumble Balzac. Enthusiasm would be followed by despair.

"I'm thirty-two, for God's sake. Thirty-two and never had a real job. I've been a graduate-student-in-training forever. I let a dumb marriage at nineteen cost me a decade." She could turn on a dime. "Maybe I should just be a wife and mother, maybe I'm not cut out for an academic career. Let's have a baby."

"Okay."

"Hah. Not always so simple."

She shifted thesis subjects, again and again, to the dismay of her advisor at Columbia. She would decide that her French was too primitive and suddenly plunge into language texts. And as suddenly drop the Berlitz initiative. Maybe she should do her thesis on Rodin as a modernist sculptor. Surprised the hell out of me. "Was he, do you think?"

"Maybe. But maybe will not cut it with the graduate committee."

Lucky for her there was a reservoir of patience at Columbia. Old man Freund was an alumnus and his name was inscribed on a building in the Law School, and a chair or two.

Some nights while I was asleep, my newborn wife would prowl. I might find her in the study at the other end of the apartment, curled up with a book on Zen. As if sleep were entirely an optional matter, she would look up at me with that sad blue-eyed gaze. "Do you think the East has much to teach us. I had this philosophy professor at Wellesley who was pushing Zen—the doctrine of no mind."

I would take her by the hand, as you would a sleepwalker and walk her back to bed. "I thought all that went out with J.D. Salinger and John Cage. I like your mind. Don't give it up." Sleepy and swiftly sensual she would flirt. "You're so glib, Zachary Roth. Come be glib in bed for a little."

Once horizontal she might turn to me: "I'm all *terra incognita*, aren't I? Everything happened so fast that you don't quite know what you've got here, right?"

Solemn, I agreed. "Not quite."

"Marry in haste, repent at leisure, is that how it goes? Everyone marries a lover and wakes up with a stranger, is that how it goes?" I knew a rhetorical question when I heard one. I said nothing.

A small search was starting beneath my pajama bottom. "Is there a child waiting in there tonight?"

"Might be. It's getting big enough."

The idea of fatherhood had played no part in my sense of destiny; but neither had living in a nine-room apartment across from the Metropolitan Museum, the promise of a visit from a Hong Kong tailor, or a job helping to restore the temple at Angkor Wat, a sinking Palazzo in Venice sheltering Tintorettos. But Grace cherished a hunger for a child, maybe two, maybe three. Every month was a cliffhanger for her.

She settled to sleep and murmured, "Maybe our German friend is both—very ambitious and a little crazy. Also, a little young." She slept, my *terra incognita*.

The job at the Grace Foundation was unknown territory, too. I felt my way. Technically, I had no supervisor, but had the sense that Arjemian, the driven director, was waiting for contributions from me, or perhaps just watching the boss's son-in-law, I had no way of knowing. I was supposed to be revving up to write grant proposals for specific projects any place in the world that held a monument, a church, a synagogue or mosque. Culture, religion, vestigial politics, take your choice. It was so wide open I had difficulty zeroing in on just one.

I went through a list of projects, underway or proposed. When I came to D—Dalleyville, a ruined monastery outside of Dublin; Delaville, the first mixed black and white church in South Africa—I stopped short at Dresden. Before the fire bombing in World War II it had apparently been a grand city. There were before and after photographs, but Arjemian was famously and angrily obsessed with Jewish projects. Why include a German city? Why include Grete's home city? Her grandparents must have endured the fire bombing.

When I came to the section on Paris and a strange-looking but familiar synagogue, I stopped again. It was in the Rue des Rosiers, not far from where I'd lived during my year at the Ecole de Paris. I'd had a tiny apartment in the Rue Payenne just behind one of those manicured small parks scattered throughout Paris, the Parc Royale. It was in the Marais, the Jewish quarter. I'd walked those ancient streets, certain that if the lunge of destiny were to happen anywhere, it would spring at me from the mysterious vista of the Rue des Quatre Vents or the long people-packed sprawl of the Rue St. Paul. The synagogue was Beth Shalom, not far from Goldenberg's delicatessen, and it was the only walled synagogue I'd ever seen. More importantly, it was the courtyard where I'd taken Grace that afternoon, a few weeks after we met.

Restless, I justified my accidental walk down memory lane by making some Paris synagogue notes with the vague idea of discussing them with Arjemian. I'd have to find my way into his gaze sooner or later. Grete's bombed and restored home city, still waited on the facing page. I closed the book thinking, no, no, thank you. Grete's German past was of no interest. Her presence was all too interesting, threatening.

The next day Freund called me from Calcutta. He always called at the office.

Freund: "It's hot as hell here."

Me: "We're having snow and rain."

Freund: "I understand you play a lot of music. Grace's mother was a pretty good pianist. Did you want to be a professional?"

Me: "I was never good enough."

Freund: "How come all those years at school, all those universities?"

Me: "I was a late-bloomer. Couldn't settle on what to do, on a destiny, so I stayed on in school. You know, extended adolescence."

Freund: (A laugh, a first) "I've read about it. I still don't know what I want to do. So I just keep doing it. Never had the knack of study; faked my way through Columbia with energy and nerve. Good preparation for business. Listen, Roth. Be kind to Grace. She's delicate. Takes after her mother, not me."

Me: "I'll be kind. I love Grace."

Freund: "That isn't always enough. She's hard on herself. Played the piano, pretty nice it seemed to me. But not nice enough for her. She quit at fifteen."

"I didn't know she played."

"There's a lot you don't know."

Dial tone.

All those questions about my college years. It was as if Freund had my resume in front of him. He'd never had the chance to interrogate his future son-in-law in the flesh, so the telephone would have to do. Except that I already had the job. And his daughter's hand in marriage. Even if, apparently there was a lot I didn't know.

The tensions in the group began to build. Within a month Tony Romano was complaining to me that Paul Dubay was getting Grete a gig at NYU.

I said, "Why not? The music's never been better. She's a real find. And she's looking to move up."

"Move up where?"

"You saw those posters she drew. Fame, fortune. Anyway she needs all the help she can get."

"And Paul is arranging this concert for her out of the goodness of his heart?"

"Tony, you're just jealous. We all saw you falling off your chair for her. All, by the way, includes Estelle."

"She didn't say anything when we got home. And I'm not saying anything against helping Grete."

"Just against Paul helping her?"

And that was that; at least until the concert at the Institute Francaise, downtown. Tony came alone, Estelle saying she had to work late at her Woman's Center Clinic, though I thought her absence said something more. Grace came; she appeared to enjoy the music more than the backstage drama. When Grete left, swiftly, at the end, with Paul, Tony Romano was in a funk.

At the coffee shop afterwards, Grace said, "Tony, Paul's not married. You are."

He stared at her, sad, and said. "What happens if I fall in love with her?"

"Easy does it, Tony," Grace said, gently as she could. "Easy does it."

I decided to beard Arjemian in his lair. Maybe some talk about Paris and synagogue projects. I would be circumspect, joke, maybe start to be where I actually was. But blunt, chain-smoking Arjemian, a dark exotic with a cap of close-cropped black curls, never let me begin.

"It's a bad spot to be in, old man Freund sticking you in here," Arjemian said. "Since your main qualification was being married to his daughter."

So it was gloves off. I was about to make some embarrassed joke about his painful honesty. But he got there first. "I'm cutting to the chase so you'll know none of that matters. What matters is who you are. Old man Freund tells me you're a musician."

"Well, I play. We have string quartets at home." I quickly added, "Amateur."

"Amo, amas, amat. The best kind. From love not ambition. How important is music to you?"

"Very," I said. "Very important."

He stood up, a long, skinny, restless cloud of smoke and walked around a desk covered with photographs, mock-up models, a scatter of books open, clipped at various pages. He poked at one. "There's a shelter for indigent girls, seventeenth century Venice. It houses some phenomenal Titians. Well, it seems Vivaldi lived and worked there. You should know that Vivaldi and Titian are both sinking at the rate of a foot a year. It has to be preserved." He swerved, "How important is being Jewish to you?"

It was turning out to be a spiritual interrogation instead of a meeting.

"It's complicated."

"It's always complicated. Barring, of course, the orthodox."

"My parents were orthodox."

"Were?"

"They died a while back."

Arjemian skipped the usual niceties, sorry etc. He said, "How about you? What does being Jewish mean to you?" He might as well have said, *What is truth?* "I wanted to set this place up as the Grace foundation for Jewish world culture—I mean five thousand years . . . but Freund, of course, being Jewish, has this thing about not being too intrusive, too exclusive. Hence world culture."

"Are you . . . ?"

"Not me. Armenian agnostic. A Jew manqué." At last a grin. A broad, mischievous grin. He sat down in the chair opposite me, then stood up quickly. The interrogation was over; no chance for me to mention Paris or synagogues, or possible projects. Then the long walk to the door, Arjemian suddenly avuncular, an arm around my shoulder. "Before we can work out what to do together, I needed to find out who you are. Not so easy. I'm not sure you know."

Embarrassed, more than a little thrown, I finally got to try a joke. "Is knowing yourself a prerequisite for the job?"

"No. I've long since given up on it, myself." Arjemian opened the door at last. "We have you in mind," he said, cryptic. "We have you in mind."

You'd think, when it became clear Grete was sleeping with Paul, that the quartet evenings would have fallen apart. But call it the pull of tradition, call it the force of habit, something reinforced the glue that kept it together, at least for the moment. Tony Romano was sulking in his tent, and I assumed a nervous Estelle Romano was hoping Grete would vanish back to the streets.

It couldn't last. And when Grete broke with Paul and finally gave Tony a glimpse of the paradise he was longing for, things began to crumble rapidly.

"Can we—you know—use your apartment for an hour or two while you and Grace are away?" Tony was sweating. These days he sweated easily. "Grete's living at a student dormitory and it's impossible . . . I don't even know how much time we have left. There are some problems with her green card . . . ."

"For Christ's sake, no," I said. "I'm not the keeper of anybody's morality but Estelle's my friend."

"So am I," Tony said, and turned away, mournful.

The first casualty was the Friday evening music. Either Tony or Paul kept canceling. It was often difficult to catch Grete at the one dormitory phone. One Friday evening she was the only one who showed up besides Tony. It was the first time I'd ever seen Grace be graceless. She made a show of serving tea and cookies and making general conversation. Only Tony and Grete were oblivious to how uncomfortable she was, hosting a friend's husband's sub-rosa romance, suddenly not so sub-rosa.

Grace was unusually quiet as we prepared for bed. But just as I was dozing off, I could sense an electrical storm brewing on the other side of the bed.

"What the hell does Tony think he's doing? At least Paul knew enough to keep the thing quiet. Tony doesn't seem to care about that. About anything."

I said nothing. Maybe she would think I was already asleep. She shook me and I said, "Okay, okay . . . I get it . . . he's crazy in love."

"He's just crazy. He's giving her money, more than he can afford."

If I wasn't awake before, I was now. "How do you know?"

"Estelle told me."

"How did she find out?"

Grace sat up, sleep postponed indefinitely. "Don't you read novels, don't you go to the movies?"

"What?"

141

"First she found credit card receipts for hotels. Then larger and larger checks . . . ."

"Good God . . ."

"Exactly."

Step by step, encounter by encounter, I was learning. At least now I knew what made this gentle woman angry: deception, betrayal. Her hair shook down around her shoulders, even her hair seemed angry. She wore it in long ripples, probably too young a style: not early thirties, early twenties, sometimes tortured into bangs which she would keep brushing from her eyes. Her hands were rarely still, flicking around her neck; hands in search of—of what? The elusive task they were made for?

The bookcase in the library was choked with Balzac, Baudelaire, Barthes, Baudrillard. Once I asked her, "Do all French writers have names beginning with B?"

"Keep going. Go forward and you get to Sartre and Stendhal; go back, turn left at Flaubert and you come to Camus."

But she kept pulling books out for a glance, then putting them back, nervously, much the same way as she played with her yellow hair. Hands in search of just the right task, just the right book, just the right set of hair to frame that oval medallion of a face.

She would disappear for hours, working at the Columbia Library, then come home and keep at it in her study, books piled in wobbly stacks on the floor. But other times she would wander through the apartment like a tourist, not quite sure where to turn next. All the while I was swimming in Foundation plans, texts, photographs; a little old for so much homework.

One night I took Grace out to dinner. Well, sort of. My freshly minted credit cards with the nicely cushioned credit limits came from one or the other Grace. Still, a few drinks, a little conversation and maybe a few revelations.

Grace: "This looks like a good menu."

Me: "Have the most expensive dish. I want to break in this American Express card."

Grace: "Is it awkward for you? It wasn't in Paris."

Me: "Not awkward, just new."

Grace: "To make it easier I see they've given me the menu without prices. Mustn't bother my pretty little head about vulgar matters. I think it's charming. I'm not complaining. Wellesley women don't complain."

"Why do I get the impression you didn't have a great time at college." It was not really a question.

It took two courses and three glasses of champagne to respond to that.

"College was hell," she said in her softest style. "I was shy and superior. My classmates thought I was snotty. I couldn't do anything right except get great grades and be rich . . . those two got me nowhere. It was hell."

She was tentative; apparently she hadn't sung this song too many times. "No sex. I was the one celibate in class. Then I met Mister Wrong, got married and lived miserably ever after, well for three years anyway."

I held my breath. But nothing more came. Just, "I haven't had this much champagne since my sweet sixteen party. You'd better carry me home."

Alcohol acted as a sort of truth serum. But not enough champagne and not enough truth.

In some ways I felt trapped between both Graces, the Foundation and the woman, neither of which I could quite understand. I'd not been married before; maybe all marriages were opaque, mysterious, at least at first. My quartet of friends had all defined themselves long before; each voice with its flavor—Suzanne dry, Tony peppery, Paul almost sweet, not without surprises but familiar. The root of that word must surely have to do with family. It would be awful to lose them. All because I was naïve enough to bring the streets of New York indoors.

I went into a terrible funk. Until now, I had been concerned, interested, but not directly involved; it was all a kind of theater, watching Grete bring first exquisite music then chaos. Friday music was, so far, the only thing I'd been able to count on. I'd slipped my new life on like a tailor-made suit. All things great and small: a batch of credit cards, office overlooking Fifth Avenue, a British couple who kept the household humming, a man named Jesse and a woman named Lesley—actually the man may have been Lesley and his wife Jesse. That confusion told everything: strange, uncertain, unplanned, out of my control. Only the quartets had been as dependable as Friday following Thursday and preceding Saturday: the now unobserved Shabbat of childhood.

Paul was first on my repair list. I would mollify, I would downplay the Tony/Grete connection, be reasonable in the face of irrational jealousy. But I couldn't find the happy ending I wanted.

Me: "You can't stay pissed at Tony forever. You weren't going to marry Grete, were you?"

Paul: "Never had the chance to find out."

Me: "But she's at the will-of-the-wisp stage. Or maybe that's her basic style. Two to one she doesn't stay tangled with Tony long."

Paul: "What do you want from me? Why are we having this conversation?"

Me: (passionate). "I want Fridays back. I want the gang back."

Paul: "And if it's too late for that?"

Angry, miserable, I thought: I can find others; New York is full of quartet players. But I wanted Tony's particular restless viola, Paul's witty violin, Suzanne's serious, strong cello, the way they brought their styles into their lives, into my life. At Columbia I once wrote a paper entirely based on one line in Joseph Conrad: "He who forms a tie is lost."

Two Fridays later: an attempt at a peace pact, another try at Friday music. Grace pleaded a sick headache until the seductive sounds of Schubert's *Death and the Maiden* drew her in. During the coffee break anybody could sense a strangeness between Tony and Grete. Some path had been closed and they were clearly not the item they'd been. Tony was acting like a teen-ager who'd been dumped. "You grew up in East Germany," he said, pushing her hard. "You probably don't even know there was a Holocaust."

"I know. I know later, not in school."

"Do you feel guilty? Where were your grandparents during the war?"

I expected Suzanne Leff to weigh in here, but she simply balanced her coffee cup and napkin on her lap, silent, watchful.

In a surprise move Grete turned to Suzanne. "Is it that people do not like Germans? Is it maybe because I'm German that I have trouble with my green card?"

"I doubt it."

"Then what? Do I need lawyer to help me stay?"

Bitter as coffee grounds, Paul said, "Why is it so important for you to stay? You can't live on the streets forever."

"Jesus, Paul," I said. "Easy does it."

Grete did not even turn to face Paul. Apparently she never looked backward, just straight ahead.

Suzanne scrambled in her purse and handed Grete a card. "I handle immigration stuff, sometimes. You can call me." Paul looked as if he'd like to drown in his coffee cup; Tony looked as if he'd like to smash his. I didn't know where to look. It was apparently too late for renewal, for mending.

Freund: "Hello, hello, hello. I can hardly hear."

Me: "I haven't said anything, Mr. Freund."

Freund: "I'm in Jakarta. Listen, call me Morris. I'll be coming back in not too long; get to know each other. I hear you found a German violinist on the street."

Me: "A lot of music students make some extra money that way."

Freund: "I didn't say it was bad. Just interesting. We have a German subsidiary. Some of my best friends are Germans. Jews and Germans should stick close."

Me: "Why?"

Freund: "Because they don't trust each other. Have to stay on guard. Is she good?"

Me: "She's terrific but complicated."

Freund: "Everything terrific is complicated. Just keep a close watch. So long, Zachary."

Me: "So long, Morris."

Freund: "What? What? I can't hear . . . ."

Dial tone.

It seemed that Grace was telling her father all sorts of stuff. From the first I'd decided not to tell her about Freund's calls unless she asked—which she didn't. But now it was as if she were using the old man to register various concerns, anxieties. Grete had not left Grace untouched either.

The following Tuesday I saw Suzanne and Grete having coffee at a Starbucks. Suzanne had Grete's hands in a hammerlock. I'd come in unseen and sneaked back out as soon I saw them; Suzanne had smudged her lipstick. A few weeks later, I encountered a sad, sobered Suzanne in the Gotham Book Mart, a copy of Camus's *The Stranger* in her hand.

"I know you saw us at Starbucks," she said. "You slunk away. Very tactful. Well, anyway, I lasted two weeks longer than either Paul or Tony."

She waved the book at me. "Camus. Paul asked me to teach a class in law and literature at NYU." And then, acknowledging the awkwardness of the moment, "Were you surprised about me? I always thought you knew. Or guessed."

"No," I said, "not that I can remember."

"I wasn't always sure myself. An in-betweener. When she suggested coffee after we met in my office she came on so strong—"

"And Germany and history became less important?" I could hear the ugly undercurrent beneath the question. It was involuntary and I was instantly ashamed.

Suzanne tucked the book under her arm. She yielded a slow smile. "Let's say it was put on hold. Anyway it's all a distant memory now."

"So are a lot of things."

"I think she was just using me to help her beat the immigration rap."

"Was there a real problem?"

"Oh, I thought you'd know. She's gone. Just vanished a couple of weeks ago. I had everything lined up for a hearing and—presto. Gone. The people at International House, the students' place where she was crashing, somebody there said she'd gone back to Paris. I'm sorry everything cracked up. I miss the gang. I miss Friday nights."

Outside in the chilly New York twilight we lingered a moment, Suzanne hefting her attaché case and the book she'd bought. "I had dinner with Paul the other day. That's when he asked me to fill in for the NYU class. Who knows, one day maybe we'll . . . ."

She turned, started to wave goodbye, then: "We used to talk a lot about destinies, who we were, all that delayed-adolescent stuff. We never talked about sexual destiny. At least I found out something about myself." A smile. "The hard way."

"And finally, it didn't matter that she was German—or about your grandparents . . . ."

"Oh, it mattered. It was like a mountain I had to climb to get to a valley. It was like holding a knife by the blade, a sharp edge that could cut you any moment. Like I said, I found out the hard way."

"Maybe it's always the hard way," I said and turned away, pulses fluttering with feelings I didn't understand.

The feelings did not go away. I became a street person myself; the slightest musical sound in the distance, a radio, some street performer even on a wind instrument set my nerves on edge. As if it might purge me, I told Grace about Suzanne's troubling fling with Grete.

"Versatile," was all Grace said, no surprise in her voice. The same Grace-cool, putting one off, holding one off. I still had no idea of how to deal with it. In any case it wasn't Suzanne I wanted to talk about, it was Grete. But I could see nothing could interest Grace less. It left me alone with an unpleasant question: why had I refused Tony's request for a trysting hour at our apartment? Propriety, or jealousy? She'd worked her way through the group, one by one—except me. She'd never shown a flicker of erotic interest; a radical critique, putting a kind of full stop to my youth. Sort of comic, if it didn't hurt so much.

I recognized how much I needed to find her when I passed a newsstand on Eighty-sixth Street and saw a German language newspaper, *Aufbau*. I was not in Yorktown by chance. It was Little Germany—a pastry place on every block. I'd hung out there for *sacher torte* and other Teutonic sweets, with the group after concerts. This was B.G.—before Grete, my first true German. But where better to look, or to listen, for her?

Why not an ad in this *Aufbau*? I recalled an oldish movie title *Desperately Seeking Susan*; why not *Desperately Seeking Grete*? Would the ad have to be in German? My stratagems were getting more and foolish. I'd already stayed away from the office too long. The versatile Grete had probably left the country, gone back to Germany, to her Conservatoire de la Musique in Paris, somewhere, anywhere in the world but here. Besides, what would I say to her? Let me make love to you, the last of the group. Make the wound mathematically healed, round it off—childish, infantile. Let me take in your energy, your belief in yourself.

Is it transferable, is it contagious, can you catch it through a kiss?

Always a sound sleeper, now I slept on a bed of nails; no place to turn. I fantasized the serendipitous meeting on a street corner.

"Grete," I would say. "I've been looking over the whole city for you. I even went to your dormitory but they had no record of you."

"I stay with friends. Why have you looked for me? Are you angry? About the others . . . ?"

I twisted around and gazed at a sleeping Grace; she slept, as always, in tranquility, a slight snore trembling her upper lip. What was going on?

Grace was love and home.

Under my gaze she turned towards me, then away, a delicate flutter of eyelids. I didn't want her to wake; I wanted to watch her, incomplete, a work in progress; a burnt child, her own Dresden needing rebuilding, restoration.

It was clear she'd invested a lot in me. All I had to go on was fragments, a mysterious first marriage as disastrous as a drive-by shooting, brief, terrible, a story she would not or could not tell. Something had happened to her that pushed her out of her orbit: graduate school, doctoral thesis, teaching. She'd stopped for ten years, picking up the pieces only about a year before I arrived on the scene. Now she was buried in writing her book—she refused to call it a thesis. "It's not going to be one of those made-out-of-plastic bookoids whose only *raison d'etre* is tenure. I got broken somewhere along the line and I have to paste the pieces together."

But if I burned myself out on this dumb quest for Grete, how much energy would be left for Grace? She seemed so alone: I knew nothing about her friends, I knew about a father away so much of the time, a mother away forever. She'd asked me all sorts of questions about Lottie and Karl Roth: as if she could borrow a couple of ghost-parents. I told her how they'd been destroyed in a few seconds on the Interstate between Ojai and Los Angeles, after borrowing the money for my Paris time, innocent of how purposeless my drifting from school to school was, how random the choice of Paris was; it was all education, and that was sacred. At least they died certain that I would say Kaddish for a year, and that their only child would never marry a shicksa. I'm not sure which would have been more important to them.

Okay, there I was and there she was, Grace Freund, in Paris. The Rodin Museum, myself a strolling eavesdropper, while Grace, the confident docent, addresses a mixed group of German and French tourists in perfect French. I assumed she was French. When the group moved into the next room I got up my nerve to ask her a made-up question in my own broken college French. The question was carefully crafted, flirtatious. It wasn't difficult, standing as we were in front of the liquid flow of Rodin's famous *The Kiss*; those two inward-arching bodies melting together, the kiss itself a creation of invisible lips.

"Est-ce-que Rodin as utilisé les modeles pour ca?"

No dope, she answered instantly in English, in that kind of waspy languid speech in which the lips barely parted, a style I'd heard from the various girls at my various schools, privileged, usually gentile. What Suzanne Leff called shicksa lockjaw.

"No, no models for this one, though for many others he used Camille Claudel, herself a sculptor and his lover."

"Any relation to Paul Claudel, the Catholic writer?" I was trying out a little fancy razzle-dazzle on her. At Stanford it had worked pretty well. She outmatched me. Flashing a small smile, she said, "A second cousin." She pointed to the famous object. "Actually," she said, "it's a sort of sentimental piece. Go see the statue of Balzac. It's something." And then moved on to catch her tour. I moved on, too, waited and hooked her into an espresso, into a long walk along the crowded Rue Jacob, booksellers becoming antique shops, becoming another café, then a hungry brasserie in Mont-parnasse talking, listening, talking. Then, as the liquid Paris afternoon light was going, she brought me face to face with the great piece, the statue of Balzac, just outside the Mont-parnasse Metro station: rotund, visionary, confident of his destiny. She looked up at the towering, caped figure. "You can keep your 'Kisses,'" she said, prophetically, "give me Balzacs."

I fell like a felled tree. It was half joy and half misery. I was positive that she was not Jewish, and I was bowled over by how important that turned out to be, caught and at the same time ashamed of the compulsion. I agonized after our first encounter, in the midst of one rendezvous after another, week after week.

All I knew was that I desperately wanted her; and I was sure she wanted me. The first kiss was all the proof I needed. I'd seen her to L'Hotel, left bank but super-elegant, costing God knows how much when, just before going in she turned to say good night, I grabbed her, inelegant, ferocious and kissed her. She kissed back as if it were a contest she had to win, mouth melting open, absolutely yielding and at the same time pushing back. It was a truly strange kiss and she clung to it for a long time, as if it were a question, an experiment.

Ash-blonde Grace, the quintessential shicksa. Or at least that was what I was afraid of all the while I felt myself falling. Blonde, discreet nose set below spectacular blue, gentile eyes, modest gentile breasts, my tribal clichés were inexhaustible. It seemed I'd lugged one part of the orthodoxy of Lottie and Karl into grown-up life, but only one. Not Kosher, no Sabbath observance, no prayers. But the shicksa taboo was burned into me so early and often that now I felt like some savage helpless in the grip of a primitive superstition. But helpless I was. Sex, okay. But love, no, and marriage—forget it! Perhaps if Lottie and Karl hadn't been killed racing back to L.A., ears and hearts full of their beloved chamber music, racing to make it to synagogue before sundown on a Friday night, perhaps then I might have been able to work some of this out. Now I was stuck.

Only lately had I gotten a glimmer of why I'd chosen Friday nights for the ritual of music; probably because every Friday night of my youth had been devoted to the big synagogue on Hollywood Boulevard, services often followed by a festive board furnished by parents of whoever was being bar or bat-mitzvah that weekend. Paralysis: No work, no travel, no phone calls, no music, either live or canned; the prison of the Sabbath loomed so large in the topography of my childhood that it was destined to be replaced by freedom; the ironic substitution of one of Lottie and Karl's obsession with another: for orthodox Judaism read music. I had done the ritual sitting Shiva, seven days of mourning, but never bothered with the obligatory year of the prayer for the dead, the Kaddish. I'd long since become a convert to the secular.

Only one prohibition—among so many—I could not shake, was not even aware of any desire to shake: No gentile women. The word *shicksa* was invested with such menace, such anxiety, that the prohibition was as powerful as a death-bed promise, extorted with a last breath; the unspoken eleventh commandment of the house of I: Thou shalt not marry a shicksa. Okay, don't become a doctor, okay, don't become a violinist, but at least stay within the tribe. Children—children must be brought up within the fold.

But Gentile/Jewish was not the only gulf to be bridged. There was also Rich/Poor, or at least Rich/Broke. Nowhere was this more easily seen than in the question of eating.

She chose restaurants way out of my league, restaurants full of stars and superior maitre d's and wine stewards with funny little cups around their necks. I thought it quite something to see the delicate, blonde shicksa tuck into a *Poulet aux Trois Moutardes*, into a mound of *Moules Mariniere*, into a *Souffle au Chocolat et Cognac*. That mouth enjoyed generous glasses of Burgundies, the tongue tormenting me with its quick little side trips to the right and left corners, the practical purpose, ostensibly ladylike, to catch errant drops of wine. While all the while I wondered how was I going to keep paying for these evenings.

The question of payment was swiftly solved, or actually never came up. You've never seen a credit card appear so quickly, with such sleight-of-hand in slender fingers, carrying two rings, both on neutral, non-marriage fingers, buff nails gleaming in the artificial restaurant twilight; the speed and subtlety and, yes I have to say, delicacy, sparing any possible protests, her gentle smile of gratitude for a fine dinner and a fine evening making it seem gross to even mention the issue. I would not be gross.

The first time was a touch confusing and was over before I realized what had happened. I'd already calculated the impossible sum from my small store of francs, but she sensed that more than one of these splurges would be catastrophic for me. The next time and the time after that were easier. I'd been single for quite a while and I expected dinner/dates to be the royal road to information, to learning lives the way you learned them from reading biographies. Grace was no exception. She was interested in everything:

art history, (her minor at Wellesley), French literature (her major), politics (liberal).

"I had a bad time at Wellesley but a good education," she said. "The danger after college is in mistaking opinions for ideas."

"Wait a minute; how about your opinion about Rodin *The Kiss* not so good, the *Balzac* terrific."

"Not just an opinion. The difference is having good or at least interesting reasons. *The Kiss* is a romanticized version of a conventional intimate act. *The Balzac* is heroic."

"One man's romanticism is another man's heroism. The way the sculptor had him stand, poised for greatness."

"But he was greatness. The *Comedie Humaine* is titanic. And *The Kiss* is an abstraction; could be anybody."

"I think that's the idea."

"A weak idea. The less specific, the weaker the idea."

She was a strong and subtle arguer. Under the pleasant pressure of discovering a nest of smarts under that nest of blonde hair, the whole unspoken shicksa issue took a back seat.

On our second outing, sated with *timbales de veau farcie*, with a sleepy-making Bordeaux, with exotic sorbets, we left Laserre and walked the two blocks to the Seine and stared silently at the blue river. I reached for her and she moved as swiftly as if it were her idea, arms curling around my shoulders. I kissed her neck then the perfumed pulse of her throat to pleasant murmurs and in a minute she was running her lips down my cheek, a trail of happy kisses. At the most I thought this might be a harbinger of gradual attraction, of growing passion. Two or three more such Olympian dinners and Seine-side walks and the real thing, bed and breakfast, might be in the offing. The folk-wisdom among my Jewish friends at school had been: with shicksas it goes more slowly. It could be days, it could be weeks, certainly not tonight.

It was not the first time that Grace Freund would surprise me.

"How do you keep that figure with Paris food?"

"I run. Also it's constitutional. My family is lean."

The figure in question was sprawled, nicely naked on her great bed in her grand suite at the Plaza Athenee, resting after making love. I did the unthinkable. *I asked her.* Lying, "all passions spent" — I forget where that phrase comes from

152

but it fits the bill—my head on her belly, face downward so I wouldn't have to see her face, I popped the question. Not the usual one you pop, that took two more days to come out, but the one that was burning me up. I unwrapped my little package of received wisdom.

Her answer began with a gentle tremor of her belly: a Grace kind of belly laugh, polite but unmistakable.

"Didn't you notice that my name is Freund?"

"Could be German, Austrian, Swiss."

"And my God, what are gentile eyes, not to mention gentile breasts?"

"You caught me. I'm not proud of this shicksa business. But I'm so damned relieved. Here, let me kiss those gentile eyes, not to mention those gentile breasts."

The very next day, in my ridiculous relief, I took her to Goldenberg's Delicatessen for lunch. It was in the Rue des Rosiers in the Marais, the Jewish quarter; afterwards we strolled and came across an abandoned synagogue surrounded by an ancient, crumbling stone wall. I no longer had much to do with synagogues, but there in the courtyard I made my move. Without money, without prospects, surprising the hell out of myself, I asked Grace to marry me. To cover my anxiety about a possible "no" or, this being gentle Grace, a "no thank you," I kissed her for a very long time: minutes, hours, days, I had no time in my head. When we finally broke apart, off-balance, I couldn't leave things hanging in the air, unspoken, a ticking time bomb—I said, "You know when I was a kid I kissed a Catholic girl, maybe fourteen years old. I remember her name was Eileen. She was terrified. It turned out the nuns at school had told her you could get pregnant from a kiss."

"I thought that, too. But I was about ten."

"You know," I said, "it's not really true."

"I wouldn't mind," she said. "Having a baby, maybe one, maybe two or three. But now I'm not sure you get them from kissing."

We laughed and married; at the wedding in New York my quartet friends held the chupa, later playing a movement of a Schubert quartet. And months after, there we were, all of us cruelly disarranged, shaken up by a German girl, a musical gift, a late-born relic of an old and terrible war.

*   *   *

Now that I'd given up the search for Grete, the unexpected gift arrived. There she was playing at the corner of Eighth Street and Sixth Avenue. Winter still held the city in its cold fingers; I froze and Grete played with her customary heat. I watched her for a half hour, shivering, my heart loose in my chest, terrified at the hold she still had on me. I wasn't quite sure if it was the actual young woman or the idea of her ferocious drive, painfully young, sexually cool, maybe even cold, that style of come-and-get-me if you can. It didn't seem to matter which. I stayed so long that she saw me, offering an impassive gaze, while spraying the air with the thrilling sounds of a Bach fugue. Fugue meant flight, I remembered from music lessons. But she hadn't fled and I was captive again.

After having refused Tony and Grete the sanctuary of my apartment, in confusion and excitement, I took Grete home with me. Grace would be safely nested for the afternoon at the Columbia Library. For the moment the coast was clear. No segue seemed to be necessary. Her thin coat unbuttoned quickly, and, at first she let me undress her like a runaway child, slender arms raised passively overhead, the blouse removed revealing a small sad brassiere, yellow and worn, a tear at the edge of one cup; the skirt stepped out of, obediently. I knelt to remove the sneakers. She let me roll her panties to her knees then took over and, finally naked, crouched before me and carefully removed my clothing, folding trousers, even shorts and socks into neat units. She'd let her own skirt and blouse find their heedless nest on the floor, like any American teenager, I thought, but I get the German treatment, neat, orderly. My eyes fixed on the slight downward slant of her lower lip, remnant of an illness? A birth accident? A scar?

As if guided by long affection instead of a chance assignation, Grete's lips opened, damp, welcoming, as if she had been as hungry as I, as if she had been desperately searching for me instead of my having stumbled on her at Eighth Street and Sixth Avenue, my lips at that crazy moment became me, what Professor Grossberg had called synecdoche, a form in rhetoric that means the part standing for the whole, my lips being, for the instant, me, yes it's okay for such abstract thoughts to drift in and out during this first kiss because, as everyone knows, the clock stops during a blind, enthusiastic kiss—there is historical, or real time, there is psychological time, not too closely measured by the order of events, witness the timeless synagogue kiss with which I'd proposed to Grace; and there is sexual time, in which either you are so concentrated on the present instant, your fingers and lips becoming eyes, your mind busily reading the Braille of body-parts or, if still lucky, but a different kind of luck, you're absolutely engaged and at the same time open to vagaries, fragments, all spelled out in the grammar of what we laughingly call desire, laughingly, that is, only after the fact when detachment returns, trailing its friends, irony and clock time.

I was gone, drowning in that first kiss in which Grace and Grete met, melted together like wafers on my tongue. Grete's tongue, like another form of rhetoric, was a question, a sensitive probe—my rhetorical over-education did not get in the way of the moist excitement, nor does it get in the way of my memory of it; maybe it helps me phrase it, telling how her hand sliding down my cheek in a caress which became a scratch, as her own excitement pushed her to the busyness of short breaths and long embraces in which entrances and exits become as natural and unthinking as sunrise and sunset.

The taciturn Grete, taking what she wanted then vanishing, the Grete who was never quite committed to being where she was—suddenly she was absolutely there, coiled around me, one leg roaming between my legs, her fingers mysteriously thrust between my lips, hesitant no more. Not since the blizzard on Fifth Avenue pouring Bach into the snow, had she been so present. Slim as she was she filled the couch to overflowing and when we were done she shrank down to herself, a sweaty slender wraith, catching her breath and hidden again behind gray eyes and a slanted swollen mouth. Tony, Paul, Suzanne, me—the quartet's finale was complete. Or so it seemed.

Why she had calmly gone with me as if she'd expected to, all along, I had no idea. Her motives were beyond secretive; I'm not sure she had what we usually call motives. Maybe Tony for money, Paul for a leg up in concerts, Suzanne for legal help: it all made some sort of weird sense except that it didn't add up. And why me?

Our conversation was not unlike the one I'd rehearsed before the discovery.

Me: "I've been looking over the whole city for you. I even went to your dormitory but they had no record of you."

Grete: "I stay with friends. Why have you looked so hard for me?" Or so I recalled my fantasied conversation. Why, indeed?

Me: "I thought maybe you'd gone back to Germany."

Me: "When I go, I go to Paris, the Conservatoire."

She glanced down at the pool of discarded trousers, skirt, underwear. "Where is your wife? She comes home soon?"

"On Saturdays she works at the library."

"She reads whole day?"

"Research. She's writing a book. Why didn't you go back. Do you have a green card? Didn't Suzanne help you?"

"She wanted, I don't know—too much. Now, I am illegal."

"What will you do? How about your career, those posters you drew: Berlin, London . . . ."

She sat up in a surround of optimistic yellow hair. "I will go back to Conservatory. My career—it will happen, *Ess muss zein*—that is Beethoven, marked on a quartet. But true for me, too." She twisted sideways to kiss me. "You are nice. You found me in the snow. Was this—" she patted the long L-shaped leather couch—"this was why you looked for me?"

Helpless, I said, "I'm not sure."

Then a sudden frenzied tossing on of clothes, a terror of capture. She stood at the door, haphazardly dressed, hair a tangle, wearing her thin, slightly soiled raincoat, the thought of her sad, yellowed brassiere with the jagged tear made my heart jump, I felt dizzy. In spite of her assurance, of her *shicksal*, in spite of her whirlwind aggression whipping through the group, in spite of her ferocious gifts, in spite of everything, she called for pity, for attention. She turned the doorknob and I said, "Where can I find you?

In a burst of loquacity, for her, Grete said, "You find me twice on street. Good things happen in three times . . . but also bad things. Maybe stop with two."

Ignoring this German folk wisdom, I would not let her go until she gave me a phone number. "They will call me. But not for a long time. I go back soon."

Unexpectedly she laughed; a new experience seeing Grete laugh. For some reason it made having a photograph of her urgent. I scrabbled for the Polaroid camera in a kitchen drawer. She posed, violin case in hand, now unsmiling; posing for a photograph was a serious matter, something she expected, publicity.

Then, the smile returned and, as if confiding a dangerous secret, she half-whispered, "On street, people give money—sometimes a lot. They think I play for them. But really I save money for going home—and I use street playing to get ready whole repertoire for Paris Conservatory recital; a contest; you must win contest today for real career." I was enthralled by this peek into a usually silent, secretive Grete. The last thing she said was, sans laughter, face frozen back into the familiar mask, "I will win!"

"*Shicksal?*" I said.

"*Shicksal,*" she echoed and was gone, leaving me holding a scrap of paper. When had the bad joke of shicksa-anxiety joined up with that other joke: the song of destiny? Wordplay was no cure for such confusion.

After I dressed and straightened up: panic; I couldn't find the slip of paper with her phone number. But it was on the floor near the couch. I wondered: did I actually bring her here, did I actually risk making a ruin of everything, marriage, job, home?

I glanced at the numbers on the scrap of paper, with a stroke through the seven in the European manner, then gazed at the photograph; already it seemed like an ancient memento, a young girl, a stranger, smiling into an uncomprehending camera.

When it was clear that she had disappeared again, this time behind the curtain of "the number you have dialed is not a working . . . ," I hit the streets again. The reality of rain corrected the fantasy of snow. This time I was not in a frenzy, I walked steadily but slowly like a man in mourning hoping for a glimpse of a ghost; a bird of anxiety fluttered in my chest. The city was still crowded with hurrying winter coats, raincoats, here and there a hat; the cold was unseasonable, people murmured in coffee shops, on line at luncheonettes picking up the morning office bagel and coffee, it's not healthy, you don't know how to dress.

I stretched lunch hours, came in late, pleaded a flurry of doctors and dentists, too superstitious to invent funerals. I needed a giant microphone, one that would broadcast every violin sound in the open air in all of New York. I envisioned Grete as a little match girl, huddled in a doorway, too sick to play. Instead it was I who had sneezes, chills heating into fever. When whatever it was wouldn't yield to tea, to around-the-clock sleep, to Tylenol, aspirin, Grace whispered to the doctor outside the bedroom door and the doctor whispered back, as if I were a child who shouldn't hear. I liked the idea, ready to be a child for a while. Flu? Pneumonia . . . ?

The fever finally yielded to time. Back to work: late at night, in the emptied-out office, I tried the number for what I swore would be the last time, the wounded-bird fluttering in my chest. Restless, miserable, I whipped through the suite of offices taking in the contents of each, here a video of an Egyptian tomb, a prehistoric cave, another Lascaux but this one near Marseille, the new Getty Museum in Barcelona; in another, grant proposals: In Peru Machu Pichu was in danger, pollution, airborne chemicals . . . the Sistine Chapel, newly discovered Botticelli frescoes in a tiny church, in Pisa where the famous tower was finally leaning too far, had already eaten up more funds than Grace had allotted. One note of irony: some ruins were in serious need of restoration, not to their original grandeur, but to their pristine state of ruin.

On Arjemian's desk there was a mock-up of what seemed to be a synagogue, spanking new: it was the fantasy; next to it were scattered a batch of photographs, the decaying reality. Photographs, videos and grant proposals. Shifting my gaze from each to each, I could understand the romance of Arjemian's obsessions: the Holocaust Museum in Washington, only a few years old but already overstressed by crowds, needing repairs, an ancient Jewish Cemetery in Tunis, crumbling in the neglect of centuries. Girona, an old Jewish town near Barcelona with ancient ritual baths and synagogues which had once been magisterial statements of faith in wood and stone, now piles of rubble waiting for a restoring hand.

Was the world always in the process of disintegrating? How was it I had never noticed it while growing up; how was it that nobody except Arjemian and his dedicated band noticed it now? I sat in Arjemian's swivel chair, dizzy with information that had been all around me, but invisible to my distracted eyes, suddenly electric with emotion, demanding attention.

Arjemian appeared, tall, hungry-thin, eternally anxious. A swarthy after-hours wraith, jumpy with surprise, a drunken whiskey-cloud of smoked breath preceding him.

"Hey, if you want my job, it's yours."

Embarrassed, I jumped up. "I didn't know you were here."

"I'm always here. Hadn't you noticed? This place is my life."

Arjemian killed one cigarette and lit another one in one swift movement. He was never at rest, all nerves,.

"I was just taking a look at some of your pet projects." Explaining felt foolish.

"I've been hoping you would sooner or later." Arjemian's conspiratorial grin. "You seemed to live on the edges, here."

Arjemian sat down, then jumped up and grabbed my startled hand. "Look," he said. He hovered over the desk top models. "This town, Girona, they've discovered catacombs. Did you know Jews had catacombs?"

"I thought Christians . . . ."

Arjmenian had no interest in replies.

"It'll cost at least two million. Which we don't have. I'll raise it. There are Jewish traces all over the world that will be dead and gone soon, if . . . ." He stopped, exhausted, stops as sudden as his starts.

I gathered my courage. "How come you, especially . . . ? I began. And Arjemian, Armenian mind-reader, said: "Because I'm Armenian. How about a drink?" He whisked a bottle and a couple of glasses from a magic desk drawer. But there was no relaxing. He poured whisky, neat, poured words: "Because Armenians grow up with their genocide, the Turkish wipe-out . . . because my Uncle Sarmanian lived to tell it, between his yellow teeth and a heavy-duty beard; he had a thousand stories, each one could sour milk or ambrosia, each one could sour your heart forever, every dinner was Passover without the Exodus . . . babies, you know what happened to babies, and pregnant women . . . no better way to get rid of more and more Armenians . . . old men, beards on fire . . . well, I don't want to sour your heart . . . you're my friend . . . ." (news to me) "nineteen-twenty-one . . . got just about all of us . . . only twenty thousand Armenians left in the world, twenty-thousand and three counting me, my Nedja and my little girl Ada. So I joined the Jews, most of who probably never heard of the Armenian wipeout . . . joined Grace and soaked myself in saving everything Jewish, anywhere . . . when there's time left I save the rest of the world . . . ."

His cheeks were flushed under brown skin full of lights and shadows, his thin lyric lips brownish and white, the white where he had sprayed with the spittle of passion. "Isn't it suppose to be a Jewish idea? Tikkun, they call it. To mend the world."

"Yes," I said. "My folks were serious Jews; I heard a lot about Tikkun."

"They didn't tell me at Cornell that art history could lead to this." He squinted at me. "You've never stayed late before. Why now? Is something wrong?"

"No . . . I don't know why," I said.

"You look down, sad." Then, out of the blue he chanted poetry:

> *All things fall and are built again,*
> *And those that build them are gay.*

The lines had an echo I couldn't quite hear. I knew they were from some poem by Yeats, but there were a bunch of other resonances, personal ones. I started to trace them but, surprising the hell out of me, Arjemian took my face between his hands, a father with a hangdog son. For one crazy moment I thought I could confide in this man, tell all about Grete and *shicksal*, about the group. Arjemian could have been our leader—he reeked of destiny: his own, Jewish, Armenian, the whole decaying world. Maybe he could take the place of the group for a moment, clip the wings of the fluttering bird in my chest. I said nothing; he just gazed at me. Then:

"Find a project that charges you up. Go with it. I'll give you any help you need." A solemn gaze with the weight of centuries behind it. "Join us. I mean, really sign on."

"I actually came in to talk about Project 345 in the Plans Book." My plan formed on the hoof, off the cuff, improvisation. "I speak French pretty well, took a lot in high school and at Columbia. There was a mock-up of that medieval synagogue in Paris, the one with the wall around it . . . ."

I was tentative, but Arjemian was ahead of me, hot for an opening. "Something you want to look into?"

"Do my best," I said. "I'm not an art historian."

160

"Not yet." Arjemian grinned as if he'd won a hand at poker. I was ready to take out the notes I'd scribbled. But he ploughed ahead. "Let's do it," he said. "I mean let's you do it. Research, site visits. Plan of action. The works. Make us believe in you." A whiff of wine-and-whisky breath followed the plea. I didn't quite know who the us was. His lyric celebration, the Armenian version of Tikkun, was oddly moving. Maybe you couldn't take the lyricism straight when the whiskey had been straight. Still, he'd touched me.

Within ten days I'd made my plan, sold Arjemian on an exploratory trip to Paris. I felt a little lousy about faking him out; his brand-new protégé running a scam: searching for a girl, under cover of nosing out some mysterious wreck of history to restore. Grete was the mysterious object I had to restore, whose provenance I had to discover. The anxious fluttering had taken its place in my chest again.

I removed the Polaroid of Grete foolishly folded to fit into the smallest compartment in my wallet for secrecy. I had thought of tearing it up at least a dozen times. Luckily, she was still there, fiddle strapped to her side, leaning sideways as if she had to dash away at any second.

Naturally, I was damned nervous about telling Grace. Some nerve of apprehension told me that she might not take something as simple as a business trip abroad with ease. I felt the need to test-drive the upcoming conversation, as if writing the scene before the fact might make it easier. I would make light of going. I would try to sense her level of ease or unease. I would have to squelch my own discomfort at playing her with a lie. But the advance fiction was not working too well. This time it felt like stepping into quicksand. I had no idea how deep I might sink.

Me: "It's just a get-your-feet-wet trip. That's all. Arjemian wants to give me a chance to stretch my wings. He's priming me to work on a project of my own."

Grace: "Why now? Isn't there somebody who could go instead of you?" A tremor of trouble. Grace was not dumb. She knew nothing about the lost and found comedy with Grete, but maybe she could feel me slipping away. It wasn't as if she had found a piece of Grete's clothing under the couch or searched my wallet and seen the Polaroid. But shivers and slivers of feelings can be almost as disturbing as discovery.

Me: "I need to give it a shot. I sold Arjemian. I can't let it go now."

Half-truths felt as rotten as lying. I told her about the Jewish Passion According To Arjemian.

Grace: "I've heard him sing that song," she said.

When the actual scene took place she looked dragged, defeated. It was not a pretty sight. We'd not been apart for a day since meeting. Now, in retrospect, it seemed odd, unpleasant. Why hadn't I chafed at such confinement; a prisoner of comfort, of safety? I'd been married to four people; now it was down to one. Perhaps that was what being grown-up was.

Grace had rescued me: security of home, job, love— could now command me. After the pell-mell rush in Paris, maybe I'd merged love and advantage all too quickly? It had something to do with our arrangement, something to do with money, how much she had and how little I had; something to do with the safe harbor at both Graces.

Then a surge of rage at Grete, that horribly young cyclone leaving only destruction in her wake. Still, I'd made my plan, or the plan had made me. It was hopeless. How did it go, *La belle dame sans merci*, hath thee in thrall. I had my passport and, in my wallet, the Polaroid of Grete waited. I was like a madman planning to flee the asylum. Nothing could distract me.

Now, here I am in Paris waiting to get my passport stamped, my one suitcase cleared. At the Rue du Dragon where my hotel waits, finding Grete is suddenly not so urgent. Peering out of the window is all, smelling, remembering the delightful alien gasoline fumes, the unmistakable rancid tinge of French cigarette smoke, the balcony hotel windows open to the muffled music of passing French conversations, the windows across the narrow cobbled street open to any gaze, all under a sea of sloping Mansard roofs.

It is nine o'clock in the morning and God knows what time it is in my head. But I will not rest. I am restless, without rest, isn't that what the word means? I have a long day ahead of me. Coffee in the Café Flore in St. Germain des Pres right next to Les Deux Magots, where I used to take lunch a hundred years ago. Then a chilly walk in the old Jewish quarter, the Marais, a half hour in the Parc Royale, where I'd found the nerve to propose marriage to Grace.

I have come to find Grete, but perversely I spend the first hours with Grace. Grace in the Rodin Museum, Grace and I walking along the crowded Rue Jacob, booksellers becoming antique shops, becoming another café, a hungry brasserie in Montparnasse, talking, listening, talking. Then face to face with the great piece, the statue of Balzac outside the Montparnasse Metro station: rotund, visionary, confident of his destiny, Grace looking up with such admiration at the towering, cape-surrounded figure.

A comedy of errors follows.

"Pardon," I say, "je voudrais acheter une reproduction d'une statue de Balzac."

Naturally the guard replies in English, "The director's office is on the second floor."

When I am admitted, I repeat my request and am told that the great man's will allows for two castings a year. There is one open this year. Five hundred thousand francs, about two thousand dollars. I tell him I had a simple gift shop version in mind and he directs me downstairs where, feeling foolish, I purchase a small bust of Balzac's head for four hundred francs. Grace will be amused, pleased.

Why am I buying gifts for Grace when I'm here to search for Grete? I'm the wrong man to ask. But I am now ready to begin my mission.

The Conservatoire de la Musique is in the Rue St. Antoine, with the spire of the Bastille as landmark. The director is Monsieur Ricaud, a tiny middle-aged man with a wisp of black beard. I gather my nerve.

"I am looking for Grete Mueller, a student, perhaps a former student. A violinist." My French is not a problem. Monsieur Ricaud informs me, carefully, that he had spent several years at Julliard in New York.

"Grete Mueller?" Monsieur Ricaud nods gravely. "We have a number of German students. We have an Inga Mueller. A relative, perhaps. But I think Meuller must be a commonality in Germany."

I produce the Polaroid. Since I'd last looked at it, the snapshot has faded to a brownish hue, has grown to represent a stranger; a haughty, humorless young girl with a forced camera-smile, a girl one would not want to know.

"Have you ever seen or heard her? She's a wonderful violinist." As if this could explain my mad mission. Monsieur

Ricaud holds the Polaroid of Grete close to his nose. He seems to turn suspicious. "She has never been a student at the Conservatoire de la Musique. Why are you looking for her? Are you police?"

"Do I look like a policeman?"

Monsieur Ricaud eases a bit. "Our students are young. They sometimes have drugs, all kinds of trouble. Yes, she was here. For almost a year. She had enormous concentration. Practiced like a devil. But she pushed too fast; we would not enter her into the competitions yet, until she had a better repertoire." Ricaud turned his hands palms up. "She left for another school. So, if you are not police then what—"

"I'm just a friend."

"Of her family?"

It is a subtle reminder of the difference in our ages. God, I think, these waters could get deep. She is a teenager, I am easily ten years her senior; this late in the life of the planet the abuse of the young by the older was everywhere. I would have to develop a more solid story. I'd not planned any further than arrival, conservatory, questions, photo followed by an address or phone number; a phone call, a knock at a door. Apparently it is not to be that simple.

"Yes," I say. "But the family has moved and, as you say, Mueller is a common name."

"You might ask at the Ecole de Musique in the Avenue Montaigne."

Mme. Laurent, the director of the Ecole de Musique, is a different cup of tea from Monsieur Ricaud, much younger; a handsome woman with too much makeup and much presence; a touch severe, not comfortable in English.

"A strange one," she says. "Greatly talented. I know, not only because of my position, but I play the violin, I have been serious, too. So I could tell quickly that she was an extraordinary musician. But I could never tell if she had the real ambition or not."

"You couldn't tell?"

"Grete transferred from the Conservatoire de la Musique. Some kind of trouble. Perhaps a boy, she is very occupied with boys. She worked hard, talked about her future, but she would not enter any of the contests." She lectured: "Contests are the main road to the career these days. The Queen of

Belgium prize, the Jacques Thibaud contest in Paris. One must win one or two of those to push, how would you say—"

"Launch?"

"Oui, launch. I am sorry about my English." Mme. Laurent now looks even more mournful. "Then she began to disappear for weeks, months. We finally had to drop her from the school."

"How long ago was that?" I was doing simple arithmetic in my head.

The director sat down at a waiting laptop on her desk. Impatient, I said, "About how long?"

Mme. Laurent looks at me, a steady gaze not without irony. She says, slow and soft, "A little patience, please." While the laptop was tuning up she said, "There was also the matter of the tuition fees."

"Didn't her family—"

"Ah, here it is: three months and two weeks ago." She closes the laptop with care. I do the arithmetic in my head. The schedule roughly matched with the first night of beautiful, frozen playing on Fifth Avenue; with the months of Friday nights and the weeks and weeks of street wandering.

"Yes, the family. I never met them, or rather him."

"Him?" I am going a little crazy with impatience. "Only the father?"

I tune down my receptors and take in only what I need— Grete's parents are divorced, the mother dead, the father an architect in Dresden, the payment for tuition irregular.

"An address," I say, "a phone number?"

"And you are to Grete . . . ?"

"A friend. We had a quartet in New York and she vanished so suddenly. I'm here on business and I thought I'd look her up."

"I have no notion of where Grete is. I'm sorry." She softens her tone. "If only she had the ambition." A cloudy moment. "I had the ambition," she says, looking away from me and holding up her long eloquent left hand. "But I had not the fingers."

The Beth Shalom synagogue in the Rue des Rosiers. A wall of some ancient stained stone surrounds it; a crazily tipped scaffold hangs from the second story, memento of an unfinished repair. Why the wall? To keep out shicksas. A bad joke is essential for my balance. This sacred ruin had been my ticket to Paris. A report would have to be written, or at least a memo.

Inside, broken benches, rubble heaped in corners, a Bima primed for prayer, except for a jagged crack from top to bottom. On the walls mosaics depicting scenes, not from the Bible, from some medieval family life; a newborn child in swaddling clothes, an old man holding onto a young woman leading him by the hand; all surrounded by richly worked gold stars of David. Strange, beautiful, the mosaic seemed to offer some consonance between the soul and the body, mysterious.

Arjemian had nailed me in my miserable state and quoted Yeats:

All things fall and are built again,
And those that build them are gay.

I sit on a filthy broken bench and gaze at the ritual stars. My report will be lyrical, I will out-Arjemian Arjemian. Experts could follow, checking dates, analyzing provenance. But in the meantime, I'd come on a fool's errand. Grete may have metamorphosed into a sad kid afraid to take the plunge, or over-ambitious, foolishly impatient for her destiny to begin. It is not clear where—or if—the true girl is to be found.

At any rate she's led me to this moment, caught by old synagogue memories, Lottie Roth upstairs with the other women, ferocious black hair folded under a silly hat, leaning over the balcony's edge to catch my eye as I sit next to my father, pretending to pray or actually praying. Karl Roth, davening in a sweet baritone; it is unclear how much of his fervor is musical, how much devout. What a strange destiny it is to be a Jew. So much forbidden, so much to follow or leave behind. And finally the comedy of shicksa-anxiety and the great shicksa-search, the comedy of *shicksal*-obsession. Wouldn't it be fine to be a believing Jew, just for this moment, so that I could turn to the exotic ruined walls and ask them to exorcise the Grete spirit which had taken me over, which would not leave.

The next morning I lug my bags and head for some badly needed coffee before grabbing a taxi to the airport. My head feels too large for my body. The night before I'd side-stepped the rain and dashed into a bistro for some savory dish I couldn't recall but I remember the Beaujolais well. I'd downed at least half a bottle and slept the night through, damp and dizzy-drunk. A sleep broken only by an hallucinatory phone call from old man Freund.

Freund: "Good idea, site visits—get your land legs. French synagogues, good a place to start as any."

Me: "Hello. Where are you, Morris? It's three-thirty in the morning here."

Freund: "Arjemian wants us to start a division only devoted to restoring synagogues. I'm not so sure. Did you know there are over three hundred synagogues in Japan?"

Me: "Is that where you are? Japan?"

Freund: "I may be home in time for the High Holidays. Depending—"

Me: "On what?"

Freund: "On the government of Japan. Think of it—three hundred synagogues for such a small place."

Me: "How many Jews are there in Japan?"

Freund: "Glad you're getting into things."

Dial tone.

Half awake, wine-dazed, I wondered, how the hell did he know where I was? He seemed to know everything—the absent, invisible God. Or what God could be if he had money. If Freund knew the real reason for my French jaunt, I was in deep trouble. Which I was, in any case.

Now in the morning I'm hunting the sidewalks for a place that will offer me coffee and anodyne for my headache. Magically a corner tabac does just that and I walk across several streets looking for a taxi *tete-de-station*.

There is a waiting line of serious, suited men, some with folded newspapers, women with umbrellas at the ready against the uncertain drizzle. One of the serious suits in front of me drops his newspaper. I bend to help retrieve a fan of wet pages and that is when I hear the sound, firm, intense, unmistakable. An old friend: the Bach "Chaconne."

Across the broad street, next to the Brasserie Lipp, a violinist is playing. Her clear blue gaze is the same as ever, fixed, the music as strong as ever. The stubby fingers, the open violin case on the sidewalk, nothing has changed, here still is the strong sound with swift, clean double-stops and chords and a vibrato almost white, perfect for Bach. The rain is now pelting. I stand, umbrellaless, cheeks streaming, like an unprotected statue of myself, watching her through the scrim of rain for a long time.

Here is Grete, violin case open, at her feet, bills and coins scattered on the purple satin lining, playing as seriously, with as much concentration and skill as if she were playing at Lincoln Center instead of on a gleaming wet sidewalk in St. Germain des Pres. The startling waterfall of bright blonde hair that used to drip below her waist is now gathered in a long ponytail. She looks even more like a teen-ager, wears only a light cloth coat against the wet. Her eyes are mostly closed as she plays. Several hurrying passersby slow down; they pay various tributes: a surprised glance, some coins, a folded bill.

I give up my place in line to move across the street where I stand in front of her. After a time I close my eyes and just listen. She has abandoned the natural independence of unaccompanied Bach and is playing the first movement of the Brahms Concerto. There is of course not the usual orchestral accompaniment, only a remembered one. It seems to emphasize her isolation. It's a feat. The long line of melody woven, compressed, then extended, the supreme song framed into discrete segments, letting the mind follow the contrapuntal argument, while the sound breaks the heart. It is like a mathematical proof that passion can be contained, can be classical, and still be passion, but without the romantic anarchy that sends birds fluttering into the chest, near the heart or instead of the heart.

Grete slams a powerful chord, rolling over all four strings. Then, for all the world like a wealthy burgher in a Schnitzler novel, perhaps on his way home from a European business trip, in rain this time instead of snow, and stopped by a little street music, moved by the sight of a young woman playing magnificently in the rain, I take out my wallet and carefully remove a five hundred franc note; finally the Polaroid, which I tear into four parts. I fold them inside the bill and place it among the scattering of coins and bills in the violin case. Then I turn away, cross the street to take my place, again, in the taxi line.

What an easiness of breath! The fluttering bird in my chest is gone. I am like a recovered paralytic who finds he can walk, like a man who had slipped into a coma, in the midst of the rush and bustle of life, and finally wakes. This moment of interminable taxi-wait, between past and future, is that inscrutable place called the present—so fragile you know it can't last. The present: this delicate breath, like the pause between movements of a concerto—the first movement finished, the last movement not yet begun.

What would it feel like to live in a reasonable way once again! I am flushed with the possibilities of mending, of picking up every dropped stitch of the past few months; I will weave them into a pattern, exploring, healing. Grace, Tony, Paul, Suzanne, Arjemian, everyone will be in play. I can redo whole lives in the suspended moment, wet and waiting for a taxi in Paris.

First Grace: Across the street from our apartment building the flags at the Metropolitan Museum will be waving at me in a warm breeze. The snowy, rainy spring seems to have changed its mind.

I will return, early evening, dog tired from the long trip, the time change. Grace takes the scene away from me. I see her holding a bottle of champagne, standing in the middle of the enormous living room, holding a bottle of Dom Perignon, the poor little rich girl. About a third of the bottle is gone. I register the danger signal.

"I'm beat. A long flight. Champagne! A special occasion?"

"Just to welcome you back. You never left before . . ."

"There isn't much 'before'. What is it, almost . . ."

"Four months and two days, but who's counting?"

We send out for Chinese and over the clutter of cartons and sauces we talk. That is, Grace talks. "I know how close to the chest I've been; how frustrated you must be. I have to tell you two things," she says. "First—"and she spins out one or another autobiographical tale: maybe the one about her first marriage to the Bad News, that's what she calls him, the Bad News. She was nineteen, he was twenty-nine; an Irish Catholic, which didn't make Daddy any too happy. But whatever Grace wants, Grace gets, so Daddy bit the bullet and came to the civil ceremony at City Hall.

This Bad News was a will-of-the-wisp, always leaving, turning on a dime, and Grace never knew if he was coming back or not—which left her not too cool about husbands going off to Paris on sudden business trips. He claimed to be a writer, claimed to have such family resources that he didn't need a thing from Grace or her father; until the crunch came—when the raggedy sixteen-year-old girl out of Dickens showed up, pregnant, and the Bad News needed money for an abortion, money to calm the girl's family, to keep them away from the police—and when Daddy took care of the girl and her family but cut the Bad News off cold, he cleaned out their joint checking account. I ask, "How did you finally . . . ?"

"Daddy got a private detective. Then they made a deal: a complete and permanent vanishing act—no charges, even let him keep what was left of the money he stole . . . ."

That, or some other disastrous early marriage story. The main thing was her coming out with it. I don't know if you've ever seen one of those sudden weather changes, the ones that seem to come from nowhere, taking trees from stillness to storm, skies from blue to black in seconds. That's what came next. Sheets of tears, awful Shakespearean moans, the kind of weeping you don't see much of in daily life: a sort of biblical wipeout leaving swollen eyes, red framing the blue. I held her until the weather changed back.

The storm purged both of us. We stayed up heedless of time, of jet lag; we swapped lives. It was one of those first dates married couples have if they're lucky; the night when they realize that the one they've married is even more mysterious, unknown, than when she was just a woman, he just a guy, before they became spouses. We traded experiences like baseball cards: the bruiser in grammar school who waited in the bathroom to beat me up; no motive, he didn't know me. The second time he bloodied my nose I did the unthinkable—I told Lottie and Karl, unthinkable for a kid to tell his folks, risking mortal embarrassment before classmates. Lottie went to school. I have no idea how she managed it but the attack never happened again.

Grace: "My mother—I was never allowed to call her by her first name—always assumed I was wrong: children were guilty until proven innocent, the way criminals were in France in Balzac's time."

Me: "Did she ever—hurt you?"

Grace: "Never raised a hand. But she had me terrified all the time, anyway. I should have been joyful when she left."

Me: "But . . . ."

Grace: "I was even more terrified. I told Daddy I wanted to be a nun. He was smart, just waited it out and it went away." (a sigh) "I'm tired of running scared."

I told her about Lottie and Karl's passion for music, their hopeless lack of money smarts.

Grace: "I never knew anything about money. It was just there, like air and water, like Daddy."

She told me of living in an enormous apartment with separate wings for warring armies. I told her how Lottie and Karl lived in each other's pockets. It was in danger of turning into a contest.

Grace: "So how come you took so long to get married?"

Me: "I don't know. Maybe the accident that took them away froze me."

Grace: "And I melted you."

Me: "Well, first you made me hard, then I melted."

Grace: "Was that an obscene remark?"

Me: "Yes."

Grace: "Good. Let's be obscene."

We told each other about masturbation. She won that one.

Grace: "Gertrude, this kid, and I used to examine each other's vaginas; we used a hand mirror. It was the Great Clitoris Hunt. Then we played with each other until one or the other of us did what passed for coming. Is that obscene enough?"

Me: "Actually it's kind of charming. When I was eleven Joey Kreizman and I used to wrestle on my bed, instead of studying for our Bar-Mitzvahs. Once or twice we went past wrestling into groping. It was very exciting so I stopped."

By now we were half-drowsing on the couch, folding and unfolding as pins and needles took various limbs.

Then a chaos of crazy confessionals, as if having opened the tap of shared memory, it couldn't be turned off. Everything, great and small: lost dogs, first loves or reasonable facsimiles, her first menstruation, terribly early maybe eleven, my mysterious lung ailment never diagnosed, keeping me in bed for a year while I read and reread, instead of *The Three Musketeers*, *The Man In The Iron Mask* or *The Count Of Monte Cristo*, I read *Love In The Western World* by Denis De Rougement, *The American Novel* by Richard Chase and the *Anxiety of Influence* by Harold Bloom. I was warming up for a nutty nonstop academic career.

. . . Grace's moment of teenage lunacy: stealing books from bookstores, and a voice of terror saying "Come with me young lady" . . . me trying to match that with library books kept for a year until people came to the house, scaring Lottie with visions of visiting days in federal prisons . . . the day I left a violin borrowed from the music school on a bus . . .

Then, like a three-decker Victorian novel, it became a jumble of loving aunts who died, of a beloved dog who took a bite of her hand, the fire that destroyed Lottie and Karl's Forty-seventh Street enclave of diminishing sales, only to start again and again. When the fountain of remembered events slowed to a trickle it felt as if we'd spent a lifetime together.

Before finally falling asleep I asked her, "Why open all this up now? And why those furious tears, before? Why is this night different from all other nights?"

She stared at her feet, embarrassed. "It's so foolish." Then, simply, "I thought maybe you weren't coming back."

We fall asleep in our clothes, like children, wordless, exhausted by old pain and fresh discovery. In the morning Jesse finds us, tactfully straightens up, brews coffee, scrambles eggs. We both eat like famished foundlings.

Over a second cup of coffee, she says, "Oh, I meant to tell you. I thought I was pregnant. But it turns out I'm not."

"So far," I said. "So far." Thinking it had been at least twelve hours since I'd thought of Grete. And this thought, itself, instead of being infused with feeling was flat; information, welcome information but nothing more.

Next: the group starting with Suzanne. Happy to hear from me Suzanne, tells me to come down, gives me a new address. She's moved, lives in Chelsea with a woman, who opens the door. An imposing figure, big and round as a Malliol. She shakes my hand firmly, holds it a touch too long, as if to establish some kind of balance of power.

"I'm Eileen. I know who you are."

From within I hear Suzanne saying, "Who is it?"

Before Eileen can answer, Suzanne appears; she is wearing gray pants and a damned dashing turban. She gazes at me, maybe enjoying my confusion. In a matter of weeks she has changed her life. Grete might have imprisoned me but she has apparently freed Suzanne. Her friend/lover is also a cellist. "We're a two cello menage," she says, happy. This is a much different Suzanne than the shy, sober Suzanne I'd encountered in the Gotham Book Mart *apres* Grete; she is not now *apres* anything. It is all forward-looking futures, including the new downtown law firm she's joined.

Eileen brews some special herbal tea and while we sip, Suzanne spins out more futures. "The group will rise again," she says, "of course with Eileen added. They can play two cello quintets. There's a ton of stuff," she says. "Schubert, Boccherini."

She is in touch with Tony Romano and Paul who, she says, had put the Grete business in a sack and drowned it in the Hudson. A phone call or two would put the group back on track.

There remains, of course, the Armenian Question. Arjemian, the fanatic of renewal. I will meet him on neutral ground: maybe the Oak Room at the Plaza. A bar feels right for an encounter with the hard-drinking Jew manqué. I will tell him I am signing on. I will do what he'd suggested. Visit, research, plan, imagine, build, rebuild.

> *All things fall and are built again.*
> *And those who build them are gay.*

I'd written one of my endless college papers on the question of sharing the word gay; homosexual, heterosexual, gay was a word with a long precious history. Yeats' old Chinese men: *their eyes, their ancient glittering eyes are gay* . . . a remembered song: *I'll take romance, while my heart is young and eager and gay* . . . Wallace Stevens: *Children of poverty and malheur/the gaiety of language is our Seigneur . . . .*

Think of the work to be done—if you couldn't enter a synagogue, pray, fast, believe—you could at least help to rebuild one that was in ruins, just start with one. Who knows where that could take you. Be a father, if not now then later, who knows where that could take you. Think of a world of men who lie and steal their way into the lives of nineteen-year-old girls, stealing their confidence along with their money, of foolish car crashes consuming parents who wanted only to live and listen to music, to play and pray; a world of time and decay which destroys Buddhist temples, crumbling Venetian buildings where Vivaldi once played, where Titian once painted. Of the whole long parade of hope poisoned, of falling things forever in need of rebuilding, of the prospect of gaining some gaiety along the way.

All this, mind you, with Grete's streetsong playing beautifully in the background. My taxi arrives. I glance back at her and decide then and there, soaked with accidental rain, that *shicksal*, this destiny stuff, is bullshit. Destiny, it turns out, is nothing more or less than what has happened.

Grete plays, but gone are all those grand concert halls, those famed conductors. I have no way of knowing if this is only a temporary glitch in a furiously young life, but I see her now as a permanent virtuoso of the sidewalks. Here is Grete's famous future—to make music appear, unbidden, unexpected, scattering notes into the streets, onto the sidewalks where passersby can pick them up, pleased by the unexpected gift of a sweet succession of sounds. Or, oblivious, continue on with their lives—as I would with mine.

Photo by Charles Mary Kubricht

Daniel Stern, Cullen Distinguished Professor of English, teaches graduate and undergraduate writing workshops as well as literature classes. His publications include nine novels, four story collections, several plays and screenplays, and more than 100 essays and reviews. Among his many awards are the International Prix du Souvenir from the Bergen Belsen Society and the Government of France, the Rosenthal Award in Literature from the American Academy of Arts and Letters, the John Train Humor Award of *The Paris Review*, the Brazos Bookstore Short Story Award from the Texas Institute of Letters, two Pushcart Prizes, two O. Henry Prizes, and publication in *Best American Short Stories*. He has taught at Harvard, Wesleyan, Pace, and New York University and lectured at the Sorbonne and other universities and conferences. He currently serves as editor of the literary journal *Hampton Shorts*.